CRYING FOR THE MOON

CRYING FOR THE MOON

A Novel

MARY WALSH

HarperCollins Publishers Ltd

Crying for the Moon
Copyright © 2017 by Mary Walsh.
All rights reserved.

Published by HarperCollins Publishers Ltd

First edition

HarperCollins books may be purchased for educational, business or
sales promotional use through our Special Markets Department.

HarperCollins Publishers Ltd
2 Bloor Street East, 20th Floor
Toronto, Ontario, Canada
M4W 1A8

www.harpercollins.ca

Library and Archives Canada Cataloguing in Publication
information is available upon request.

ISBN 978-1-44341-036-6

Printed and bound in the United States

LSC/H 9 8 7 6 5 4 3 2 1

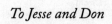

To Jesse and Don

PROLOGUE

DECEMBER 7, 1970

Monday night, drunk, Maureen started hysterically accusing Bo of going with someone else, and if it wasn't the one with the withered arm in the next apartment, it was someone. She knew he was out catting around. She called him all the big betrayers in the book, every heartbreaker, every whore-hopper, and once she started, she didn't stop. Bo hauled her out of bed, pulled her hair out, blackened her eyes. He wouldn't even let her sleep on the couch; he wouldn't let her sleep. He just kept dragging her around by her hair and kicking her and spitting at her and yelling.

She couldn't remember much else because they'd both been really, really drunk. Tuesday morning, she got up, hungover, bruised, miserable, without a thought in her head. Then her eyes lit on the big industrial-sized brown glass bottle of chlordane, a chemical exterminator used 1:50 to kill cockroaches and all other manner of insect life, which the ditzy buddy from Orkin had forgotten after he'd sprayed their apartment for earwigs. Next to the bottle was the Flit gun that he'd also forgotten, filled with the 1:50 chlordane-water cockroach and earwig killing mix. Not really present to herself, dazed and stupefied, she picked up the Flit gun, went directly to the fridge and Flit-sprayed on everything that wasn't covered—on the half tomato on the plate, on the deli turkey in the gaping plastic, on the cheese, on the sad piece of leftover pizza; she Flit-sprayed them all. Then she spotted the orange juice. She could see in her mind's eye Bo hungover, padding out from the bedroom on his big, thick, hairy hobbit feet, pulling the fake crystal fancy stopper out of the bottle and drinking straight from the decanter, probably downing the entire contents. Maureen went over, picked up the huge bottle of straight chlordane and poured the poison right into the orange juice, put the fancy stopper back in the bottle, put it back in the fridge, put on her clothes and, quiet as a mouse, left the apartment.

PART I

CHAPTER ONE

WHEN MAUREEN GOT OFF THE PLANE AT TORBAY Airport on July 15, 1967, of course the Sarge was not there waiting to pick her up and welcome her home, but Carleen's big sister, Joyce, and her mom were there. Carleen's mom was crying and Joyce was trying to calm her down. They wanted Maureen to tell them all about Carleen and what was going on in Montreal. Mrs. Maynard seemed out of it somehow and was really mad at Maureen, which Maureen thought was so unfair on the one hand, but on the other, she felt so guilty about Carleen, she knew she deserved it. As she was standing there, she was uselessly wishing that the Sarge and them had come to pick her up, but of course Maureen's family didn't have a car, and the bus that was going to drop off all the girls who weren't picked up by their parents was blowing its horn, waiting on Maureen, so somehow she got away from Joyce and Mrs. Maynard and got on that bus. She'd known they were going to blame her, because they thought they were better than her, better because Maureen didn't have the kind of *Father Knows Best* family from TV, or the David and Anne in the

Grade One reader good, decent, Catholic kind of family that most of the other girls in the glee club seemed to have. Maureen had a hard-drinking, hard-living, working-class, sell-your-mother-for-a-bottle-of-beer, downtown St. John's family who lived on Princess Street. If they'd been any further downtown, they'd be in the harbour, and those were the facts, but oh, sometimes Maureen just wished and hoped and dreamed and made up and pretended that she didn't have her kind of family at all. She desperately wanted that other kind of family, because as much as Maureen was always getting on like a rebel without a clue, a little tiny part of her knew that all she really wanted was to belong, to be "in," to be one of those "in girls," one of those girls with the dad and mom and little brothers and sisters and the car and the house in on the tree streets, Pine Bud Street or Maple Avenue or Chestnut Place, one of those girls Maureen could see from the window of the bus, being welcomed back home from Expo. *Fuck 'em, fuck 'em, fuck 'em! I don't care. I don't give a sweet fuck*, Maureen's mind said, but Maureen's heart knew different.

MAUREEN HAD BEEN DYING TO BE PART OF THE CHOIR, mostly because it would be going to Expo, but also because there was a part of Maureen that longed to be able to sing. Every year at the Kiwanis Music Festival, Maureen was one of the girls who had to stand at the back of her class choir, clasp her hands in front of her chest and silently pantomime the words to the songs. In January of 1967, Sister Mary Catherine, tall, patrician, cold, was auditioning girls for the choir that would be travelling to Expo. Anyone in the school could try out, but that day she was dismissing most of the wannabe choristers because their voices were too small, too weak. She was looking for altos with strength and power.

When Maureen got in front of Sister Catherine, she opened her mouth and gave her all to the note.

"Oh . . . ," Sister Catherine said. "Again." And, once again, Maureen put all the power she had into that one deep note.

"Good, very good," Sister Catherine said. "Go stand over there with the altos."

Maureen adored Sister Catherine and hated her just as much. She'd always known, though, that if she could just get in with Sister Catherine, become part of her inner circle of singers, she would drop her hatred like a hot rock. Sister Catherine was just like all the other nuns, of course, a sucker-upper and a kicker-downer, totally nice to the rich girls and so unbelievably mean to—or, at the very least, dismissive of—the poor girls.

It was still months before the choir would be going to Expo, so Maureen had to play a very clever game. Many times during those months, Sister Catherine would say, "There is something off. Something is wrong in the altos." Maureen knew, of course, that it was her who was wrong, who was off, and whenever Sister Catherine said it, Carleen, Maureen's friend, would look at Maureen, raise an eyebrow and start to tut-tut until they were both reduced to helpless laughter. That would irk Sister Catherine even more than the off-key singing in the altos, and she'd banish them from the auditorium until they'd gotten themselves "under control." A couple of times, being sent out of the room saved Maureen, because some days, when Sister Catherine heard the off-key alto, she would get up from the piano, push back her starched white guimpe to free her right ear and listen to each girl in turn in order to catch the culprit. On the days Maureen wasn't out of the room, she would wait until the moment Sister Catherine was standing right in front of her and, using the force of her will, sing strong and loud and, most importantly, on-key. Most days, as long as Carleen sang right into Maureen's ear (without, of course, ever letting on that she was doing it), Maureen could just manage to stay on-key. It was the stupid music that made her sing off-key.

At last, in July, Maureen found herself in Montreal at Expo 67, mortified. Everyone in Montreal had a bouffant, while Maureen had plaits. It was the Summer of Love, and everyone who was truly groovy was in bell-bottoms or had gone all mini mod, while Maureen was trapped in the awkward, obsolete, itchy wool serge Our-Lady-of-Mercy-Convent-for-Girls school uniform with the horrible white buttons down the front and the hideous plastic collars and cuffs, which set her apart for all to see as someone who was truly not "with it."

The choir was staying at a convent in Old Montreal. Right away, Maureen hated Old Montreal; it was a real downer, all that stone . . . all that grey, weighty and oppressive stone. Maureen was all for gutting the old. She was all for not trusting anyone over thirty.

The first night, after they'd all knelt in the corridor and said the rosary, after Sister Mary Imobilis had checked each room to make sure the girls were all in bed, Maureen and Carleen snuck out of the dorm and went to The Rainbow Steps bar on Crescent Street. Carleen's sister Joyce, who'd lived up in Montreal and gone to McGill, had told Carleen that The Rainbow Steps was full of poets and singers and that even Leonard Cohen sometimes went there.

Crescent Street that night was alive with people and music and life—real life, life like Maureen had only read about in magazines—and as soon as she set foot on that street, she felt herself come alive with all that endless longing, all that real hunger to be part of "It," all those feelings she usually kept underneath a blanket of "I Don't Give a Fuck." But now, all that achy yearning rose up and almost swallowed her, and she knew she couldn't wait one minute longer to start her real, grown-up, sophisticated Montreal life.

The bouncer at the door of the club wanted to see their ID, and Maureen's real Montreal life was almost stopped dead before it even began. Carleen and Maureen put on their best country hick act and said they were from Newfoundland and just visiting and had left their ID at the hotel. They were ready to get down on their knees and beg the guy to let them in. But then a nattily dressed man in shiny white shoes and a dazzling white suit stood in the doorway. As soon as he heard they were from Newfoundland, he whisked them past the bouncer and right into The Rainbow Steps; they would be his guests. He introduced himself as Perry Johns, the owner and operator of the bar. Right away, Maureen didn't like the look of him, didn't like all that white. Sure it was okay on that guy Trudeau: he was so cool he could get away with it. But buddy? She didn't think so.

Inside the bar, he introduced them to another Newfoundlander, a young fella he was starting a business with, he said. There were a bunch of them, "Newfie up-and-comers" Mr. Johns called them, giving the young fella, Fox, a hard smack on the back as he said it. It turned out that Wade "Fox" Albert knew Carleen's sister Joyce— his face lit up when he realized who Carleen was, and he asked anxiously how Joyce was and where she was. Maureen got bored; she wasn't up in Montreal to waste all her precious real-life time answering questions about Carleen's big sister. Mr. Johns, "Oh call me Perry," was telling them how he had opened a couple of bars in St. John's, the El Toro and The Stone Mill, and was going on about how much he loved Newfie girls. He was definitely putting the makes on Carleen, and after a few drinks, she looked like she was warming up to him, but Maureen couldn't believe that Carleen could be so easily sucked in. "Oh my God, Leonard Cohen! Leonard Cohen! Look! He's here," Maureen said.

"He's always here," Perry said flatly, unimpressed.

Maureen struggled to get up the nerve to go over and talk to him. She'd fallen in love with Leonard Cohen while watching *Ladies and Gentlemen . . . Mr. Leonard Cohen*. It came on the CBC in the afternoon, after *Take 30*. It came on so often, Maureen's mother, Edna, or "the Sarge," as everyone in the family called her, was moved to remark, "Jesus Christ, that crowd at the CBC, they got that on a loop or something? What, they got nothing else to put on? Turn it off, I'm sick to death of listening to him jawing on. Oh, he thinks a lot of himself he does, and then look at the size of the conk on him, my God." Maureen borrowed *The Spice-Box of*

Earth and *Let Us Compare Mythologies* from the Gosling Memorial Library and even read *Beautiful Losers*, which she loved, wishing she was Catherine Tekakwitha, the first Canadian saint, and now there he was ... *Oh Jesus!* Maureen stood up from the table. Carleen called out to her, but Maureen was on a mission and could not be turned aside. She ignored Carleen and walked straight across the room to where Leonard Cohen was standing at the bar. She stood there without a word in her mouth for what seemed like hours. At one point, Cohen turned toward her and gave her a quizzical look. Still Maureen couldn't think of a thing to say.

"How'd your hair get so long since *Beautiful Losers*?" Maureen blurted out finally.

Cohen looked at her and then simply replied, "It just grew."

At that, he turned back to the bar and his glass of wine. Maureen stood there, feeling so stunned to have asked such a half-assed question when she could have said anything. For one brief moment there, the world had been her oyster: she'd had Leonard Cohen's attention, for God's sake, and then ... God, why was she so stupid?

Having fucked up her chance with her hero, Maureen was more determined than ever that she was going to live the high life here in Montreal and so kept drinking. After a few more drinks, every time Maureen looked at Carleen, Carleen would say, "Da feet, da feet," the punchline of an old joke that just killed them in Grade 9—dead Jesus, up on the cross, and little Jimmy down below, Jesus saying, "Jimmy, take the nails out of my hands and feet and you will join me in heaven for eternity." Jimmy scrambled up the cross and took the nails out of Jesus' hands ... Our Lord falling forward, screaming, "Da feet! Da feet!" And that night, again, Maureen and Carleen started in laughing until they laughed so hard that big tears rolled down their cheeks. And then in a blink, before Maureen even realized it was happening, Carleen was sobbing and laughing and sobbing and laughing and switching it up so fast that Maureen was terrified "it" would happen again.

She tried to get Carleen to go back to the convent, but Perry kept insisting that he would take her upstairs and that she'd be fine.

"I'll just bring her upstairs. No need to worry," Perry said. "You get back to the nuns, Maureen." And with that, Perry led a laughing, sobbing, shaking Carleen away. Maureen didn't know what to do. It was already eleven o'clock and soon they would have to leave and get back to the convent because Sister Catherine had warned them that the nuns were going to conduct a bed inspection at 12:10. If they were caught, well, she couldn't even imagine what price Sister Catherine would exact. At the very least, they'd be thrown out of the choir and sent home in disgrace. And the other one, Sister Imobilis, or "the Mob," was always in a red rage anyway, and she'd probably just beat them to death—or at least until they begged to die.

Maureen started to stumble after Perry and Carleen. Just as she was heading up over the stairs marked Private, that guy, Fox—Carleen's sister's friend—stopped her.

"Are you all right, little one?"

"What?" Maureen was totally flustered.

"Are you all right?"

"Oh no, no, I'm good," Maureen said.

"Where are you going?"

"I'm going to find Carleen."

She tried to push him aside.

"Perry said upstairs is off-limits to everyone. That's his apartment." Fox put his hand under her chin and put his face close to hers and in a not unkind way said, "No exceptions."

"But I'm her friend and I need to see if she's all right."

"She's fine, she's with Perry. Sit down. Have a drink."

And Maureen thought, *Yes, a drink. Maybe it'll help me think and give me a bit of courage to get up over those stairs and get Carleen out of there.*

"Can I buy you a drink?"

"Sure," said Maureen, trying to be as nonchalant as possible. "I guess, I got nowhere else to go, might as well."

"Well, gee. Don't put yourself out on my account."

"Oh! No, no, no . . . sorry." Now she was going to have to worry about him, how she might've hurt his feelings or something. "Sorry, sorry. Sure, sure—I'd love to have a drink."

"Okay . . . ," Fox said. "What'll you have?"

"Well, what are you having?"

"A Quebec beer."

"All right, that's what I'll have too then."

"Yea," said Fox, "they're called 'mighty beers.'"

It was the first time she'd ever had one of those Big Tallies, Quebec quart beers. She didn't really like it. Bill, Maureen's father, always called beer "old bellywash" and that's what it tasted like to Maureen, too. So to get rid of it fast, she decided to chug it. Buddy,

Fox, seemed impressed with her chugging ability, and Maureen, who always longed to impress, longed to be the best at something, anything really, kept at it, steadily gulping back the beer that Fox kept buying for her. Soon, she found herself in the centre of a group that was encouraging her and chanting, "Chug! Chug! *Descendez un!*" Before she knew it, she was loaded. It occurred to her that she hadn't seen Carleen in a while, and then, just as she had the thought, there was Carleen, sidling up to her, looking sheepish or embarrassed or something.

"Perry wants you to come upstairs."

"Okay . . ."

"He . . ."

"What?"

"Perry, he wants"—Carleen could barely look at Maureen—"*it.*"

"It? What *it?*"

"*It*, it."

"Jumpins, Carleen! What do you mean he wants *it?*" Maureen said, starting to stand up.

"With the two of us."

"What? What are you—" Maureen was stopped dead by a sudden realization. "Oh God." The heat rose all the way to her hairline. "Oh Christ on a crutch." She was beet-red, she was mortified, and the queer thing was she was even more mortified that she was caught being mortified. But really, she had never, never even suspected for one minute that actual real people would ever be at *that* kind of dirt. A ménage à trois, that's what they called it; Maureen knew that because she'd read it in a Harold Robbins book. She stood up, outraged, and fell back on Fox's lap, stood again and then . . . everything started to spin.

She came to with a splitting headache, a mouth as dry as the Sahara, and the realization that she had no clothes on. She was afraid to find out where she was, but she made herself turn slowly and look, and she saw Fox lying next to her, grinning from ear to ear.

"I'm your first time and you're my first virgin."

"It wasn't my first time," she said angrily, "not by half."

He pulled back the covers to show her the bloodstained sheets and winked at her. Maureen felt herself turn crimson from the tip of her toes right to the top of her head, that same old shame. With the sheet pulled back and her whole body exposed, Maureen's mind didn't have time to feel sorry that her first time had turned out to be so nothing, so no big deal. Her mind was too busy noticing how white and flabby and repulsive and disgusting her actual body was—not just the each gross part, but the totally hideous all-together.

"I was having my period," Maureen mumbled.

She grabbed the covers and pulled them over herself, but then it struck her: the convent. Oh Christ. She had to get back to the convent. Had she already been caught? The choir was singing today at the Place des Arts with choral groups from all across the country.

She leapt up, wrapped in the sheet, and began the tortuous process of trying to get her clothes on without letting the sheet drop.

"Where are you going, Maureen?" Fox said.

"I'm singing. I gotta go. I'm late already."

"You're a singer?"

"No."

"But you said you were singing—"

"Yea, yea, yea, yea, yea," Maureen said, desperately trying to keep the sheet around her and get on her bra at the same time. "But I can't sing really. I'm in a choir. They're going to slaughter me. Our Lady of Mercy girls' choir from home." Maureen couldn't believe she was stuck there answering his stupid questions when she should be back at the convent by now.

At last, she started for the door. She half expected him to say, "When can I see you again?" but he didn't say it. He didn't say anything. That stopped Maureen. He didn't want to see her again? Well, Maureen thought, she'd definitely better make plans to see him again, and so she had to say, "When can I see you again?"

"I'll be at The Rainbow Steps tonight," he said.

"Okay," Maureen said. "I'll be there."

She flew down the street without even knowing what street she was on, her mouth so dry it got in the way of her breathing. She asked the way to the convent and, mercifully, it was close—eight or ten blocks back the way she'd just come. *Idiot, you idiot.* Maureen's mind started in with the same message it replayed all day, every day. *Stupid idiot, how can you be so stunned, you idiot?*

She got back to the convent. The alarm had gone up at breakfast that she and Carleen were missing. So she lied and lied and lied and kept on lying. She said she'd gotten up early; she said she'd gone out to see the sights; she said she'd walked around Old Montreal.

"It was just amazing, and those wonderful little streets, just like being over in Paris, France, or somewhere," she said.

MARY WALSH

She could tell that Sister Catherine didn't believe a word she said, but Maureen could see her decide to let it go for now. Sister Catherine told her to hurry up and go get changed for the concert.

Where was Carleen? God, where was Carleen? Anything could have happened to her. It was Montreal, Sin City. Maureen was frantic. Halfway up the stairs, Sister Imobilis, who was an alarming sight at the best of times with her flaming red wig that didn't even try to pretend not to be a wig, and no eyelashes, no eyebrows, no facial hair of any kind—the girls in the choir had started calling her the Pig with the Wig—stood, wig askew, her anger burning with the white-hot intensity of a thousand suns, stopping Maureen and telling her that Carleen's parents would have to be contacted and that the Montreal police had already been called.

"You are the last person who saw her. She must have said something to you!" she spat at Maureen.

"Promise soul to God, Sister, she never said anything to me."

Imobilis's hand darted out and slapped Maureen hard, right across the face.

"What?" Maureen stammered out.

"Don't you, you dirty, filthy little girl, call forth the holy name of God to back up your sinful lies. Holy God doesn't want your soul, you good-for-nothing little streel. Now get out of my sight."

"Gladly," Maureen muttered.

"What?" Imobilis roared.

"Nothing, Sister," Maureen said as she backed away.

After the concert at the Place des Arts, Maureen went back to The Rainbow Steps. She was in such a rush to tell Carleen that her parents knew she was missing and the nuns had called the cops that she didn't even bother to change out of her stupid navy blue serge uniform.

The bouncer let her in and directed her upstairs. When she opened the door to what she imagined was Perry's flat, she saw what looked like a cross between an office, a warehouse and an apartment, and there sat Carleen at a desk, typing away prettily, looking for all the world like the cat who'd just eaten the canary. She was wearing that big man-sized watch on her wrist. It was Carleen's father's watch, and he'd given it to her for luck before they left for Montreal. Maureen didn't know why, but seeing that watch on Carleen's wrist made her feel angry or uncomfortable or . . . something.

Looking up at Maureen, Carleen said, "What you got your uniform on for, retard?" She didn't wait for an answer. "I'm Perry's secretary now. I'm gonna help him run the business, and I'm gonna live right here, too, and—"

"What? What? You're nuts, Carleen! Your parents are gonna come up here and—"

"I'm seventeen—"

"Sixteen!"

"—and I'm doin' it."

Maureen distractedly picked up a tape dispenser from the desk and turned it around in her hands.

"They are going to skin you alive, Carleen." She looked at the dispenser. It was in the shape of a penis. She dropped it like a hot rock and then looked at the rest of the stuff on the desk. A lot of things were penises, or else they were breasts, or they were shaped like naughty monks with their robes held up by their erect cocks, or nuns with their tits out.

"What kind of business is it that Perry is in?"

"A catalogue business."

"What kind of catalogues?"

"Mail order, sort of porny stuff."

"Porny stuff?"

"You know."

"No, I don't know."

"Jokes, you know, and balls you shove up your bum, and plugs and dildos and all that stuff."

Maureen didn't know what to be more ashamed about: all that stuff or the fact that she didn't even know what a lot of that stuff was. "They've called the cops on you," she said after her face had stopped burning so hot.

"I'm sixteen, the cops can't do anything. I'm allowed. I'm starting my real life now, away from all that bullshit."

Maureen looked at Carleen helplessly.

"Look, I know for a fact that no one is gonna let you get away with living your 'real life,' so you might as well come back to the convent with me now."

Carleen sat there like a rock, unmoving and unmoved. Nothing Maureen said shifted her. When Maureen picked Carleen up underneath her arms and dragged her physically toward the door,

Carleen went limp and let herself collapse to the floor, but still Maureen kept dragging her. Then Carleen started to laugh and said Maureen was tickling her, and she was laughing so hard that Maureen got nervous.

Her mind went back to when she and Carleen were sitting in the auditorium at Our Lady of Mercy Convent, watching the movie *A Tale of Two Cities*. At first, they were just sitting there, bored stiff, talking, saying the movie was a real dweeb-fest, but then they found themselves sucked into the emotion of it, and by the time Sydney Carton was taking other buddy's place on the guillotine and saying, "It is a far, far better thing that I do, than I have ever done . . . ," they found themselves sobbing uncontrollably. They were so moved by his love and devotion to Lucie Manette that the both of them were inconsolable and crying and sobbing so hard that when they looked at each other, they laughed at how foolish they were being, and they laughed so hard, they started to cry again.

The crying and laughing went on right through the credits, but then Maureen started to slow down. She wiped the tears from her eyes, hiccuped, coughed and tried to catch her breath. But Carleen was still really crying in earnest, big air-gasping, heart-broken, gut-wrenching, chest-heaving sobs that just went on and on until she flipped and started laughing hysterically again, and then in a blink, she was sobbing, then laughing, then sobbing. She was switching faster and faster between crying and laughing and laughing and crying, and finally, Sister Mary Virginia had to deal with what was from then on referred to as "the incident."

Maureen stopped trying to drag Carleen out of the apartment, and Carleen just got up and went to sit behind her new porny desk again, looking at Maureen defiantly.

"Well, I'm going then," Maureen finally said from the door.

"Well, go on then," Carleen said.

"I mean it, Carleen. I'm really going—back to the convent."

"Yea, all right."

"I'm just going to leave you here, all by yourself."

"Yea, but I won't be all by myself, will I? I'll be with Perry."

"Okay, but they're calling the Montreal cops."

"Let 'em," Carleen said.

Maureen opened the door.

"This is your last chance, Carleen."

"Okey-dokey," she said, not even looking up.

"I mean it, come with me now or . . ."

"Or what?"

"Or . . . don't," Maureen said, finally resigning herself to the fact that there was nothing she could do.

After "the incident," after Sister Virginia took Carleen out of the auditorium, Maureen didn't see Carleen again until she hesitantly visited her on the seventh floor of the Grace Hospital, the psych ward, where they kept Carleen for a full month. Maureen only visited once and that was in the first week. She always meant to go back, she really did, but Carleen was in a ward with a whole bunch of crazy women—well, Maureen couldn't say for sure that they were crazy, because she was so afraid to look at them, afraid she might see something that she'd never be able to un-see, and afraid that once she clapped eyes on crazy, really "locked-up crazy," she'd just naturally go crazy herself. So that day at the psych ward, she kept her eyes firmly on Carleen, who looked different, altered, dozy, not like herself, not like the Carleen who played Simon & Garfunkel's *Sounds of Silence* and Gershwin's *An American in Paris* and Aaron Copland's *Appalachian Spring* over and over and over again until she almost wore the records through.

It was Maureen who'd discovered the Gershwin and Aaron Copland albums. She'd read about them in America's Teen-age Magazine, *Seventeen*, in a music column that had been squat in between a long "Facts about Your Bosom" article and "Posture Pointers to Make You Prettier." She and Carleen had found the records and loved them and, even more, loved that they loved them. It made them feel so grown up, so above the fray, so sophisticated, to be listening to music that was almost classical; they were not just a couple of teenyboppers grooving mindlessly to VOCM's top-ten hit parade.

But now this person, the one lying so listlessly, so limply, in the psych ward, was not the same Carleen at all, not a bit like the Carleen who always "died" at that Lenny Bruce album, the one with a picture of him having a picnic in a graveyard. *The Sick Humor of Lenny Bruce* it was called. This new Carleen was lying there unable or unwilling to be interested in much of anything. Maureen only stayed a few minutes, and she never managed to make it back there. She didn't know why, and she always felt so bad about it. She knew that no true friend would ever do that. Something about Carleen had always made Maureen feel a little bit ashamed, like Carleen wasn't good enough. Not that she wasn't good enough for Maureen—she was more than good enough for Maureen—but what would they think of Carleen, especially now that she wasn't just odd but certifiably nutty? Carleen's weird, crazy, unpredictable self, Maureen knew, would not be good enough for them, the all-knowing, all-seeing, all-powerful them who always sat in judgment and whom Maureen was always trying to live up to and please.

After leaving Carleen at The Rainbow Steps, Maureen went down to the Park of Islands all by herself because she hadn't even been to Expo yet. She managed to see the big Imax thing, which was . . . well you know, it was big and all, but then again, so what? In the Czech pavilion, while Van Morrison was singing "Brown Eyed Girl" over the loudspeakers and big, fat, humiliating tears were pouring down Maureen's face, she thought, *Here I am, wandering around, standing in line at this stupid world's fair, all by myself,* and a guy caught her eye and sidled up to her.

"My brown-eyed girl?"

"I got green eyes, actually."

He smiled at Maureen.

"Well," she explained, "hazel . . . so there is brown in there, technically speaking." She continued, though she didn't really want to: "Kind of a shitty brown, not that warm, velvety brown that people go cracked for, you know, the whole swim-in-the-pool-of-your-eyes kind of brown, I was just . . ." She couldn't seem to stop talking.

"The song," he said, "I really like Van Morrison."

". . . I would love to have brown eyes and brown skin as well," Maureen went on, as she wiped the tears from her eyes. "And for all my freckles to just magically melt together and become a deep tan, or . . . I'm probably talking too much, am I?"

"Yea."

"I like Van Morrison too," Maureen lied. She'd never heard of Van Morrison, but now she was going to buy all his records.

"Wow, are you wrecked?" the guy said to Maureen. "Do you think it's time to have another draw?"

"Yea, okay. Let's have another one."

And with that, Maureen had her first-ever toke of hash.

Laughing, laughing, uproariously laughing at everything. The world was a funny old place. Then they were walking, and then they were at his place. And buddy was all over her. *Well, I already did it last night*, thought Maureen. *Who am I to deny someone something they so obviously, so alarmingly and so desperately want?* Maureen didn't feel she had the right to deny anyone that. She didn't feel it was her place. So, she thought, the best thing at this point would probably be to just keep giving it away now that she was ruined anyway and they seemed to want it so much, to want her . . . so much—well, the use of her body anyway. *I mean, it would be mean just to keep it, wouldn't it?* And so she and the Van Morrison buddy just did it, but of course Maureen didn't let him touch her or anything in any of "those places." Maureen thought that because "it" was a definite mortal sin and doing "it" was so dangerous because you could get knocked up and your life could be totally over forever, so in a way just by doing "it" you were already being punished, or potentially being punished anyway. And since almost everything that went along with doing "it"—French kissing, intimate touching, even dry humping, someone had told Maureen—was, according to the Church, a mortal sin, Maureen figured why pussyfoot around? It was definitely more valiant, more courageous, to just let buddy stick it in, get the deed done, commit the big, dangerous sin and move on. From what she could tell so far, doing "it" involved no pleasure whatsoever, so it stood to reason, if there was no pleasure and there was great danger and, on top of that, it was kind of disgusting and grunty, she was probably already paying for the sin right here on earth, so why would she have to burn in hell for eternity for doing something that was so grody anyway? *I would love to know, though, what all the big fuss is about*, Maureen thought. *Just more bullshit*, she guessed. She'd never actually, to that point, heard the term "foreplay," but she knew she was against it—against it ever since Mr. Kearsey . . . Maureen didn't let her mind go there. It was all bad enough.

The guy from Expo fell asleep. She lay there for what seemed like hours, bored out of her gourd and a bit sore. This wasn't what Maureen had had in mind at all when she dreamt of the worldly delights she'd enjoy in Montreal. *This can't be it, just lying here in the cold on a dirty old mattress on the floor, next to someone I don't even know.* She crept out of bed and dressed and made her way on foot through Old Montreal to The Rainbow Steps on Crescent Street. She wasn't giving up on bringing Carleen back to the convent with her.

CHAPTER TWO

THE ONLY PERSON SHE RECOGNIZED AT THE RAINBOW Steps was that Fox guy from last night. *Oh shit!* thought Maureen. *Now what am I supposed to do? What about if he wants to do "it" again? Am I obliged because I did "it" last night with him? But then I'd be doing "it" with two different guys on the same night—the absolute height of slutdom.* Though Maureen felt ashamed, she also felt kind of elated, because, after all, if she was going to leave virginity, holiness and goodness behind her, she might as well do it with a bang—*two bangs in one night, actually,* Maureen's mind interjected.

She asked Fox to go upstairs and get Carleen for her.

"Can't. She's not there."

"She's gotta be there," Maureen said.

"No, they're gone up to Perry's other bar up on Sherbrooke. Why don't you sit down, take the weight off your feet and have a drink with me?"

What weight? Maureen thought. Was he calling her fat? God, he'd actually seen her actual gross body. Yuck.

"No, I've got to go. What's the name of the bar?"

"Le Parc," Fox said. "But sure, I can drive you up there after. Why don't you . . ."

Maureen didn't even reply, just tore out of The Rainbow Steps and practically ran up to Sherbrooke Street. She dashed back and forth, looking for the club. When she finally found it, the barman said that Perry and some little dolly had already left. Maureen ordered a drink. For a moment, it seemed the bartender was not going to serve her, or was going to ask for her ID, but the moment passed and he put a rye and ginger in front of her.

After a lot more to drink, Maureen ended up with two old farts from the bar, at a party in Westmount. Maureen had never seen a house in such a state: mouldering newspapers were piled up as high as a person, and when Maureen touched one of the drapes, it crumbled in her hands; it was rotted through. *Everything here is rotted through*, Maureen thought, or she just felt—she really wasn't capable of thought anymore. She had so many feelings and they were bumping around, banging up against each other, and some of them were so big she thought she might explode if she didn't . . . if she didn't have another beer and . . . *Oh my God, Carleen! Where was she?* She'd left Carleen in trouble, in the arms of an old perverted wholesale pornographer who wanted to do it with the two of them—*ugh, oh God.* Then she was upstairs on some mouldy old bed, in the arms of some mouldy old guy who was lying on top of her and wheezing in his sleep.

☠

WHEN THE BUS FROM THE AIRPORT DROPPED MAUREEN off at 17 Princess Street, the door was locked. She banged on it. Her mother came to the door, yelling, before she opened it.

"Jakey Young is at number 7."

Jakey Young was the bootlegger. Princess Street used to be full of bootleggers one time, but now there was just the one left, just poor old Jakey, blind since he was ten from drinking moonshine from a Javex bottle.

"Mom, it's me, Maureen!"

The Sarge opened the door. "Keep your voice down, for Christ sakes! Himself is passed out in the front room. Don't you go upsettin' that hornets' nest today."

Maureen tiptoed in, dragging her suitcase behind her. She stood there in the hall, looking at the Sarge.

"Well, can't you even ask me how it went?"

"All right, I'll play your foolish game. Let me ask you, Maureen, how did it go?"

"Jumpins, Mom."

"Well, how was it?"

"All right, I suppose."

"All right? Well it cost enough, you gallivanting around the world and leaving me here, dealing with that." She pointed to Maureen's father, who was sprawled across the chesterfield. "Not to mention Kathleen. And Raymond got me drove half-cracked. Go on up and see her—oh, she's gonna have a fit when she sees ya. She knew you were comin' home today. Oh, she's a cruel fool, Kathleen.

I told her, though, not to dare set foot out of that room till you got here or I'd cripple her."

Maureen went up over the stairs and into the room she shared with her older sister Kathleen. Kathleen was twenty-five but she was retarded. "Retarded when it suits her," their mom used to say. "She don't miss a trick, and if crucifying and mesmerizing and old fuckery was any kind of skill that was worth anything at all, Kathleen would be worth a fortune. She'd be on the cover of the *Fortune 500*."

Kathleen came lunging at Maureen. "I made it for you, Maureen. I made it, I made it, I made it myself, I made it for you. Here! Here! Here! I made it! I made it!"

"Okay, okay, that's great! Thank you!"

It was a little tiny picture of some trees and a blue sky crayoned on the back of a butcher's bill from Halliday's Meat Market. They always got their meat from Halliday's, including the T-bone roast they had every Sunday, which was "expensive but worth it," Maureen's mother used to say, because "it was quality and she knew quality." She'd been a cook at the City Club and at the Newfoundland Hotel before she "threw her life away for that big drunken galoot and his pack of snot-nosed youngsters."

"But we're *your* youngsters too, Mommy! We're your youngsters too!" Kathleen used to say when they were little.

"No, you're not. You've got nothing to do with me. I don't know what hole your father helped you crawl out of, but you never crawled outta me. You're not mine, not even Raymond, who's the best of ye. Come over, Raymond," she said, pulling him down on her lap. "Mom's little pet rabbit. What does he want to be? Mom's pet rabbit, Mom's pet hen or Mom's pet trout?"

"Mom's pet rabbit," Raymond would say. Maureen could still feel her heart come up in her throat and her eyes begin to fill up with tears of rage at that. God, Maureen hated Raymond. He got away with everything because the Sarge loved him. They were all the Sarge's, every last one of them. There was only Maureen and Raymond and Kathleen left home now. The rest of them were living away, in the army, down in the States, up in Ontario, so there was just the Sarge, Raymond, Kathleen, Maureen and, of course, Maureen's old man, who was now in passed out on the chesterfield. William "Bill" Brennan, worked Longshore. At one point, he told Maureen, everyone in the middle of town worked Longshore. Now the union members were dwindling, machines were off-loading cargo and he said he felt like a dying breed. Shure the city had already torn out half the centre of town, torn down Tank Lane, half of Carter's Hill, Brazil Square gone, a lot of New Gower, even the other half of Princess Street. Though Bill was the union steward, he complained often that his heart wasn't in it and cursed the day he'd left the silversmith his mother had gotten him apprenticed to when he was thirteen, for the paltry sum of one dollar a month. He was young then and wanted more money, and he knew he could get it working Longshore or shipping out on the salt fish and rum trade boats. Bill told Maureen that in the old days in the centre of town, the men would go down to the harbour at six in the morning and come home, walking up over the hillsides, for a second breakfast at nine o'clock, and you could watch them if you were up on Long's Hill or Cabot Street, a wave of working men, a steady stream, watch them climb the hills, climb up from the harbour to their breakfast. But that was all gone, Bill said, and it wouldn't come back again. Bill still had the traditional big khaki-coloured Longshoreman's winter coat with the special pockets that the Sarge had sewn in so that he could bring home "found" items from the wharf: loose tea, dishes, good biscuits, car wax, sometimes pockets full of fresh crab. Lots of times, his big rubber boots would be loaded up with flasks of rum.

Bill never said much except when he was loaded, and then he wouldn't shut up. The Sarge had no time for Bill and treated him even worse than she treated the youngsters. She knocked him around, hit him, smacked him. A couple of times, she took his shoes and burned them. She just generally treated him like dirt, and Maureen, Raymond and the rest of his youngsters followed suit. One time, the Sarge burned Bill's one good suit of clothes when he made the mistake of going down to the Ritz Tavern after she told him not to go. Maureen and Raymond were outraged, but they didn't say anything—they didn't want the Sarge to turn on them. For days, they couldn't even look at their father, they felt so bad, but they never did say anything—they didn't want to be caught out loving such an obvious loser. That time, even Kathleen seemed leery of listening to her father or even of being in the same room with him when he started going on about rounding the Cape of Good Hope, or saying, "I've been everywhere . . . Mozambique, fuck it, Madagascar, fuck it, there's no place like Newfoundland." Seventeen Princess Street was a house divided, with most of the house living in fear over on the Sarge's side and Bill left standing all by himself on the other.

Oh, but Maureen loved her father. She knew he was boring and old and drunk and useless and a dirty big bastard and no good for nothing and an old fool—all the things that the Sarge called him—but there was a picture of him when he was young and in the Merchant Navy, and he'd been heart-stoppingly handsome. Even though she was careful not to be caught talking to him when he started in on one of his all-night stories, a part of her longed to know the full story of the time the Captain gave Bill and the crew a quarter of a bottle of rum as they were rounding the Horn—"One tot per day per man"—and about the time he ended up on a Greek tramper because he got drunk and missed his boat in the Mediterranean and he was six months at sea and nobody else on board spoke anything but Greek. But she never let on that she felt that way, because she'd never want to face the Sarge's scorn.

Her mother roared out at her up over the stairs, "Sister Catherine called. You're thrown out of the choir. I knew that was gonna happen. See, I said that. Shure you can't sing. You can't sing for Christ sakes. Anne was the only one of ye crowd who could carry a tune, and shure that was only when she was drunk."

As her mother walked into the room with Maureen and Kathleen, she added that Sister Catherine had said that Maureen was lucky to be just thrown out of the choir and that she'd only made it into the choir by the skin of her teeth.

"Sister said your behaviour in Montreal was shocking. What did you do?"

"Nothing. I never did nothing. Shure Carleen, she never even came home."

"I never asked you what Carleen did; I asked you what you did."

"Nothing. I stayed out late one night. That's it."

"You got thrown out of the choir for that?"

"Yea, you know what the nuns are like."

"They wouldn't throw you out of the choir for nothing."

"Mom, the nuns? Remember? Suck up and kick down? If I lived up on Circular Road and not down here on Princess Street, I'd still be in the shaggin' choir. You know that! You know what they're like!"

"You always got an answer for everything, don't ya," the Sarge spat at her, but Maureen could see that she'd gotten to her. She'd seen her face darken at the mention of the suck-up-and-kick-down Sisters of Mercy.

"Well, you're as good as any of that crowd on Circular Road," the Sarge muttered as she walked out of Maureen's room. "Hurry up and get unpacked out of it."

CHAPTER THREE

ON SEPTEMBER 5, MAUREEN WENT BACK TO SCHOOL, and if going back to school without Carleen there wasn't bad enough, it turned out that the Pig with the Wig, Sister Imobilis, was her new homeroom teacher. Maureen knew this year was going to be a real drago dragini.

It was only the first day and already Imobilis was up on bust. Maureen started to feel kind of sick during first period, Religion. She tried to get Sister Imobilis's attention so she could go to the bathroom, because she was definitely going to hurl. Finally she was forced to make a dash for it, but Sister Imobilis grabbed her by the arm, twirled her around, and then . . . that was it. Maureen barfed everything she'd had for breakfast right down the front of Imobilis's stiff, white wimple. Maureen was sent immediately to the Prefect of Discipline's office. She sat there in the office with the eagle eyes of Sister Virginia, the Prefect of Discipline, focused directly on her. Good God, she was practically boring holes in Maureen's skull. Maureen was in the blood sweats she was so nervous.

Maureen finally said, "I couldn't help it! I never did it on purpose. I just felt right sick and then Sister Imobilis wouldn't let me go and I had no control over it. I mean, it's not like I want to be throwing my guts up in front of thirty-seven girls and onto the Pig with the—I mean Sister Imobilis!"

Sister Virginia, deliberately and without speaking, took Maureen's wrist, found her pulse, looked directly in Maureen's eyes and said, "What did you do last night, my child?"

"Got ready for school, S'ter."

"Do you know any boys, Maureen?" Sister Virginia asked calmly, looking at Maureen so intently that Maureen felt even sicker. She was terrified she might hurl again. She could feel all the blood in her body rushing up to her face. "Why is your pulse quickening my child?"

"I don't know, Sister," Maureen said, but thought, *Because you are terrifying the crap out of me, you heartless old bat.* She felt herself getting swept up in that nameless swirling fear that threatened, on an almost daily basis, to swallow her whole. She felt her heart leap up into her throat, tears filled her eyes and a flood of water pushed and burned just behind her pupils. *Oh no!* She panicked. *I can't cry! If I start crying now, I'll never stop.* So she began systematically shutting herself down. She knew she was getting that look on her face, that stubborn, stupid, vacant look that so enraged Sister Virginia and pretty much every other grown-up on the planet who'd had to look at it. This time, it worked in Maureen's favour, though, because Sister Virginia was so angry she stopped taking Maureen's pulse, which was a bit of a relief anyway.

"Maureen, tell me the truth: Are you in trouble with God?"

Maureen looked back at her blankly.

"Are you in trouble? Have you committed the sin of impurity? Impure thoughts? Words? God forbid, deeds?"

Maureen just sat, stubborn as a rock.

"Young lady, know this: you are going to sit there until you give me some answers."

So Maureen sat there.

At 3:15, Sister Virginia finally let her go, but she insisted that Maureen be back in her office at ten to nine the next morning.

When Sister Virginia opened the door of her office to her the following day, Maureen immediately and without any forethought whatsoever threw up on the floor. Sister Virginia was horrified; so was Maureen. There was orange with red bits and the undigested egg she had had for her breakfast just half an hour ago. Normally, Maureen didn't vomit; she wasn't one of those people. She could usually keep everything down. When she was sick, she just shut down. She didn't empty out from all ends like some people, and so this new letting go, this opening up, this quite literal spilling of her guts was shocking to Maureen.

Sister Virginia manoeuvred her around the vomit, sat her in a chair and buzzed for Mr. Martin, the janitor. When he came in, Maureen automatically stood up, and she found herself more embarrassed by the standing up than even by the throwing up. Our Lady of Mercy Convent girls were supposed to stand whenever priests entered the classroom or auditorium or even the gym, and since priests were usually the only males who were ever seen,

Maureen just automatically stood up whenever any man came in the room.

Sister Virginia snapped, "Sit down, Maureen, for pity's sake. Thank you, Joseph, if you could just take care of this for us."

"I'll just be a minute, Sister," Mr. Martin said.

He came back in with the bucket. Sister Virginia and Maureen sat in uncomfortable silence during the long process of getting Maureen's insides off the floor, and it was only after Mr. Martin had sprinkled that red stuff, that special janitor's absorbent stuff on the floor, and swept it up and withdrew, that Sister Virginia spoke.

"Maureen, my dear, physically . . . do you feel any different?"

Maureen just sat there, still stubbornly determined not to speak. Sister Virginia sighed and looked at her almost with pity, and that look really worried Maureen.

"I fear, Maureen, that your immortal soul is in grave danger, my dear, and you have started down a path of sin and sorrow off which you may never have the spiritual strength to stray."

Maureen looked at Sister Virginia blankly.

"Maureen, how many mornings have you thrown up?"

Maureen met Sister Virginia's gaze and suddenly she knew. *Of course . . . I'm up the duff, knocked up. I'm up the stump. Montreal. Oh shit, oh no! Montreal.* She felt a deep sense of shame and thought, *Oh shit, I am fucked in so many ways. I don't even know who the father is. It could be that guy Fox or the other fella or that old guy. I don't even know their names.*

"I'm afraid that you will have to leave school."

"But," Maureen protested, "I'm only in Grade 11, Sister. I . . ."

"I will contact your parents."

"Oh no, Sister. Please, please, let me tell them." She almost fell to her knees, but she could see from the look on Sister Virginia's face how useless her begging would be. *Okay then*, she thought, *I'll just have to kill myself, I guess, but I don't even have a gun or drugs or anything. I am so useless, I don't have any way to kill myself. I can't cut myself—I'm too afraid. I'll just jump to my death off Signal Hill.* It was settled, then. Before Sister Virginia would even get a chance to tell the Sarge, Maureen would be washed up, dead, at the foot of Signal Hill and everybody would be devastated. A young girl cut down in her prime, in the flower of her youth. Everyone knew it was better to be dead than to be pregnant. It was way better to be dead than for everyone to know that you were nothing but a slut and a loser and a lizzie too probably on top of that. And that's what they'd call her, because once they started calling you a slut, they automatically called you a lizzie. Maureen didn't know why.

"Gather up your things and go home now, Maureen, and may God have mercy on your immortal soul."

Maureen looked at Sister Virginia. "Did you say 'and may God have mercy on my immortal soul,' Sister?"

"No, my dear."

Maureen knew she was lying.

She stumbled down the corridor, unscrewed one of the emergency lights and smashed it in the waste bin just for old times' sake. She tried to beat the door off her locker so no one else could use 321 ever again, but she attracted the attention of Sister Mary

Monique from Room 207, who came out and asked Maureen if everything was all right.

She was such a sweet nun that Maureen almost caved for a second, almost sought the solace of falling sobbing against Sister Monique's enormous bosom, a set of knockers so huge that even the starched white wimple could not hide them. It was said that her own mother had predicted that Sister Monique would either have to join a convent or have breast reduction surgery because her breasts were that big, those were the only two options open to her. When Maureen had heard the story, she'd quipped, "Or become a famous stripper like Chesty Morgan or Watermelon Jones," and ever after, every time she clapped eyes on Sister Monique, Maureen had a disturbing vision of seeing Sister Monique peeling off her habit in the most provocative and cheesy way. Today was no exception.

"Stupid door on the stupid locker is stupid stuck, Sister! Stupid!" Maureen said, hitting the offending door with each "stupid."

"Well, keep it down to a quiet roar!" said Sister Monique, rolling her eyes as she stepped back in her classroom and firmly shut the door.

Maureen flew out the front door and almost ran into Dicey Doyle and her friend Sam—two-thirds of the Three Musketeers. Dicey and Sam were laughing uproariously as they sailed down the steps of Mercy Convent to freedom. The girls were going on the pip, and they somewhat grudgingly invited Maureen to join them.

The first time Maureen had gotten in tack with the Musketeers was on the steps leading down from the basilica one Sunday

morning as she was escaping the end of 12:15 Mass. According to
the Rules of the Mass, you could get away with coming into Mass
as late as the Gospel and tear out of there right after the Conse-
cration of the Host and still manage, just by a hair's breadth, not
to commit the mortal sin of missing Sunday Mass. That Sunday,
Maureen had ducked out and was racing down the basilica steps,
thinking how they were too narrow for two footfalls but really too
wide for one—weren't there any step rules? Weren't they supposed
to be standardized? Wasn't it kind of dangerous for them all to be
different widths? Maureen was working herself up into a bit of a
fit about how half-assed city council was, when she almost banged
right into a girl, a tall girl with coal-black hair, who was standing in the middle of the steps, smoking what looked to be a rollie.
Maureen had never seen a girl smoke a rollie before, and this girl
was spitting loose tobacco off her tongue. She was wearing a black
trench coat, pegged Newfoundland tartan pants, black short boots
and a white turtleneck. Maureen had never clapped eyes on anyone
decked out quite like that before. Newfoundland tartan pants?
Pegged? Short boots? Nobody wore short boots anymore, not since
people stopped wearing Beatle boots. It was all so wrong, but on
this girl, it was all, somehow, so right, right and true. It turned out
her name was Dicey—well, really her name was Patsy Anne, Patsy
Anne Doyle, but her father used to call her Dicey when she was
little because she was always so thirsty and drank so much milk,
she was just like the Old Woman in the Irish song who drank too
much, Dicey Riley. The name stuck.

That morning on the steps, Dicey, of the small mouth and the crooked teeth and the great big brown eyes, had a bruise on the side of her face, which she made no attempt to hide. She'd been up on Signal Hill, parking—"car-free parking," Dicey said, "all the fun with none of the expense," and laughed. Maureen laughed too, just to be polite. She had no idea what Dicey was going on about. Dicey must have read the confusion in her face.

"You know, how everybody goes parking up on Signal Hill?"

"Yes," Maureen said, but she didn't really know.

"Well, me and Roger went parking—without the car. Kind of 'grassing' really . . . Yea, we were having a fight and he pushed me and I fell right down over Signal Hill."

Maureen was kind of horrified at this news, but Dicey seemed almost proud and shrugged off her trench coat to show Maureen the scrapes and cuts on her arms and shoulders. On her upper arm, cutting into the generous amount of flesh she carried, there was a huge, thick copper bracelet—a slave bracelet, Dicey called it, saying an old boyfriend had gotten it for her. Dicey offered Maureen her pouch of tobacco and rolling papers, and Maureen about died of shame as she clumsily tried to roll a cigarette. Dicey rolled one up for her using just one hand. Watching her do it, Maureen's gob was well and truly smacked. Dicey finished off by striking a Sea Dog strike-anywhere match on the back of her heel and lit up Maureen's rollie for her. Dicey lived just over the road from Maureen on Bell's Turn, and Maureen couldn't believe she had never before run into this extraordinary creature. Was it because Dicey went to Presentation Convent, the other girls' school, which most of the girls in Maureen's neighbourhood attended? Maureen had never understood why she had to go to Mercy Convent. All her other sisters had gone to Presentation. The Sarge said that the five bucks a month they had to pay for Maureen to go to Mercy Convent meant that Maureen was getting the best quality of education, but with the same breath, the Sarge would mercilessly torment Maureen, accusing her of putting on airs and thinking herself above everybody else just because she went to Mercy Convent. The Sarge called Maureen "the five-dollar-a-month girl." But it turned out Dicey went to Mercy too. She was a year older than Maureen, but still Maureen couldn't believe she'd never met her.

That Sunday morning on the steps, Dicey asked Maureen if she wanted to come down to her house. Dicey, her sister, Sharon, and her mom and dad lived in an apartment on Bell's Turn, and after that first morning, Maureen tried to spend as much time as she could there, drinking Mrs. Doyle's tea, which was kept going in a pot at the back of the stove all day long. It was so strong, it was thick. That tea and a cigarette made Maureen sick every Sunday morning, when, for the rest of that year, she went to the Doyles' instead of going to Sunday Mass, thus damning her immortal soul for eternity. Maureen thought it was worth it. Mrs. Doyle was so nice. She had short white hair and looked just like what you thought a mother should look like. Mr. Doyle went to sea and only came home every fortnight. Whenever Dicey had a little cough, he would give her and whoever was with her a sip of London Dock, the 140-proof rum he was so fond of. Dicey and Maureen were always coughing in the most unconvincing way, but Mr. Doyle didn't seem to mind and always gave them a sip of rum anyway.

Sam Fleming and Sara Browne were Dicey's friends and they called themselves the Three Musketeers. By association, they kind of became Maureen's friends too. Sam, Sara and Dicey were the kind of girls who hitchhiked to all the grown-up dances up the shore in Kelligrews, Manuels, Long Pond and out at Power's Court, where there were always rackets. They even hitched as far as the street dances out in Brigus. A couple of times, they hitchhiked out to Gander—two hundred miles away—where, they told Maureen, they'd done nothing except eat a plate of chips, dressing and gravy and turned right around and hitchhiked back to town the same day. Maureen thought them amazing, but she was a bit afraid of them too. They were so tough and fearless and always blazing some new trail, leaving Maureen stumbling along after them.

The day Maureen was thrown out of school, she, Dicey and Sam walked down to Water Street and started trying to hitchhike to Mount Pearl. They were headed out Waterford Bridge Road when they got a ride with an old, fat, creepy salesman type, who kept on with the "I suppose lovely young ladies like yourselves wouldn't be interested in an old fella like me?" following on the heels of "Sometimes us old fellas fool ya. We're all go, you know what I mean." He actually turned his head and gave them a nod and wink when he said "full of spunk."

"Okay," said Dicey, who, as the biggest and fiercest-looking of the Three Musketeers, often led the charge, "that's it. Let us out here. This is where we're going."

"But sure," fat, old and baldy persisted, "I didn't mean nudding by dat. Spunk—life, energy."

"STOP THE CAR!" Dicey screamed at him. "Stop the fucking car and let us the fuck out!"

They'd only gotten as far as Bowring Park.

"You sick old fuck!" Dicey screamed after the car.

"Full of spunk," Sam said, outraged.

"Spunk," Maureen said, and she almost giggled until she remembered what she was actually full of—the consequences of spunk—and her heart fell. *Spunk! Spunk! Spunk!* It was an extraordinarily funny word if you said it often enough.

When they finally got to Mount Pearl and piled out of the car they'd hitched a ride in, they ran into Spider O'Rourke and Spook Wakeham. The boys had just bought a car up in Holyrood for fifty bucks, a real shitbox with the floor in the front passenger side gone and no seat in the back. Dicey and Sam got in the back and Maureen ended up in the front seat. She had to keep her feet up on the dashboard and was scared to death to look down through the hole in the floor at the road that was careening by underneath. Spider drove them to the dump where everybody from Mount Pearl went parking at night. But it was early afternoon, so they had the place to themselves. Just as they got there, the junk-heap car sputtered out and nothing that Spider or Spook could do would make it sputter back in again. Maureen, without being fully conscious of how she got there, ended up on the hood of the stalled and useless car with a ball-peen hammer she'd found in the trunk and was beating in the front windshield while Dicey and Sam were smashing out the back window, and Spider and Spook were banging up the doors. It was glorious. The whole time they were at it, Maureen forgot all about her predicament. She had never felt so alive and so a part of something—all of them working together, lifted up and out of themselves by their united act of destruction.

When they'd finished smashing the car to bits, they hardly knew what to do. They were suddenly uncomfortable and shy; they were having a difficult time looking at each other. Something made them want to get away from each other—it was like they'd been too intimate, too close, too open to each other or something. And so, not talking at all, they walked out of the dump, across the Experimental Farm and back down to Park Avenue, and the girls left.

When Maureen walked in the door, a shoe hit her over the head—not a stunning blow, but it hurt.

"What, Mom! What?"

"Dicey's mother called me. The principal called her. Ye weren't in school today. Out curb-crawling, were ya . . . ," she went on, but Maureen just zoned out. She was still safe; the Sarge hadn't got the call yet from the Prefect of Discipline. Sister Virginia was giving Maureen a chance to tell her parents. Just as she had that thought, the fucking phone rang. Maureen knew right away it was Sister Virginia. Now the shit was really going to hit the fan.

Maureen's mother stopped the "we're not running a whorehouse" attack just long enough to answer the phone. Maureen stood there, trapped like a rabbit in the headlights. There was nowhere to go, nowhere to hide. It was all coming down, and coming down fast. She started up over the stairs but thought better of it. What was the point? They'd come up too. So she just gave up and sat on the stairs, waiting for the inevitable shitstorm. It came. All her father said was "Well, there's not much point in locking the barn door after the horse is out"—this after her mother had called her all the big whores in the book and swore that Maureen would never step outside the door again.

That night, Maureen went to bed and dreamed and dreamed and dreamed, first of smashing cars and then of bulldozing St. John's, driving everything before her into the sea. In her dream, she was full of rage, nothing stopped her and the more she destroyed, the more joy she felt, and so she rose up in her dream, full of beauty and destruction and swollen up with life, but when she woke in the morning and looked around the crummy room in her crummy house on the crummy street on the edge of the crummy world, Maureen just wanted to go back to sleep and keep dreaming her dreams of destruction. She heard her mother's footsteps and pulled the covers over her head and pretended she was still asleep.

"Don't think, my dear, just because you got yourself knocked up and thrown out of school that you're just gonna lay there in the bunk all day, doin' nothin'. Get up outta that bed and get down over them stairs." She hauled the covers off Maureen.

"Jesus, Mom, what are ya doin'?" *You old bag, you big bitch, you ugly, syphilitic old whore* . . . All those names, all those bitternesses were going through Maureen's head, but she dare not, of course, breathe a word because the Sarge would kill her. That was a certainty. She would actually kill her, not just beat her within an inch of her life, but totally beat the life right out of her. The fact that

Maureen was carrying a new life would do nothing to stop her.

"Go down to Water Street and don't come back to this house till you got a job of work."

Well, at least she'd be out for the day and not home listening to the name-calling and the screeching and the bawling and the tears and the recriminations and the hatred. If Maureen's life were a TV show, Maureen's TV mother would blame herself, go all weak in the knees wondering where she'd gone wrong, say if only she'd loved Maureen more. Then she'd tearfully embrace Maureen and say she'd always love her no matter what, and everything would work out for the best in the end. Unfortunately, they didn't make any TV shows in St. John's in 1967 except, of course, for the news; and no stories of knocked-up sixteen-year-olds whose lives were totally fucked, never to be unfucked again, ever found their way onto NTV or CBC News. Oh, if Maureen didn't feel so mad, she might lie down and weep and never, ever get up again.

That day, she got a part-time job at The Agora, a discount place downtown, locally owned, full of stuff that had been bought at various fire sales in Montreal. That's what she felt like too, like she was the victim of a Montreal fire; she would fit right in. But, of course, she didn't. All the girls who worked there were that hard crowd who could—magically, it seemed to Maureen—see right through her tough act and see that she liked books and thought way too much of herself. They could see that even though she felt she was worth nothing, she still thought she was better than all of them, and she could tell right off the bat that they were going to set her straight on that little misapprehension. She pretended to the owner, Mr. White, whom she'd convinced to give her the job, that she was still at school and could only work Thursday and Friday night and all day Saturday. She would have gone for a full-time job, but Mr. White had assumed from the start that she was looking for part-time work and that's what they needed, part-timers, so she went along with him. *Will that old cunt*—oh God, she couldn't believe she'd even thought that word, the ugliest word in the entire English language; she would never, ever think that word again—*will the Sarge want me to get another part-time job or is one enough to shut her up for the time being?*

The Agora—a pretentious name for a dump. Maureen started off on the floor of the ladies' department, tidying and folding bins of cotton bras by size and colour, black, white and beige. God, how mortifying Maureen found it to be out in public, touching over-the-shoulder-boulder-holders. And even more humiliating to have the actual boulders stuck on your very own chest, poking out at the world, always just a B-cup step ahead of you. Folding up those bins of bras was kind of like the myth of Sisyphus: no sooner would Maureen have one bin tidied and in good order when a flock of Portuguese sailors—"the Gees," that's what the girls on the floor called them—would descend on it and, in a flurry of looking for bras to fit their wives and girlfriends back home in Portugal, would totally obliterate all of Maureen's careful folding work. The Gees were generally not popular at The Agora. Maximum mess for minimum spending—and they smelled on top of that, you know, exotic, like different kinds of cigarettes, Maureen thought, and different food and, of course, fish. Good God, the dreaded smell of fish. The entire island was up to its neck in the stink of fish, and everyone worked overtime trying to get away from it and at the same time pretend it wasn't there.

"The wife. This one," said one of the older Gees, holding a white cotton bra to his chest, the bra with the butterfly inset under the breast. Just being in bras made Maureen want to break out in boils, let alone having to watch some guy pretend to wear one. Breasts, boobs, boobies, knockers, gazoombas, jugs, hoohas, tits, titties—good God, even the words were like some big advertisement of shame.

Mrs. Lee, the head of the department, spoke loud and slow, as she did to all the foreign sailors, like they were deaf as well as stunned. "How big is she, your wife? Is she a big woman like me, or small, like you are?" After a few more bawls at him, the Gee held his hands out in front of him, way out in front, making the universal sign for big tits.

"Oh my," said Mrs. Lee, "that's big! You'll probably have to find somethin' up in Yard Goods, in the fabric department, to fit her!"

Every Thursday and Friday night, and all day Saturday, Maureen worked at The Agora. Nobody said anything about her getting bigger. Everybody who worked at The Agora got fat eventually anyway—blown up from sadness, Maureen figured.

Three months after she started working there, the management took the doors off the toilets, and that meant that when the staff, who were 99 per cent girls, were sitting in their lunchroom, having their bite to eat, they had a full view of other girls going to the toilet. Management said it was to cut down on the girls stealing pantyhose and underwear and whatnot.

Though the morning sickness had passed, just the thought of having to gawk at someone else going to the toilet made Maureen too queasy to even go into the staff lunchroom. So, on her break, Maureen had to sit at the public lunch counter, where, through some weird alignment of the stars or something, there happened to be another Maureen Brennan, working in the snack bar. This one was from Torbay, big-boned and raw and graceless. Three times a day, people thought Maureen was her. Maureen was shattered. Okay, so she had always been "a big girl for twelve," granted, but she had a certain . . . *Oh, I don't know*, Maureen thought. Even though she was ashamed to think it, she still thought, *I don't look . . . poor, not like this other Maureen, with that raw look and her big hands and feet and her big, strong, thick upper back and neck, almost like she was built especially to haul a plough through the fields. I've got long legs, and my ankles are quite delicate. I do have little, sort of meanish eyes and a thin mouth, but overall I have a good bone structure, big cheekbones and a strong-but-not-too-strong chin. I definitely do not look like that other Maureen Brennan. No, not one bit. I look destined for better things. Yea, destined for better things, like bringing another little bastard into a world already rotted out with poor little bastards and straightening out bins of bras that have been flung about by poor, stinking sailors—poor Portuguese sailors lost in a foreign land, where no one remembered anymore that the Portuguese led the Age of Discovery and that their great explorers had opened up the world. But now the world has left them far behind. They're no longer the Kings of the Sea, but just the butt of some shopgirl's contempt.*

One night, while lying awake, unable to get back to sleep because now, in the second trimester, with her belly as big as it was, it was getting harder and harder to find a comfortable way to sleep, she had a thought come to her out of nowhere: she'd do something about what management was putting the girls through in the lunchroom. Maybe she'd make some cartoons. Of course, she wasn't what you'd call a natural cartoonist. For one thing, she couldn't draw, and on top of that, she didn't really think in a cartoony kind of way. She tossed and she turned and she finally went down to the front room. Dad's paper, *The Telegram*, was there. She turned to the editorial page and saw a cartoon of a guy in a prison cell. He was skinny, done in, and he was counting off, with strokes on the wall, his time left in prison. Maureen found a big sheet of tracing paper in Raymond's bookbag and traced out the cartoon. She wrote, "In the Agora lunchroom," put a few strands of hair on buddy's head and replaced the caption with "Only three more minutes before lunch break is over." She did all that again, and she was going to do it again, but she'd used up all the paper and couldn't find any more. Sometimes paper was hard to come by in the house on Princess Street, and it was hard to find a pencil or a pen, never mind something like a sharpener. Always with a big kitchen knife, that's how they sharpened their pencils. One big knife was pretty well Edna's only household tool. It served as a hammer, screwdriver and beer bottle opener and was driven down into the top of the can of milk to make the two holes. It cut the bread, it buttered the bread and it could usually be found stuck in an industrial-sized jar of jam in the middle of the table. Of course, it was also an excellent

MARY WALSH

weapon. It should have its own K-tel ad on television: The Amazing Big Knife, the household tool that can be put to any use. They could even use it to chop wood if they had to.

There never was a pair of scissors in that house. They had a lack of everything and a glut of nothing. Of course, they never had anything like glue. The covers they made for their school books were stuck together with canned Carnation milk, so their books always smelled like sour milk, and no, this was not the life Maureen wanted, not now, not ever. She wanted art supplies. She wanted the kind of house where the mom put up a pencil sharpener, like a school one, in the kitchen. Some people even had desks in their rooms and "oh mind out you don't swell" books. Maureen's father had the odd book. Sometimes he'd just stay in bed days on end and read Louis L'Amour or books with pictures of big four-masted ships on the covers, coming down over the stairs to get something to eat before going right back up. He wouldn't even go to the bathroom, just piss in an empty Captain Morgan bottle. He'd buy second-hand paperbacks at John D. Snow's. Maureen used to go with him to Mr. Snow's store when she was little. Mr. John D. Snow was pale, the palest kind of pale, even his lips had no colour. His hands were dry and papery, and he had no hair, no discernible lips and definitely no eyebrows. The store was toppling with junk, endless paperbacks, glass bottles, old bits of mouldy clothes, broken lamps. Nothing in that store seemed to have any colour. Maureen believed that Mr. Snow had somehow sucked the colour out of everything—even himself.

Maureen's mother read too—Harlequin romances mostly.

Maureen remembered her mother sending her to the drugstore one September when Maureen was small, far away from the house, Ricketts' drugstore. *"Success to Private Ricketts, our gallant native son, he proved himself a hero, the Victoria Cross he'd won. He was only a boy from Newfoundland . . . "* Maureen couldn't remember the rest of that song, but it was about buddy who owned the drugstore. That day at the drugstore, there was money left over and it was the Sarge's birthday, and so Maureen bought her mother a Harlequin romance. The woman in the drugstore wrapped it up nice, and when Maureen gave it so proudly to her mom—yes, admittedly, she was a bit puffed up, but she was only seven years old, for Christ sakes—all Edna said was "A birthday present? Shure you bought that outta the change from the money I gave ya. What kind of a gift is that?" Maureen had mistakenly thought that giving her mother a birthday present would make her happy, but when it came to her mother, Maureen realized very early on that she didn't have a clue. She was endlessly trying to figure her mother out. She twisted herself into knots trying to become whatever it was this terrifying mountain of flesh called Mom wanted her to be.

"Maureen, Reenie, Reens . . . Whaddya at?"

Maureen almost jumped out of her skin. Kathleen was standing at the bottom of the stairs, rubbing the sleep out of her eyes and talking loudly in a stage whisper.

"Shh . . . SHHH! You are gonna wake up the whole house. Shhh . . . Look. I am drawing a cartoon—look!" Maureen whispered at Kathleen.

"Let me draw. I can draw." Kathleen sat down next to Maureen on the chesterfield, picked up a pencil and started to colour in or scratch out—Maureen wasn't sure which—one of the two cartoons Maureen had managed to trace out. Maureen made a grab for the pencil, but Kathleen just held on. "Let me draw. I'm the one who draws. Let me!" she said, grabbing the tracing paper from Maureen's hand.

Maureen lost it. She yelled at Kathleen—something she'd done a lot when she was younger but something she had promised herself she'd never do again. "What's wrong with you, you moron?"

Kathleen was crumpling up the paper.

"Look! You're ruining it, just like you ruin everything. I just spent an hour on that. Here, give it to me."

As Maureen grabbed to take the cartoon back, the flimsy piece of paper tore in two.

Maureen was yelling, Kathleen was crying, and then there was the Sarge, barrelling down over the stairs.

"What in the Joe Jesus is going on down here? It's three o'clock in the Christlyfied morning and you've got all hands . . ."

Kathleen kept crying. Maureen didn't care. She'd already gone so far, calling Kathleen a moron—something she'd sworn she'd never do again—she figured she might as well just keep going.

"IT'S NOT ME, IT'S STUPID ARSE. She just wrecked something—I was down here working on something. Why can't I ever have anything? Why does she have to wreck EVERYTHING?"

The look on Kathleen's face stopped Maureen in her tracks, and she reached out and put her arm around her sister, drawing her close. The Sarge was still going on at her. "Shure you were always half-cracked, Maureen, but now with that youngster coming, you're worse than ever. Up all night, in the bunk all day—the whole house up on stilts. You're liable to do anything. You should be locked up is what you should be."

"Yes," said Maureen, smiling at Kathleen. "We should all be locked up in a big family-sized rubber room, where we can't do damage to ourselves or to each other."

I am so sorry, she mouthed at Kathleen.

CHAPTER FOUR

SHE NEVER EVEN GOT IN TROUBLE ABOUT THE CARTOONS she put up, the protest cartoons, which just showed how effective they were. She spent the next two months working at The Agora, but by April, she was too big to work, and so big that even the Sarge didn't say anything mean to her, which was alarming in and of itself—how different had this new monster body made her?

Bill borrowed a car from the union steward on the Longshore, and after giving her one of Edna's Miltowns, they told Maureen they were just going for a ride up around the bay and would maybe stop to get an ice cream cone in Furey's in Holyrood. Of course, that should have made Maureen suspicious, but she was so fat and so uncomfortable and so swollen up with the baby, she didn't say anything. She laboriously got herself into the back of the car and somehow failed to notice her already packed hospital overnight bag being put in the trunk. When they sailed past Furey's, Maureen was truly taken aback. They took her out to the Carbonear cottage hospital, where Maureen's dad had been born, brought into the world by the famous Dr. Young. They told Maureen that she was being taken to the hospital in Carbonear to have her baby, and that all the arrangements had been made. The way Edna said "arrangements," the set of her jaw and the hard looks she kept giving Maureen let her know that the fantasy world she'd been living in for the last couple of months—where she'd hoped and even prayed that Cuba might launch a nuclear missile that would hit directly on Princess Street, or that she'd die down dead before she reached nine months, or that the house would spontaneously combust and all hands would succumb to smoke inhalation, or, most ridiculous of all, that she would get to keep the baby, who would be brought up by Edna and Bill—was just that, a fantasy, and it was never going to be anything else. Arrangements had been made to give her baby away.

Maureen cried the whole way from Furey's in Holyrood all the way to the hospital. She couldn't stop. Of course, she knew that no one in their right mind would want the Sarge to be the mother of some poor innocent baby—and what help had Bill ever been to any of them?—but better the devil you know. How could she let the baby go, even though she'd prayed for its disappearance day after bloated day? But it was her baby; she'd been growing it, and, for the past month, growing it was all she could manage. She had spent days just sitting there, a huge mound of pulsing, throbbing, kicking, growing life. She was on a train where there was no getting off. She was a huge, ever-expanding blob of non-thinking. She was too big to think; all she could do was hope. She just hoped senselessly that everything would work out. Part of her wanted Edna and Bill to keep the baby, but part of her wanted the whole thing to have never happened, that somehow, magically, the last eight months had been a dream and that, through some sorcery, her life would go back to normal, and the baby would . . . Her mind wouldn't let her go any further down that road, but now it was obvious that the Sarge and Bill had already, without ever talking to her, made their "arrangements" and that the baby, her baby, was going to be taken from her. She knew that in some secret, unknowable part of herself, she had been longing, right from the beginning, for this baby, because this baby would love her the way she wanted to be loved. She couldn't stop crying—all the way through Bay Roberts, Clarke's Beach, Spaniard's Bay—though she knew that no amount of begging or crying or effing or blinding was ever going to change their minds now.

"My dear, you've got to stop crying. Your water'll never break," her father said. "Shure you got no water left in ya *to* break, you're after cryin' it all outta ya! Stop! Stop now! You're just gonna make yourself sick, Maureenie!"

"THIS IS KIDNAPPING!" Maureen screamed from the back.

"This is happening for your own good," said Edna. "Yes, that's all you need now—and you a little bit of a thing—is a youngster hanging off ya. Shure you're as wild as a billy goat already."

Before Maureen drowned in a pool of her own tears in the back seat of the borrowed car, they arrived at Carbonear hospital and Maureen met the great Dr. Young. Bill's people had been in service to the famous Dr. Young's crowd. Maureen's Gran was the house-keeper, and her Poppy, Ambrose, had looked after the grounds for the Young family, and that left Bill feeling like he was a serf and that

Dr. Young was the lord of the manor, and when you were a serf and you had a problem, you could bring that problem to the seigneur, and that's what Maureen's parents were doing now: bringing her, the problem, to Dr. Young, who was so old he looked like he was barely alive. But he had gone ahead and set up the whole adoption thing. The baby would be taken by a couple from up on the mainland.

Maureen's mother explained, "They're doctors, maybe both of them, or maybe a doctor and his nurse, and they'll know how to look after a little infant baby better than some chit of a child like you, 'cause let's face it, Dr. Young, she can barely even look after herself."

Since Edna had first found out about the pregnancy and had gone mad for a day or two, this was the most she had ever said to Maureen about the baby. Though someone was always talking on Princess Street, no one ever really said anything—not about anything that mattered anyway. Nothing was said about Bill's drinking, or about what would happen to Kathleen, or about Edna's hysterical cruelty, which exploded daily around their house like shrapnel, or about Maureen and the baby. Not that Maureen ever broached the subject herself. She was as cowardly as the rest of them, fearful of what someone might say to her, or even worse, what she might say to one of them.

"A baby . . . havin' a baby," her mother kept saying over and over and over again until Maureen finally screamed, "STOP IT!" They gave her an epidural and then put her on a drip. They asked her to count back from ten. Maureen was saying, "But I don't want to be drug . . ."

☠

MARY WALSH

At some point, Maureen dreamed that she came to—or maybe she actually did come to—and saw a nurse take a swaddled baby, a baby with a shock of flaming red hair, out of the room. When she really did wake up, her mother and father and old Dr. Young were at the foot of her bed. Her father, who she knew really resented Dr. Young, was standing next to him, all smiles. Bill practically had his forelock tugged right off his head. Maureen took this in before she opened her mouth and started screaming.

"For the love and honour of God, keep your voice down! Don't mind the child, Dr. Young. She's just, well, you know, she's been through a good bit," Edna said, giving the doctor her best servile smile.

Maureen kept screaming. Dr. Young, without batting an eyelash, bent down and smacked her hard across the face, which, of course, had the desired effect and immediately shut her up, but not for long.

"Where's my baby? Where's my baby? Mom, what have you done with my baby?"

"Now, Reenie, you gotta put all that old nonsense behind ya. Doesn't she, Dr. Young?" Maureen's mother had on her wouldn't-say-shit-if-her-mouth-was-full-of-it voice, giving the old doctor ingratiating nods, grateful smiles and apologetic looks. "Now, Reenie, you got a chance, a chance to start over."

"WHERE'S MY BABY?" Maureen screamed.

"And that's what you're gonna do, isn't she, Dad?" the Sarge continued, totally ignoring Maureen's screams, and smiling and nodding toward Dr. Young. "That little baby is gone on to a better place, Maureen."

"What? My baby's dead?"

"No, foolish arse. It's gone up to the mainland somewhere with its new mommy and new daddy, who will take good care of it." Again, the phony smile for Dr. Young.

"It? It? What did I have?"

"Shure what odds what you had, it's done now, over and done with, and as soon as you're healed up . . . 'down below' . . . we're going back home. Now, say thank you to Dr. Young. Go ahead, say thank you to the man who helped you out. Even though God alone knows you don't deserve any help."

Maureen's mother was forgetting she was in the presence of the great Dr. Young. She was forgetting her mommy act and was talking more like her real self.

"WHAT DID I HAVE?" Maureen screamed.

"Shure you're out beatin' the street all hours of the day and night like a common slut, up there in Montreal at the Expo, welcoming flags of all nations. I suppose God alone knows what it is you had."

"It's a baby, Mommy."

"Yes, a baby, and good riddance to bad rubbish."

"Keep your chin up, young lady," Dr. Young said as he made his way out of the room. "You've got your whole life ahead of you."

Then her mother and father left too, and for the first time in at least the last six months, Maureen felt like she'd been left completely alone. She was empty—but emptier than just not having the baby inside of her, empty in a way she didn't understand. She didn't know how she was going to go on now. The last few months had been all about the baby and now the baby was gone—gone out of Carbonear, if she could believe her mother, gone off the island of Newfoundland, gone . . . she didn't know where. How was she ever going to find her baby again?

PART II

PART II

CHAPTER FIVE

MAUREEN DIDN'T BOTHER TO GO BACK TO SCHOOL THE September after she'd had the baby. There didn't seem much point to it; her life was over anyway. Everyone knew she'd had a baby, and you might as well just say everyone knew she was a "good-for-nothing slut" and just get it over with, and if they were going to go around treating her like a slut, Maureen thought, she might as well start acting like one. There was really no point in saying no to anyone now. So Maureen went to see a Dr. Divine on Duckworth Street. She'd heard he'd give you the pill even if you weren't married. He asked her how old she was and then asked what she thought she was doing at her age looking for birth control. Maureen cut him off: "I already had a baby."

It was the first time she'd said it out loud to a stranger, and she thought it would probably be the last time, too, because Dr. Divine gave her such a look—contempt? scorn?—it made her feel as low as she'd ever felt. She tried to brazen it out, answer him back, but even her voice deserted her. Her big, booming, able voice had jumped ship. It was deeply ashamed too, apparently, and so she said nothing, and in the end, he gave her the birth control pills. All he said was "Take these until you have your period."

Maureen kept taking the small, pink pills, but she never got her period. She kept taking them for three months . . . No period. And so, she was sure she was knocked up again. She went to a brand new doctor on Freshwater Road, out near the mall. He gave her an internal, took her pee and called her back to his office after Maureen had put in a few anxious days.

"Apparently, the rabbit lived," he said when Maureen walked into his office.

"What? What does that mean?"

"Oh, it's an old joke about rabbits. They were supposed to die when a pregnant woman's urine was injected into the rabbit's ovaries, but actually, the rabbit always dies when they do that procedure."

Maureen just looked at him. "Yea. Funny," she said flatly. Really funny.

"But when they test the dead rabbit's ovaries, that's how they can tell if you are pregnant or not, and you're not pregnant."

"So why don't I get my period?"

"Are you on medication?"

"Yea." Maureen showed him the disc of birth control pills.

"Well, when you stop taking these, on the twenty-first day, then you should get your period."

"What? . . . He said to just keep takin' 'em till I got my period!"

"Who?"

"Dr. Divine."

"I doubt that, my dear. No, you take these every day until the twenty-first day, at which point you stop, which brings on your period, and after day twenty-eight, you start in again and you should be as regular as clockwork." He spoke to Maureen as if she was an idiot.

"The old bastard," Maureen said.

"I would thank you not to use language like that in this office, my dear. This is a family practice."

Well, imagine that old frigger, Maureen thought as she hitchhiked home. *He didn't even bother to tell me how to use them . . . He had it in for me 'cause I had the baby.* She couldn't get a ride, and she was in by the university anyway, so she stopped into the Spanish Café in the Student Union Centre. She sat down and got busy pretending she was a student at the university and in no way just a loser who didn't even have her Grade 11 and who had a baby on top of that. She tried to sit there like she was her best self, the self she so desperately wanted to be: the quiet, languid, mysterious, enigmatic blond self with perfectly straight hair, no freckles, pale olive skin, beautiful large brown eyes, dressed all in white—not the real Maureen, not the mousy-brown-haired, freckled, brash, fat, big and loud Maureen who was always telling everyone everything whether they wanted to hear it or not. As she made every effort to sit like the Ideal Maureen in her lumpy winter coat, one of the Three Musketeers' brothers—Sara Browne's older brother, Trevor—came by. He sat down with Maureen.

"What are ya doing in here?"

"I'm . . ." She was going to say that she was studying biology in her second year, but then she remembered that Trevor would know she wasn't in school and that she'd only be in Grade 12 at Mercy if she was, and oh Jesus, he probably knew all about her having the baby and everything. No point in pretending. Maureen didn't know what to say then.

TREVOR WAS IN HIS THIRD YEAR OF UNIVERSITY AND WAS part of a frat. Sara's father had given her a T-Bird as soon as she'd gotten her licence, on the condition that she give Trevor rides whenever he needed them, and sometimes the Three Musketeers and Maureen had to share the car with Trevor and sometimes pick him up down at that frat, Alpha Delta Phi. Trevor had a nickname: Bo or something. They all had nicknames at the frat, and they were overwhelming in their confidence, their cute nicknames, even their teeth, for God's sake.

One night, Maureen had gone to the frat with Sara and the other two Musketeers to pick up Trevor, and there was a party on. Everyone at the party seemed to be pretty and grown up and like they were part of a country club or at least played tennis or something, and they were definitely Protestant with that perfect Protestant hair. Maureen was only fifteen then and desperate to look grown up, to look at least eighteen, and she was hoping one of the frat boys would offer her a drink. A short, stocky, shambolic, drunk fella with a blond buzz cut came up to her.

"Jack Dunne," he said, putting out his hand. He then proceeded to roll up his sleeves and say, "Look at that forearm. Pretty massive, isn't it?"

Maureen, trying to be polite and act as a college girl might act—a sorority sister, though God alone knew how *they* acted, since she'd never really met one, only read about them in Mary McCarthy novels—thought the best thing to do was to just agree, though really, she could give two shits about his stupid fucking arm size.

"Yes, yes, it is," she said, smiling, polite as cat shit.

"You know how they got that big?" he said.

"Well . . . no, I don't," said Maureen, still smiling, thinking it was something she should know, something that only middle-class girls knew. Should she pretend to know?

"Hauling myself!" the blond flat-head said, laughing.

Maureen, her smile dropping, moved away in utter confusion. What was wrong with her? Why would people talk to her like that? Would they talk that way to Muffy Fitzpatrick or Pinky Doyle or Trevor's girlfriend, Fluff Dawe, or any of the other girls whose very names proclaimed their class and superior position in the dating order? Oh, they had the right names, the right hair—always perfect—the right clothes. Fluff Dawe's mother was said to have knit Fluff fifty-two angora sweaters, all in different styles and shades, in summer and winter weights, one for each Saturday afternoon skate at The Stadium—for both ice and roller skating. All those girls had the attitude too—they truly did seem to feel they were worthy. And why wouldn't they? Their clothes always matched, their leather boots were never spongy with slush, they never had cold sores. Pimples and whiteheads were forbidden to take up residence on their perfect faces, and you'd never see them cut their own bangs. They all lived in around the back of town and couldn't walk to their houses from the school. They had to wait to get the bus and were always accompanied by Davy, or Ronny, or Johnny, or Jerry, or some other highly desirable fella. They always had a boyfriend.

There was a time when Maureen used to wait for the bus even though she lived on Princess Street, which was just down over the hill from the school. She stood at the bus stop alone, clasping her binder with the names Grant or Keith or Joe written in pink nail polish and then marked out, replaced with some other Eric or Rob, not a member of the adorable names-ending-in-*y* crowd, just some non-cute dork Maureen thought she might be able to get to like her. She waited, pretending she lived in on the tree streets, until everyone had gotten on their bus and only she was left after telling everyone she wasn't waiting for the Loop or the Number 10. Sometimes she lied herself into a corner and had to get on Route 2 and ride around until everyone she knew got off. When everyone else had got on their bus, she'd toddle on down over the hill and home to her totally *not*-like-TV-home home, with the Sarge ruling the roost, and her dad half afraid to say anything and Kathleen rushing to the door, her face all lit up to finally see Maureen, saying, "Mo, Mo, Mo, I'm on a diet! I'm on a diet! Mom! Mom! Ask Mom. Mom, I'm on a diet, aren't I, Mom? Mom, Mom, Mom, I'm on a diet! . . . She put me on a diet, Mom did."

Lost in her own thoughts at the frat party, she banged right into someone, a carbon copy of the offending hauler, except his hair was kind of long and a bit blonder.

He passed her a drink and said, "Smile. That's my brother, Jack. He's not all that bad, not once you get to know him."

"I'll take a pass on that," muttered Maureen, but she gratefully took the drink and tossed it back. It burned all the way down, but when it hit, it immediately made her feel a little bit better, a little more relaxed. But it didn't completely take away the feeling Maureen had that everyone could see *her*—the real her, not the her she was trying to pretend she was. Everyone seemed to know that she was no good, that she didn't fit in, and that must be why *they* always managed to find her.

When Maureen was eight, an old man named Mr. Kearsey befriended her. He lived by himself up the road from their shack in Tors Cove. A lot of men who worked Longshore, like Maureen's father, had fishing shacks up around Tors Cove or Mobile and they'd go there for part of the summer, but Mr. Kearsey was from Tors Cove and he lived there all year round. He was really, really old and really nice. He had been part of the 1914 Great Newfoundland Sealing Disaster, when all hands were trapped in a storm on the ice and seventy-seven men perished. Mr. Kearsey wasn't even supposed to be aboard the *Newfoundland*, but he had missed his own ship and ended up on the ice without proper clothing. He had had even less to keep him alive than most of the other men there but, somehow or other, managed to live against all odds.

Mr. Kearsey was Maureen's friend. They'd walk up to the pond to go fishing just after supper; you'd see them any evening, walking up the road hand in hand. Then one night, they were watching TV in Mr. Kearsey's front room—Maureen and them didn't have television in the shack—and he touched her under her underpants. Maureen knew it was a very, very, very bad thing, but at the same time, it felt good, and Maureen knew somehow that *that* was the worst thing, that it felt good. She knew she was a very, very bad girl doing a very, very bad thing, and yet that very, very bad thing made her feel good. She stumbled home that night and never spent any time alone with Mr. Kearsey again. But she could remember how sick with shame that good feeling made her, and so Maureen made a vow that she would never, if she could help it, let herself feel that good feeling again. And though she constantly broke pretty well all the promises she'd ever made to herself, for some reason or other, she kept that vow.

Just remembering all that, Maureen blushed to the roots of her hair there at the Student Union Centre.

"What's wrong?" Trevor, or Bo, asked her. "You're as red as a beet."

"Hot flashes," Maureen said, not thinking. Bo laughed and then Maureen laughed with him, relieved that he thought she was funny. A lot of times when people laughed at what she said, she was actually being deadly serious, but if people laughed, she'd just go along with them and pretend she'd meant to be funny all along.

"Sara's picking me up in a couple of minutes. We'll give you a ride home if you like," Bo said.

"Sure, great."

Then Maureen didn't know what else to say. It was like she was struck dumb. She just sat there in the blood sweats for what felt like hours, trying to think of something to say, something smart or interesting or engaging. He didn't speak either. He just kept staring at her, so she started looking around the room, but there wasn't much to look at. There were breeze blocks on the wall, garbage on the floor, a drug deal going on at the next table—oops, she shouldn't be staring at that, so back to the breeze blocks. Finally, she couldn't take it anymore, couldn't take the pressure of sitting there with nothing to say.

"Look, I've got to go. I've got to—"

"Sara'll be here in a minute. Sit down, sure."

She knew that if she sat there for one more second . . . Well, she didn't even bother to think what might happen if she sat there. She just couldn't, and so she bolted.

Oh great, now he knows you're a retard, Maureen's mind said.

I don't care. I'm not interested in Bo, Maureen said back to her mind. Fuck Bo. That's what I say. Fuck Bo and the tiny T-Bird he rode in on.

But what if Bo likes you? He seemed interested.

What? Really? Do you think?

Why do you care? You don't even like him.

Well, what difference does it make how I feel? He might like me!

Well, you screwed that anyway, running away like a baby, like a little youngster. You're an idiot. You're so stupid. How can you be so stupid? How can you always be so wrong, wrong, wrong, wrong, so stupid, stupid, stupid, such an idiot, idiot, idiot?

Maureen flagged down a huge Chrysler LeBaron with some old guy in a suit at the wheel. He dropped her off right at her door after the usual leering and lecherous remarks. "You don't mind thumbing a ride, young one like you? You don't know who'll pick you up . . . ," leer, leer, ogle, ogle, ". . . Wouldn't give your phone number"—hand moving across the seat—"to an old fella like me . . . blah blah, woof woof."

Maureen flung open the door when they got to Princess Street and looked buddy right in the eye. "You're right, I'm not going to give a dirty old ram like you my phone number. You can't have my phone number, but you know, I might have given you a blow job if you asked me."

She laughed at the look of shock and hurt on his wrinkly old face. Old fellas like him went around like horny old goats, but if a woman, especially a young woman, said anything about sex, well, it'd leave them breathless. Horny old hypocrites. Finally, the voice in Maureen's head shut up for at least a minute.

WHEN MAUREEN RAN INTO BO AGAIN, HE WAS LIVING IN A bedsit on Gower Street with a whole bunch of guys and one girl, an extraordinary girl, Freda. Freda was from Montreal, had short hair and big eyes, drove a motorcycle and wore a motorcycle jacket. She looked like a beautiful lizzie and, most astonishingly to Maureen, didn't, for some unfathomable reason, care that she looked like a lizzie. How Maureen longed to look more like Freda and not like the pasty-faced Princess Street brat that she was. Bo used to go out with this motorcycle-riding, rebellious beauty. She was from some prominent Quebec family; her name was the name of some legendary French noble family like the Bourbons or Huguenots. She was in all ways extraordinary, and Maureen quietly grew to hate her.

She would actively look right past Freda every time they met. Not that Miss Big-eyed Beautiful Motorcycle Rich Bitch ever noticed. She was cold and haughty and always held herself aloof. Maureen hated those qualities in a person, especially in a woman. But, oh, how she longed to have those qualities herself and embrace them on a daily basis. Outwardly, Maureen tried as best she could to be polite, friendly, chatty and girlishly full of cheer—full of shit, really, because Maureen hated everyone. She'd just as soon get aboard a bulldozer like in her dream, start in back on the tree streets and drive everything ahead of her right into the harbour, knock every-thing down, demolish the whole works, lay the whole fucking thing to waste, all the time smiling that phony smile and saying with that high, bright voice, "Hiii, Freda, love your boots! . . ."

That day, Maureen was walking past the house Bo lived in, when he leaned out a window and called down to her, and then there he was, standing on the street in front of her, and before she knew what was going on, he had wordlessly swept her up in his arms and was carrying her up over the stairs as Van Morrison's *Astral Weeks* blared out of someone's stereo on the ground floor.

He threw her onto the bed . . . and then . . . But, as usual, "it" was awful. Of course, everything around "it" was fabulous. It was so extraordinarily romantic to be swept off her feet and carried up over the stairs. How wonderful that the decision was out of her hands. How delightful it was to be just ravished. But then, ulti-mately, "it" was so unsatisfactory and disappointing—dispiriting in a way. She didn't let him touch her, which didn't really seem to bother him, and in his defence, neither had it seemed to bother any of the other young fellas she'd let fuck her. Bo seemed to be quite carried away by the excitement of it all and came quite loudly. Maureen just copied what he did, and tried to breathe like him. At one point, he said, "You're breathing heavy—you are a hot little girl, aren't you?" Maureen was embarrassed and wanted to explain, "No, I'm just breathing along with you," but then she thought she'd just keep her mouth shut and go along for the somewhat painful ride. She made what she thought were the appropriate noises, and he seemed well satisfied. He rolled off her, lit up a smoke and looked the very picture of smug contentment. They started living together soon after that.

CHAPTER SIX

Bo got *ESQUIRE* AND *TIME* MAGAZINE IN THE MAIL. Maureen read them cover to cover. He almost had his B.A. He read the *Gormenghast* trilogy and books by Carlos Castaneda and Ayn Rand. All of them were impressive to Maureen, but she found them almost unreadable. It was not the kind of writing that Maureen had ever been exposed to, and she imagined that it was worldly and scholarly. Maureen thought she didn't like those books because they were too smart for her. Later on, she realized she didn't like them because she didn't like that fantasy stuff, and nobody past the emotional age of ten could actually read and take Ayn Rand seriously. But when she was living with Bo, she didn't think she had the right to say what she liked and didn't like, because, let's face it, she was damaged goods. That's how she felt after she had the baby—that she was ruined, that she was finished, that her chances of ever becoming that idealized girl were gone for good. So for Maureen to even have a boyfriend, let alone a boyfriend who had a car and almost had a degree, who read all the right books and seemed to be on the fringes at least of the totally cool crowd, was WOW. She was just so grateful, really, to have anybody, not to be shunned, cast out, cast aside. Just to get in out of it, out of the aloneness, and finally be paired up, she almost didn't care with whom, as long as it was with someone.

That first Sunday and almost every Sunday after, Bo took Maureen out to his parents', out to Paradise, for dinner. Not real Paradise—they weren't dead, just living up in Conception Bay South, in the town of Paradise, which was not the least bit paradisal. Bo's mom, Mrs. Browne, looked like a sweet, small, girl version of Bo but with all the lights turned out. Vera Browne (née Nichol) was Scottish and a war bride and had married Bo's father, Art Browne, when Art was overseas serving with the Newfoundland Foresters. Vera was an orphan from Gorbals, who, against all odds, had gotten a scholarship to the University of Glasgow and received a Bachelor of Science. But because of the Depression and the general lack of tolerance toward girls with Bachelor of Science degrees, she had to go to work at Pringles department store in management training, and that's where she met and fell in love with Art Browne. It must have been the Foresters uniform, Maureen came to think, because what else besides a smart uniform would have been attractive about the arrogant blowhard, the paranoid know-it-all with the short temper and the long wind.

The first Sunday Bo took Maureen to meet his parents, Mr. Browne flirted with Maureen about her long legs and said he'd always been a leg man. Maureen, pleased to get the attention, really liked Mr. Browne—until they sat down at the table and he boasted long and loud and made much of the fact that he was having lobster while the rest of the family was left having to share a measly chicken.

"It is only right," Mr. Browne said. "I'm the man of the house after all, and I bring home the bacon—or, in this case, the lobster." He laughed. "I deserve it, don't I?" He turned to Bo and challenged him to say different. "Don't I, Trevor?" Bo muttered his ascent and looked down at his plate, but Mr. Browne wouldn't let him get away with that. "Speak up. What, are you afraid in front of the new girlfriend, are ya? Don't let yourself be whipped, boy. Now, what do you say?"

"Yes," Bo muttered again.

"What? I can't hear you."

And he kept at that until Bo, in a rage, stood up from the table and yelled out, "YES."

"Sit down. Pull yourself together. You got to learn how to take a ribbing and stop getting hysterical like a little girl." And then he winked at Maureen, and she felt sorry for Bo having to grow up in the shadow of that man. She almost said something, but Sara, also over for Sunday dinner, grabbed her hand, squeezed it and begged her with her eyes not to open her mouth. Mrs. Browne listlessly pushed the food around on her plate and didn't say anything.

After dinner, Maureen was helping Mrs. Browne clear the table, when Mrs. Browne, laughing, turned to Maureen and said, "Awright, Maureen? When I married Mr. Browne, you know, I was so excited about moving to the New World. I thought I was going someplace like New York—maybe even somewhere better." All this was said in a very thick, what Vera called her "Glaswegian," accent.

"Art's family were from a little wee place called Open Hall in Bonavista Bay, a heart-stoppingly beautiful place, but a good ways back from the back of beyond." She put her hand over her mouth and said, "Oh, don't let Art hear me say anything against Open Hall. It's the Browne natal seat and must only be spoken of with solemnity and respect."

She giggled. Maureen could see she was nervous. Bo came in then. He looked with suspicion at his mother and Maureen laughing. Later, Maureen understood that Bo was the type whose first thought if he heard someone laugh was that they were laughing at him. Vera waited for him to leave, but Bo stubbornly stayed in the kitchen, and so with some hesitation, Mrs. Browne continued to tell Maureen how she got from the slums of Glasgow to Paradise.

"When I got off the wee boat in 19 and 45, aye, it was '45, in St. John's, I thought I'd reached the end of the known world, but no, far from it. I still had to board the wee train and ride that all one day to the town of Trinity. But I still hadn't gone far enough, and it took two dog teams, tearing through the frozen tundra, until I finally reached—"

"And you never really got over it, did ya, Mom? She's been half-cracked ever since," Bo said.

"Get off Mom's back, will ya, Bo," Sara said, coming into the kitchen and putting her arm around her mother. "Don't mind him, Mom. Since he's going for his B.A., he thinks his shit don't stink. Yea, B.A. from MUN—that's the two little x's you put after your big X when you sign your pogey cheque."

"Go fuck yourself, Sara."

"Oooh, touchy."

The smile had left Mrs. Browne's face and she was back to drying the dishes. She didn't have much else to say for the rest of that Sunday.

On the drive back to the apartment, Bo told Maureen that his mother was often in and out of the mental. Nobody really knew what was wrong with her. They kept changing her meds and hoping for the best. But she seemed to be getting worse.

"Worse how?" Maureen asked.

"I don't know. She wants to be dead all the time or something," Bo said, not taking his eyes off the road. "They are going to try shock treatment on her."

Maureen had read Kesey's *One Flew Over the Cuckoo's Nest* and was terrified to think of little Vera being put in a vegetative state like Ellis or one of the chronics. But when Maureen said as much to Bo, he got mad and said they might as well shut up about it because there was nothing they could do anyway.

Bo was often mad at her and Maureen hardly ever knew why. She started to suspect that he didn't really like her, especially when she talked or if she was feeling emotional about something. The first time Maureen got drunk with Bo, she went on a crying jag about the baby, and he just got up and walked out, leaving her there in Chamberlains. Maureen had to hitchhike home by herself.

A few days after that Sunday dinner, Mrs. Browne went into the mental, and three Sundays passed before they went back again for dinner. Maureen couldn't believe what she saw: all of Mrs. Browne's front teeth were missing. There had been some kind of accident during the electroconvulsive therapy. From then on, Maureen very rarely saw Vera smile, even when they were alone in the kitchen, even after she had gotten a new set of "choppers," as Art called her oversized false teeth.

Maureen asked Mrs. Browne why she had let them go ahead with the shock treatment. Vera looked at her, her eyes dull, and said, "I needed it." But later on, after she made sure that Mr. Browne was in his room with the door closed, she told Maureen that in the late 1950s, the doctors and Art had felt that a frontal lobotomy might do the trick. "But I had just enough spark left then to stop them."

Maureen thought Mrs. Browne was amazing. Despite everything, she was always taking night courses at the university, she spoke six languages, and she somehow continued to survive around that house, quiet as a mouse, terrified to disturb Art in any way.

CHAPTER SEVEN

ONE DAY, ALMOST A YEAR AFTER THINGS STARTED TO GO terribly wrong between Maureen and Bo, Maureen found herself alone in their apartment, and just on a whim, began poking through his stuff. Just snoopin', not looking for anything in particular, no biggie, just looking for . . . what? She didn't know.

"Nosy Parker," the Sarge used to call Maureen whenever she'd catch her going through the stuff the Sarge kept poked away in the trunk room. "Curiosity killed the cat," she'd say, giving Maureen a smack to the back of her head. Yes, Maureen had always been a bit of a snoop. It's just that she always felt safer knowing what other people were keeping secret. She was just looking to see if there was anything she *should* know. Maureen had an abiding and overwhelming fear of not knowing and of being caught out as a fool. Maureen thought that knowing stuff would protect her. "I knew that already," Maureen imagined saying when she found herself humiliatingly taken advantage of. Maureen didn't trust anyone.

Maureen started flipping idly through Bo's bank book. She saw the two-thousand-dollar credit in September for his student loan, the fifty bucks a week his old man paid him to do candy and confectionery deliveries. But where did the three-thousand, four-thousand and five-thousand-dollar deposits come from? Every week, multiple thousands were going into his account. The money appeared just after Bo had started working for DAFT. Maureen's first thought was, *That cheap fucker. There he is with thousands and thousands in his bank account, and he makes me go halves on cheeseburgers out at the Pioneer.* She'd had a pretty good idea, of course, that when he started working for the DAFT crowd, he'd be at it with the rest of them—dealing marijuana and whatnot. But he'd never said anything to her, and though he must have gotten all that money from dealing drugs with the DAFT boys, he'd never really splashed out like the rest of them, with their vans and their leather coats and always throwing dope, and lately even coke, around everywhere. Bo still lived like he was making fifty bucks a week. According to his bank book, he was making a small fortune working for the DAFT boys. But even having that much cash didn't make him happy. Only a few days ago, after they had gotten through three-quarters of a bottle of Glenfiddich, Bo was in the bathroom with the door open—he never shut the bathroom door, no matter what he was doing—saying, "I'm too fuckin' volatile to be a fucking partner with that bunch of fuckin' whack jobs? And that fuckin' little psycho Deucey had the nerve to say to me that I was too fuckin' volatile. Volatile? VOLATILE? Fuck them and the boat they're riding out on."

He worked himself up into a red rage. When he came out of the bathroom and stood, totally naked, at the foot of the bed, still going on about how unfair the DAFT boys were, he started to jump up and down with anger, to actually dance with rage. Maureen could hardly breathe, she was so terrified, but at the same time, some secret, small place inside her was laughing—he looked so ridiculous in his frenzied, berserk toddler's flip-out, with his package flopping up and down. "Volatile! I'll show them vola-fuckin'-tile!"

Maureen heard Bo at the front door and quickly put the bank book back where she'd found it.

"Maureen! Reenie . . ."

"Just in the bedroom, Bo." She tried to keep the resentment out of her voice.

"What are we gonna eat?" Bo called out.

"Why don't we go out and eat for a change?" *You cheap fucker*, she added under her breath. She heard him come to the door.

"Jesus," Bo said.

For one terrifying, awful instant, Maureen thought he'd overheard her, but he went on. "I forgot we gotta go in to Mom's. And by the way, did you hear? Deucey's gone missin' and Big Jack is havin' a conniption. Couldn't happen to a nicer pair," Bo said, smiling smugly.

Maureen looked at Bo, concerned. "Deucey? Where is he?"

"Well, how the fuck should I know?" Bo said, turning on Maureen with such rage that she instantly took a step back, hit the desk and almost took a tumble. That made Bo laugh.

"Yea, stupid question," Maureen said. "Of course you don't know. But where do you think he is . . ." Maureen didn't go on. The look on Bo's face put a stop to any further conversation.

CHAPTER EIGHT

Soon after Bo and Maureen had started living together, they went to a party at Roger "Booman" Tate's. It was a kind of big, open warehouse space up over a law firm on Duckworth Street. Maureen was really chuffed to be there at that party with those guys—it felt like she was finally making it, becoming part of the happening, all the peace, love and groovy stuff she read about. If she wasn't so self-conscious and if she'd had a tam, she would have thrown it into the air and sang out *The Mary Tyler Moore Show* theme.

Booman was part of DAFT, a company that started dealing drugs on a small, friendly basis and then got more serious and even started a legit business as a front for their dealing. DAFT stood for Dunne, Albert, Furlong and Tate. The boys were heroes to the local counterculture scene. To Maureen, at that time, they were the closest things to revolutionaries she'd ever seen. There they were, right in the middle of boring old St. John's, living an alternative lifestyle, doing what everybody wanted to do but didn't have the guts to do, setting up their own rules, sticking it to the man, living high off the hog. They were just selling marijuana and that was natural—it grew in the ground, for God's sake, and it was good for you. They—the government and them—just didn't want people to get high. They didn't want people's consciousness to expand, because then everyone would start seeing how foolish and stupid the whole big phony system was, everybody working nine to five, the war in Vietnam, all the oppression and all the vast structures of bullshit it took to keep everyone with their heads down, going into their shitty little offices every day, doing their shitty little stint of meaningless shitty labour, and driving home to the wifey, who was going around in a coma, out of her mind on Miltowns and boredom, and the two and a half kids they were brainwashing, crushing them until they were ready to step up and take their turn on the big treadmill of bullshit. The DAFT boys were boldly and courageously saying, "Fuck that shit!" and starting a new life, a different kind of life, a peace, love and groovy-acid-trips kind of life. It was a fucking shining city on the hill they were building, on marijuana and freedom and equality. Of course, now they were dealing a bit of cocaine, which, according to *Time* magazine that week, was really bad for you and dangerous and rotted out your brain on top of that. But, sure, that's what they said about weed, and that was just lies, so they were probably lying about the coke too. Bo had just started working with them, doing carpentry work, building packing cases—not for dope, he assured Maureen, but to send legit stuff around the country.

The party was packed and loud, and it was the first time Maureen saw whole green garbage bags full of marijuana, and Nescafé jars of cocaine. There were gallons of liquor, and Maureen got drunk, of course. She couldn't find Bo. She went reeling around the loft, but there weren't that many places to look. Turned out he was holed up in the bathroom, necking with red-haired Marina Halley, a girl Maureen had gone to kindergarten with. Maureen physically pulled Bo out of the bathroom, and then there she was at the top of the stairs, punching him as hard as she could in the face.

"Just do that once more," Bo warned her, and so she did. By the end of it, Maureen was at the bottom of two flights of stairs with an eye that was rapidly swelling, handfuls of hair missing from the side of her head and what was feeling like a broken rib. She was on her knees, sobbing, crying.

"Look . . . look what you did . . ."

Bo started to walk away from her, saying nothing. She stumbled after him, desperate for him to acknowledge what he'd done, to beg her forgiveness, to address this unbelievable, unbearable situation. Part of her hoped and prayed that he could change it somehow, make it better, make it go away. He shouldn't be walking away from her, she shouldn't be running after him, but she couldn't just let him walk away, could she? Some attention had to be paid. She followed him back to their apartment on Livingstone Street.

That was the first time he hit her, and of course, it wouldn't be the last. There were lots more black eyes and bruised ribs and rackets every weekend. For a while, foolishly, she thought she could take him, that she had the physical strength, that she could go punch for punch. She wouldn't let herself be beaten down like this. But after a while, she stopped fighting back altogether, hoping, thinking, that would make a difference. It didn't. She tried to give up drinking, but that failed miserably. She tried to control the amount she was drinking, the kind of liquor she was drinking. Beer was all right, but inevitably beer led to whisky, and whisky seemed to drive them into a frenzy of fists. Nothing she tried worked, and half the time she felt too useless to even try. She blamed herself and she kept it as secret as she could. Somebody, the Sarge probably, said, "Once it starts, my darling, it never stops. Why should it? Shure if he got away with it once, why wouldn't he do it again the next time he got mad, even if it's only to prove just how mad he is?"

Lots of times she ran away from him, back to Princess Street. But one night, Maureen's father tried to push Bo out of the house. Bo started pushing back, and then there was Maureen's father on the floor, fighting with Bo. The Sarge broke it up with the help of a broomstick. She called the cops and they hauled Bo down to the station. Maureen went with him, and the whole time she was there, she felt that's where she belonged, and after that, she didn't even have Princess Street to run away to.

The more she lost or cut off ties with her family and friends, the deeper she got into the violent mess with Bo, the more draw the mess seemed to hold for her: she'd spilled blood for this relationship, and she'd lost family—even Kathleen didn't want to see her if she was with Bo. She was too ashamed to have friends and Bo didn't want anyone in the apartment, so this was it: the big love they wrote about, giving up everything for love.

Secretly, Maureen knew she hated and feared Bo. He made her feel sick. More than one person asked Maureen, "The sex must be great though, is it?" That question left Maureen speechless. What were they thinking? Because she was so bloodied and bowed, because there was so much anger and instability, because the violence was so bad, the sex must be good? It was unfathomable to Maureen that the kind of shit-kicking she was getting could be, in some people's minds, the door to pleasure.

Maureen could not think her way out of it, and she could not feel her way out of it. She just wanted to die, but at the same time, she wanted to make Bo pay in some way or at least admit how wrong he was, and she held on to that hope month after miserably unhappy month.

CHAPTER NINE

SOMEHOW, EVEN THOUGH SHE FAILED HER CIVIL-SERVICE exam, Maureen got a job as the assistant to the film-strip librarian at the Department of Education Film Library. Gerry was the film-strip librarian, and he was old, but as old as he was, he didn't really need an assistant for the simple reason that no one ever wanted to borrow film strips anymore.

A cute but dorky guy named George, who was doing a master's degree in English at the university, worked in the film library, humping around those big heavy cans of film, checking them out and restacking them on the shelves when they came back. There was a steady stream of films being borrowed and brought back, but George always found time to hang out in the tiny film-strip library room to talk to Maureen—talk at Maureen, really. He talked at her about Raymond Chandler and Mickey Spillane, about Philip Marlowe, Sam Spade and Mike Hammer. Maureen could not be less interested. She dismissed all those books as penny dreadfuls, mindless pulp, but George was doing his master's thesis on mid-century American hard-boiled detective fiction. He'd say,

"Don't be a bunny," when he meant, "Don't be stupid." He called money "cabbage," and when he referred to Diana Ross, he always called her "the canary." It could have sounded cool, Maureen guessed, but it just didn't. Gerry didn't say anything, but whenever George was perched on the edge of Maureen's desk, talking a mile a minute, Gerry would give Maureen that goofy "oh, he likes you" nod and wink, which managed to make Maureen feel even more low-minded than she already did.

Of course he would like you, said Maureen's mind, *because he's a dweeb and you are like a gravitational force field for dweebs. They cannot resist you.*

At least someone likes me, Maureen said to her mind.

Yea—'cause they think they've got a chance with you. Who else are they gonna like?

Oh, shut up.

Maureen tried to lose herself in restacking the shelves of film strips, which were unmoved and untouched since she restacked them two days ago.

Sometimes, Maureen didn't show up for work. It was a hard job to believe in. There was really nothing for her to do. Sometimes, her bruises were too visible, and sometimes, she couldn't get up out of bed. Bo was working with his father, a wholesaler who supplied Groc and Confs across the island with bars and chips and soft drinks, and Bo would occasionally have to travel out to Grand Falls or Corner Brook or as far as Port aux Basques to make deliveries for his father. Maureen thought that driving a truck full of three-for-a-cent candy—coloured jujubes, green leaves, bananas, jawbreakers,

Bazooka gum—not to mention all those different delicious Vachon cakes—May Wests, Lune Moons, Flaky buns, Jos Louis—would be a job that would lighten the heart and lift the spirits, but Bo often came back crankier and even more unhappy than when he left. Sometimes, on the days he was travelling, Maureen didn't bother to get up at all. She just stayed nailed to the bed for twenty-four hours, rarely eating, just drinking juice, reading, not thinking, staying as still as she possibly could. During those marathon bed-ins, probably from a combination of semi-starvation and not moving for three days (that's what Maureen put it to, anyway), she would find herself in a kind of trance, seeming to have risen above herself and looking down from a great height at her own inert form lying dead still on the bed below, not thinking, not feeling, not planning. Then the two of them, the real Maureen and the Maureen who was watching the real Maureen, would share a moment of, if not peace, at least emptiness.

Then Bo would come home and Maureen would be forced to get up and step back into the thick of that mad and painful storm that had become her life. She was sure that other than choosing to lie there dead to the world, that this life, the life with Bo, was her only choice. She was damaged goods. There was no other life open to her. She had nowhere to go.

SOMETIMES ON FRIDAY EVENINGS, BO WOULD PICK HER UP after work and they would go out to the Pioneer Drive-In and Restaurant, out past Topsail. On those Fridays, she felt like she was normal and that this was what regular people did. He'd pick her up in his little red Renault—*Red for anger, black for death*, her thoughts would chant—and they'd be just like a real boyfriend and girlfriend celebrating the weekend by driving out to the country and having supper, but she was drowning in misery, choking with unhappiness. She was only eighteen—what was wrong with her? Why didn't she leave Bo? She was no good—that had been proven to her finally and irrevocably. She just was no use; she was totally use-less, "a total useless waste of skin," as the Sarge used to call her when she was little. She didn't like to think about that sort of stuff, because she didn't want to emotionally cash in on that whole "my mother was so mean to me blah blah blah" thing. She had no time for *those* dreary sob sisters. She was getting on with her life, not whining and complaining all the time about what her mom did to her. She was moving forward—well, when she wasn't staying in bed twenty-four hours a day, or picking herself up off the bottom of some staircase, or too beat up to do much of anything. When she was drinking, though, just before the racket rose, before she and Bo would take that fatal turn, she'd start snotting and bawling about the Sarge and about her lost baby.

Maureen was afraid that her life without the baby had no meaning. Sometimes she thought that being hit, punched and hated and still holding on gave some awful meaning to her otherwise empty existence. Sometimes, she thought that her pain, her flesh and her blood, sacrificed on the Altar of Love, would somehow redeem everything. But mostly, she didn't think like that. Mostly, she didn't think; mostly, she was just afraid. Afraid of everything—afraid of Bo, afraid of Bo leaving, afraid Bo would never leave, afraid of keeping her meaningless job, afraid of having no job, afraid of the Sarge, afraid of her father, afraid of people in the streets and in the shops, afraid of the baby whom she secretly called Nora, afraid that everyone could see her worthlessness, that it was written all over her.

She was shoplifting like crazy, smashing in the odd window, sometimes pulling a scattered fire alarm, and one morning, letting the air out of all the tires on Riverview Avenue, an upscale area in town. At one point, during a Turtles concert at the Student Union Centre, she even put a big wad of chewing gum into the perfect long blond hair of the girl in front of her. She was so beautiful, thin, ephemeral and spacey, one of "the Vague Sisters"—that's what they called the three Fardy girls. She was the youngest, Leanne, and was dating Wayne Furlong, a member of DAFT. She was everything Maureen longed to be. She loved Leanne's ability to appear uninterested in everything, her mysterious vapidity. Maureen wanted to be just like her.

"Oh my God!" Maureen said when Leanne started to cry. "Oh my God, what a mess. Here, let me see if I can get it out for you."

Leanne declined Maureen's help and sobbed that she would have to cut it out. Her pupils were like tiny pinpricks. *She's on acid*, Maureen thought. *A real bad trip, what a sin!*

After the concert, as she was lying on the couch, reading every last word of *Esquire*, desperately trying to avoid having sex with Bo, Maureen thought it was no wonder that she often felt so bad about herself. *I am just bad. Who would do something as mean as*

that? No one, that's who. Even in books, it's only the really, really bad
people who commit the mean acts of petty cruelty like that. I am a real
bad person.

"No, I'm still reading," she said to Bo's inquiry as to whether or
not she was ever going to come to fucking bed out of it. Sex had
gotten even worse since about a month before. Maureen had been
walking home from another mind-numbingly boring day at the
film-strip library. She hadn't gotten to work until 11:20 that morning, and just as she was settling in, Gerry sat down across from her
and said, "Maureen, nine-fifteen, nine-thirty okay, even ten . . . ten-
thirty is pushing it, but it's still all right. But after eleven? Coming
into work after eleven in the morning is not acceptable—even if
there is nothing to do." Then he just smiled a somewhat painful
smile at her and went back to his desk.

So Maureen stayed late that day, and she was just slogging up
Military Road through the ice and slush at five-thirty. Her new
leather boots were so soaked that her feet actually squished. Usually, Bo picked her up, but he was playing bridge at a tournament
down at the hotel. She had nothing pressing to go home to, and
the big picture window under the sign "The Women's Centre"
caught her off guard. She could see a bunch of women inside, sitting around in a circle in big, comfortable chairs, talking, and it
seemed particularly warm and inviting. March had come in like a
lion and was continuing to roar all month long; the cold of March
was more penetrating and bitter than even January. Maureen knew
you could just drop in the big, open office for no other reason than
that you were a woman and this was your centre. When she got

inside, though she was relieved to be out of the biting cold, she immediately felt uncomfortable and was overwhelmed with a feeling of being out of place. They were having a consciousness raising. One really smart-looking woman with glasses and Angela Davis hair—even though she was white—stood up and gave Maureen her armchair. But Maureen knew right away she didn't have any of the right kinds of things wrong with her for this crowd. And when they started discussing whether their orgasm was clitoral or vaginal, Maureen sat mute, because, of course, she'd never had an orgasm, not ever. She'd never said it out loud, because you weren't allowed to. It was all bad and shameful enough without having to admit to that. It was all part of the big bullshit life story, and you could never let on that you saw through the tissue of lies, all the big fat fibs that everyone told about "The Family," about the inherent virtue of the Holy Roman Catholic and Apostolic Church, about true love and romance—and orgasms.

Listening to the women defending their vaginal orgasms, talking about pleasure, talking about being in charge of their own orgasms, Maureen couldn't help but think this was just another crippling fiction, another tall tale told to keep you in your place and thinking it was all your fault if your family life was a nightmare, if the Church was up to stuff too evil to even think about, and love and romance were a big crock of fairy tale nonsense, and now it was your own fault if you couldn't find pleasure in the old in-out. Maureen dismissed them as just another crowd of bullshitters. She was in a rage at the whole phoniness of the consciousness raising, but at the same time, later that night, after she'd had sex with Bo and she'd done the half-hearted, heavy-breathing, nails-scraped-down-his-back job of finishing the hideous encounter, something made her say in her smallest, phoniest voice, "I feel it's only right to tell you this because, well, I feel it's just so important for us to be, you know, honest with each other . . ." As her lips were engaged in this pseudo-earnest heart to heart, her mind went mad on that last remark about honesty. *Oh yes, it's so, so, very important to speak honestly to each other. It's crucial that the torturer and his victim be open and truthful, one to the other, for Dr. Mengele and his patients to speak honestly to each other.* "I'm afraid I haven't been totally honest with you . . ." *You big hairy-arsed, slope-headed, ham-fisted, childish, moronic, violent motherfucker!* her mind screamed with more vehemence than Maureen thought she might be able to contain. "I have to say it: I've never had . . . actually had, you know . . . I've never actually had what you might call an orgasm."

"What?" Bo said, looking a bit like this news was really, really going to piss him off.

"No, no, no, no, I'm not saying it's your fault. No, no, no, it's not your fault at all. It's me! It's me! I've never, ever, ever, I've not ever in my whole life, I've never had an orgasm, not ever."

"Well, what was that just then?"

"Well, that was me . . . I was making out that I'd had one. Pretending."

"Why?"

"I—I—I don't know."

"Oh," he said, and turned his big, hairy back to her and went to sleep.

MARY WALSH

Maureen would live to regret this brief burst of honesty, as sex with Bo became even worse and more relentless. There was a singular ruthlessness to it now. He was going to make her come "supposing he had to fuck her right out through the other side." He actually said that, or something very close to that anyway, and Maureen got the picture. After about a month of what seemed like ceaseless and really quite painful sex, she started back on the heavy-breathing, back-clawing, squealing, squalling act again.

Bo said, "But how do I know that that one is real?"

"Because . . . because the sex was just so good," Maureen said, almost robotically.

It turned out that heartfelt performances didn't really matter anyway. Bo heard what he wanted to hear. He smiled smugly, rolled over, turning his hairy and now *Oh Jesu joy of man's delivering* pimply back to Maureen and went into a deep sleep.

Things got worse from there. Ever since that party at Booman Tate's, it felt like Maureen and Bo were engaged in a kind of nightmare war scenario. It was like Beaumont-Hamel, Maureen thought, with her continuing to go bravely over the top, always hoping the German machine guns were misfiring. But just like the Newfoundland Regiment, Maureen just kept getting slaughtered. It was a nightmare, a war zone, where she and Bo daily exchanged fire, made treaties, promised each other they would not drink or would only drink moderately, promised they'd use a safe word, "pickles," when things seemed to be headed down the bad road, but not once did it ever work. If they promised they'd only drink a flask of whisky, before that flask was even finished, they'd be driving to the liquor store to get another, and then one of them would say, "Hey, might as well get a twenty-six-ouncer while we're here."

But as the year got older and the days lengthened, Maureen felt less and less like she was engaged in war, and more like she was being held prisoner in one of those dreadful Japanese prisoner-of-war camps you saw in the movies, with the daily beatings and the brainwashing and the humiliations and degradations. It became clear to Maureen that as the ice was cracking up, so was she. The constant fear with which she was living, always waiting for the next blow, was a pain worse than even the physical beatings.

CHAPTER TEN

MAUREEN KNEW SHE WAS CRAZY, BUT IT WASN'T CLEAR to her *why* she was so crazy. She had no explanation for her actions. For instance, one day she came to herself just as she was halfway through cutting up Bo's one suit, and she saw then that she'd already shredded all his shirts—all with a tiny pair of nail scissors. She hadn't felt angry while she was doing it. In fact, like usual, she'd felt nothing; she just felt numb.

One Sunday during a particularly violent week, he moved quickly and she instinctually flinched. He hit her for flinching, and she didn't leave or even think about leaving. But as he was going out the door, she screamed at him that she'd cut the tie rod end in his Renault. She didn't do it; she wouldn't know if a tie rod end was fit to eat. Yet, by unlucky happenstance, that very afternoon, the tie rod end broke as he was driving over the bridge on his way to visit his mother in Paradise. The Renault broke through the bridge and tumbled down into the rushing Paradise River. Bo survived the crash and was completely unharmed, and when he came home, he punched her full in the face. She knew it was useless to say she'd been lying about cutting the tie rod end, but she said it anyway, which just angered him more, and so she got a few extra knocks and kicks. Of course, he thought she was lying—who wouldn't?

It was so weird, though. Here she was, powerless against him—if she stood up, he beat her down; if she pulled back cringing in fear, he hit her for getting on his nerves—and yet that afternoon, just her words had apparently had the power to cut through a tie rod end. She was so confused and confounded. Inside the bubble of her world, nothing made any sense; it was just horrible and meaningless.

One Monday night in December, almost a year to the day after that first night of violence at the Duckworth Street party, Maureen, drunk, had been awake for hours, waiting for Bo to come home. She'd finished off a flask of Captain Morgan Dark, and when she heard his key in the door, she swore to herself that she would say nothing. She would just lie there and pretend to be asleep. But as soon as he stepped over the threshold, Maureen's feet were on the floor of the bedroom and propelling her forward as her scream-ing voice accused him of sleeping with someone else. Bo looked at Maureen with drunken contempt and didn't bother to reply to her accusations. He just pushed past her to the bedroom.

Maureen had known for a while that Bo was banging someone else, and she knew she should be relieved. But a part of her felt that because she'd suffered so much, because she'd put up with so much, she surely had some rights, just by the dint of her pain. She followed him into the bedroom, calling him all the filthy names she could think of—a whore-hopping cunt; a knob-gobbling, motherfucking Judas; a heartless pin-dicked prick job. She ran out of words before she ran out of anger. Bo turned on her, knocked her down, hauled her out of the bedroom, pulled her hair out, blackened both her eyes. She thought he was finished. She crawled onto the couch in the living room, hoping to sleep it off, but he came out of the bedroom again and hauled her off the couch. She curled up on the floor, trying to protect herself from the blows. He wouldn't allow her to sleep, not even on the floor. He just kept dragging her around the living room by her hair and kicking her and punching her, spitting and yelling and raging. The last thought Maureen had before she lost consciousness was, *This time it won't stop. I really will be dead this time.*

But Tuesday morning, there she was, not dead, so she got up off the floor, hungover, bruised, miserable, vaguely surprised that she was still alive. That's when she saw the big brown industrial-sized glass bottle of chlordane and the Flit gun next to it. And without thinking, she took the Flit gun and sprayed the poison all over the open food in the fridge. The glass bottle was heavier than she'd thought, and more slippery too. She almost dropped it, but managed to get it to the fridge and upend it, straight chlordane, into the orange juice. She couldn't remember leaving, but she knew she did because she found herself knocking on George's door that Tuesday morning.

CHAPTER ELEVEN

MAUREEN TOLD GEORGE EVERYTHING AS SOON AS SHE arrived on his doorstep at four in the morning, and then she stayed up the rest of that day, not talking, not thinking, not feeling, just existing. When night came, she crawled into George's bed and went right off to sleep as if she was a person who had nothing on her mind, as if putting poison in someone's food was an everyday occurrence for her, like she was one of the Borgias or something. Just as she drifted off into a deep sleep between George's comforting flannelette sheets, Maureen thought that maybe she was like one of them, and that maybe she lacked some kind of strong moral . . . zzz.

On the second morning that Maureen woke up next to George, he turned to her with concern.

"Okay, put me wise. How ya feeling now?"

Maureen sat up in bed, gingerly touching her swollen left eye. She had tried to gauge her feelings earlier that morning, but, like testing a rotten tooth with your tongue, the action, though almost irresistible, was too painful to continue. Now she looked at

George, and though she really didn't want to say anything at all, she found herself inexplicably opening up. And once she started, she couldn't stop.

"First off, I don't even know what I'm feeling, and"—she could hear a catch in her voice—"and at the same time, I'm afraid of what I *might* be feeling." She really did not want to cry, so she picked up speed: "And so really, I'm just as happy—if *happy* is a word you could use under these circumstances—just as happy not knowing how I feel . . ." Maureen was talking so fast, she could barely keep up with herself.

George interrupted her.

"You know, you just opened your lamps. You just woke up and now you're getting yourself all worked up. You're blowing your wig. You might feel a little better if you just slowed down, if you stopped bumping your gums, maybe. Could you do that?" he asked, looking at Maureen with even more concern.

"I can't believe you just said that. I can't believe you want me to not talk. Already, and it's the first time we've gone out, for Christ sakes."

"Well, put the kibosh on that right now, 'cause technically, we've never gone out," George said in that infuriating way he had of insisting on the facts but missing the point altogether. "We've just stayed in one night here in the cave. And I didn't tell you *not* to bump your gums. I just asked you if you *could* . . . you know . . . stop talking."

Now the catch was gone from Maureen's voice. She no longer felt like crying. She was back on safe ground, or at least on familiar ground: she was angry.

"Well, where everything hurts and where my heart is split into two, that kind of makes me worked up. I guess I'm weird like that, and turns out, when I'm worked up, I talk a lot."

George just looked at her. He had a kind of sad, pitying look in his eyes. That made Maureen even angrier. She didn't want anyone feeling sorry for her. It just made everything worse. It just confirmed for her what she already knew about herself: that she was a sad, useless, beat-up, knocked-up loser who was too stupid to ever get anywhere, even out of her own way, though she burned with ambition, with wanting and needing . . . something. George looking at her like that made her feel exposed and stupid, and so she struck back as hard as she could.

"Of course, I can do it; I just choose not to do it! There is a difference, and you probably just want me to shut up so you can, once again, tell me even more boring details about *The Big Sleep* and what Raymond Chandler really meant when he called somebody a Bruno or any of the other stupid, irrelevant stuff you go on about. That's really why you're against talking, because you talk so badly. You're boring! Yes, you are. You're a boring, balding"—Maureen could see that "balding" had really hit home—"piece of oozing, mainland self-satisfaction, and you're doing your very best to make everyone you come in contact with feel as miserable and as failed as you do. Fuck you!"

Maureen felt maybe she'd gone a bit too far. She was a guest in George's apartment; he'd taken her in when she had nowhere else to go. But she was just so angry—where was she going to put that anger? Sometimes, it just came out and spilled all over whoever was next to her. She felt so done in, so failed, so ashamed and so guilty, all she could do was lash out.

George gave Maureen a long, hard look, stood up and said, "It's time for me to blow this pop stand . . . I gotta drift. Maybe I was a bunny to take in a frail like you, Maureen."

"I don't even know what you just said, retardo," Maureen shot back.

He was mad, she could see that, and the only way she knew how to respond to mad was to get madder. Maureen watched him put on his jeans.

"What are you doing?"

"I'm pinning on my diapers so I can breeze off."

"What?"

"I'm going."

"Where are you going?"

"Out."

"Out where?"

"Out where there is nobody throwing an ing-bing."

Maureen let the "ing-bing" go.

"When are you coming back?"

"Well, because you are tearing off the track, acting all Section 8, I'm going to let you have the joint for the next few days."

"Oh my God, you're leaving me here? How can you leave me now? Look at me: I have two black eyes, and I don't know, something could be broken . . ."

He was still intent on getting dressed.

"And I may have poisoned someone!"

George looked at Maureen with some alarm and then turned away and continued to dress. He spoke quietly but with conviction. "Let's face it, Maureen, you're always going to have a kick about some jam or—"

Maureen couldn't help herself. She spat out, "Could you just speak to me in plain English? Could you do that . . . please?"

"Okay, is this plain enough for you? Stuff happens. Something is always going to be going on. Sometimes, things are bound to go wrong. That's life. It's how you handle it—that's what matters."

"How am I supposed to"—Maureen made vicious air quotation marks—"'handle' it? I'm a battered woman! Maybe a murdering battered woman! That's a pretty big 'something,' don't ya think?"

"You're really angry with me for some reason I am not even aware of, and I just can't take that. I'd rather be on the nut in a flophouse, because I just don't want to live like this, not even for a week."

"I don't care. I don't care what you want."

"Exactly."

"Oh, for God's sake! I don't mean that; I mean, what about me? It's just—look, I'm mad . . . I don't know why . . . Well . . . one thing is . . . I just keep thinking that I'm going to have to sleep with you because you let me stay here. And even thinking about having to 'do it,' being under an obligation to 'come across' just makes me mad."

"Wow. Just thinking about sex, you know, Maureen, makes a lot of people happy and relaxed or—"

"Well, I'm not a lot of people, am I?"

There was a long silence. Maureen thought about how relieved she'd been to have somewhere to go when she'd arrived at four in the morning a couple of days ago, and how she knew right from the moment she knocked on the door that sooner or later she'd have to "do it" with George because he'd been actively attracted to her for so long, the whole time they'd been "friends," and it only seemed fair that if he was going to let her stay at his place, she was definitely going to have to fuck him.

George moved toward the bedroom door.

Maureen wanted to reach out to him but she couldn't. Instead, she sat there, lost in bitter thought.

"I don't want to feel like I have to have sex with . . . anyone, really. I don't want to feel like I *have* to do anything. Just the thought of being obligated to have sex with someone makes me upset and angry and tense. But, at the same time, I can't take it if somebody is mad at me, and I do not want to be left, abandoned. I'd do anything rather than that—even have sex. Oh God, I hate this dance. Here I am, beat up and fucked up, and I'm still thinking I've got to come on to someone and try to seduce them because I'm so desperate not to be left, and that makes me really hate them for putting me in this position—not this position physically, but the position of feeling like I have to do what they want in order to manipulate them into not being mad at me and not leaving me, and do my best to suck them into staying with me always or at least until I find someone else better—"

"Maybe now is when you might wanna stop talking because—"

Maureen gasped.

"I said that out loud? Look, I didn't mean that. That's just internal thoughts . . . Private, internal thoughts. Crazy, private, stupid, internal thoughts."

Maureen got up and started to put her clothes on. *Where in the fuck will I go now? Oh, did I say that out loud too, or was that just in my mind?*

A quick look at George convinced Maureen that it was only in her mind.

Storming toward the door, hauling her jeans up and buttoning her blouse, tripping over herself thinking, *Well, fuck him then!* and wondering why even the thought of sex made her so angry—sure, she had gotten off to a bit of a bad start with the whole sex thing, what with Mr. Kearsey and all that—Maureen pulled open the apartment door and saw two RNC cops standing there, just about to knock.

"Maureen Brennan?"

"Yea? . . . What? What do you want?"

"Have you been cohabiting with a Mr. Trevor 'Bo' Browne at 231 Livingstone Street?"

"Why?"

"Just answer the question, Miss."

"Yes . . . well . . . no. I was, but I left."

"When?"

"Two, maybe three, days ago."

"Oh. Well, I'm afraid we have some bad news for you, Miss Brennan. Mr. Browne is dead."

"What?"

Maureen felt the ground open up beneath her feet and she almost fell.

The older policeman put out his hand to steady her and then said, "Miss, I'm afraid we're gonna have to ask you to come down to the station with us."

George stumbled out of the bedroom.

"Excuse me. What're you bulls doing here?"

The older cop gave George a look.

"We're just bringing Miss Brennan down to the station to answer a few questions."

"Nix nix on giving her the third. Are you bringing her down to the clubhouse? Are you clamping her?"

"What?" the older cop asked with irritation.

"Are you arresting her?"

"No. Not really."

"Well then, she doesn't have to go, does she?"

The older policeman fixed George with a baleful look.

"We are conducting a murder investigation."

Maureen's heart actually stopped and fell to the pit of her stomach and wanted to go further.

"As far as we know, Miss Brennan was the last person to see the deceased alive, and there is a history of violence in Miss Brennan's relationship with the deceased, the police having been called to the scene on a number of occasions. So, I think it would be better for all hands if she just came down to the station."

The younger cop piped up, "But she don't have to go, right, Sergeant Kent?"

"No," the older cop said with notable exasperation. "No, McCarthy, she don't have to go, but I think it would be in Miss Brennan's best interest if she co-operated."

George stepped in front of Maureen and said, "I think it would be in Miss Brennan's best interest if she stayed right here and you bulls took a powder."

The older cop, having lost patience with George, said, "And who are you, a Philadelphia lawyer?"

"No, I'm an English major, actually."

"Well, don't let us keep you from your busy work of parsing sentences, et cetera."

"I'm writing my master's thesis on Dashiell Hammett, the founder of the hard-boiled school of noir detective fiction."

The older police officer, totally ignoring George, took Maureen's arm and propelled her out the door.

CHAPTER TWELVE

THE TWO COPS LEFT MAUREEN TO SIT ALONE IN THE interrogation room for over an hour, left her just sitting there. And the longer she was there and the more she thought about what she'd done, the more Maureen became convinced that she had to confess. She had to do the right thing.

Sitting there, she kept coming back to the inescapable fact that no matter who did what, she, Maureen, had poisoned him. Right there in the interrogation room, it hit her like a punch in the stomach, the knowledge that she was a bad girl. For a minute, she couldn't catch her breath. Suddenly, she knew that despite all her rebellion and all her acting out, all she ever really wanted to be was a good girl. But good girls didn't get knocked up at Expo, good girls didn't fuck everybody in sight, and good girls definitely didn't poison and murder their violent, abusive boyfriends. All her life, Maureen had clung to the belief that, despite the world conspiring relentlessly against her and her total powerlessness over all the bad stuff that happened, inside, she was fundamentally a good girl, and that had kept her going, even through the worst of it. And so now, she didn't know how she could go on. There was no question any-more: she was a poisoner, a murderer. A bad girl.

The interrogation room was empty and desolate. *And so am I,* thought Maureen. For the past two and a half days, Maureen had kept the chlordane out of her mind. What she'd done was almost surreal, so unlikely, so outside the realm of what was possible, that she'd stopped believing she'd done it. And now she was faced with the awful consequences. Bo was dead. She hadn't really thought of Bo dying, of him actually being dead by her hand. What would Mrs. Browne think? What would she do? But really, who knew she'd tried to poison Bo except her and George and . . . *and maybe Bo, I guess?*

Finally, the two cops came back into the interrogation room. They sat down across from Maureen. The small, stupid one asked Maureen for her full name, address and where she was employed.

"Maureen Brennan. I'm nineteen years old. I did live at 231 Liv-ingstone Street, but now I live, well . . ."

"Where we picked you up this morning?"

"That was just a friend's place," Maureen said.

She was ready to spill her guts, but before she could confess, the little cop said, "Friend?" He leered at Maureen, and then he actually did that thing where you make a hole with your thumb and your forefinger with one hand and poke your other forefinger back and forth through the hole—the universal sign for screwing. But the little cop jammed all the fingers of his left hand through the hole in his right and then slowly and with great difficulty forced them in and out, in and out.

Maureen went hot with shame.

"Friend?" the little cop said. "Like Trevor 'Bo' Browne was your friend? You don't take much care of your friends, do you, Maureen? We found Mr. Browne up on The Brow, dead, trussed up in the trunk of his car, and you never even bothered to report him missing. Not that friendly, if you ask me."

"That's enough, McCarthy. That's enough," the older cop said, stepping forward. "Now, Miss Brennan. Do you know why you're here?"

Oh yes, Maureen definitely knew why she was there, but suddenly she didn't want them to know—not yet, anyway. For one thing, the older cop seemed so decent, in a way that made Maureen want him to like her and not know what a low-life, murdering piece of scum she really was. And so, she said simply, "I s'pose you want to talk about what happened to Bo."

The older cop let Maureen's answer just sit there in the air, and he gave her a piercing look, like he might be able to see right through her. Maureen, who always tried to fill every silence, who was terrified without noise and chaos, immediately wanted to blab out the entire sad scenario, but the younger cop answered the question.

"We want to talk to you because you are a person of interest, my maid. We talked to a lot of people about what happened to Mr. Browne, and all the pieces are starting to fall together quickly. So, if you had anything—anything at all—to do with this . . ."

The older cop shot McCarthy a look and he shut up. The older cop then looked back at Maureen and waited. Maureen tried not to say anything, but she could feel her stomach come right up almost to her throat. She was the kind who couldn't go on a roller coaster, because when she got to the top, she was so choked with fear she just wanted to jump and get it over with. The mounting terror of waiting for her inevitable death was too unbearable, and she felt she would do anything to make the terror stop. It was the same way even on a simple Ferris wheel or at the edge of a cliff. It was better to get it over with. That's how she felt now. She opened her mouth to tell them everything.

A really cute young guy—cute for a pig—stuck his head in the door.

"Sergeant Kent, sorry to interrupt. We just got word from Dr. Hutton in Pathology. They're all backed up. It's going to be a few days before they get to Mr. Browne."

The older cop walked with menace toward the young fella.

"Thank you, Constable. That'll be all." He quickly shut the door.

So far, they didn't know about the poison. They had nothing on her yet . . . God, she was even thinking like one of those murderesses on TV, on *The Defenders*, or like one of those awful blackwidow killers who murdered their loved ones in one of the books George was studying. *Oh fuck, that's right, I am!* she thought with a sinking heart.

Maureen knew that she was guilty. She was guilty as sin, but if Bo died from being poisoned, how did they find him in the trunk of his car up on The Brow? It didn't make sense. Did he, in his poisoned state, drive the car, stumble out to get something out of the trunk and collapse into it, and somehow or other the trunk closed on him and . . . yes! A perfectly reasonable series of events if this was *Get Smart* or *Herbie: The Love Bug* or some shit, but this wasn't Walt Disney—this was real.

She had put the poison in Bo's orange juice, but if he drank the poison, how did he get in the trunk of his car? Maureen's mind scurried around, trying to find a logical explanation. Had someone come to the apartment, found Bo dead and then, for some unfathomable reason, stuffed his dead body in the trunk of his car, drove it up to The Brow and abandoned it there? Why would anyone do that? Was it someone who was trying to protect her? Was it George? Or was someone trying to frame her?

"All right, Miss Brennan, why do you think somebody would do this?"

"Do what?"

"Murder Mr. Browne."

"Murder? Why do I think someone would murder Bo?" Maureen said, stalling for time.

She was thinking, *Why wouldn't someone?* He was like a magnet for a racket. He just caused trouble and destruction wherever he went. Once, she and Bo were just walking down the street and a crowd of little boys swarmed Bo, kicking and punching him. In restaurants, he often took umbrage and tossed insults and sometimes a nickel or dime at the unlucky waiter, and because of that, they'd once found themselves outside a restaurant, circled by the kitchen staff, all wielding their chefs' knives. With a few drinks in on the right day, someone could just bump into Bo and that'd be it: the place'd go up. There'd be punching, cursing, bleeding, and Bo would be always in the middle of it.

Now Maureen thought, *No, I am not gonna tell him. I don't want to anymore, because I am gonna get out of this room and take off and join the French Foreign Legion, or I'll be like Audrey Hepburn in* The Nun's Story *and devote my life—my stinking, meaningless, murderess life—to serving the poor, the leprous, the babies with the flies in their eyes.* Without knowing she was going to do it, she heard herself blurt out, "Well, he was working for DAFT, you know."

"No, my maid, we don't know," McCarthy said. "Why don't you tell us."

Jesus, if he didn't stop calling her his maid . . . Christ, stupid and a bayman on top of that.

"I don't know. I never really thought about it, but . . ."

The old detective sergeant had Maureen back in his sights. She desperately tried to break eye contact with him but couldn't.

"DAFT, you know. They're a company. Bo built boxes for them—crates and stuff. They were all in the same frat at university. The boys got an import-export kind of company, and Bo . . . he worked for them. I mean, but he would've rather be workin' *with* them . . . You know what I mean?"

"And?" said the detective sergeant, his eyes still locked with hers.

"And, you know, he was mad at them—a lot. He said they were making a shitload of money and they weren't cutting him in on it, and he was working his bag off for them and wasn't getting nowhere doin' it. He was real mad at Jack and Deuce Dunne. They are a twin—"

"Yea," said McCarthy. "Jacky and Deucey were with the Caps— St. John's Capitals. They were the best defencemen we ever had. When the two of them came at ya, ya pretty well knew you were fucked." His eyes darted over to Kent. "Sorry for the language, sir. They almost got drafted to the NHL, but they were not quite violent enough, I s'pose, to make the grade."

"But one of them did get drafted, didn't he?"

"Yea—that's right. I forgot that, sir. They did try to draft one of 'em into a Junior A team up in Toronto. It'd be his ticket to the NHL, but he wouldn't go without the brother."

Maureen just stared at McCarthy.

"Forgive McCarthy's language, Miss Brennan. He grew up in Harbour Main. Hard crowd. Sell their mother for a bottle of beer."

"Shure little Miss Brennan grew up on Princess Street with a bootlegger either side of her. Bad language, shure that'd be the least of this young maid's worries. So, you're tryin' to point the finger at Jack and Deucey Dunne, Maureen?"

"No, no," she sputtered. "You just asked me why someone would have . . . done this. And, well, Bo, when he was mad at you, you know, he might put the boots to ya. And maybe he was so mad at Jacky and Deucey that he mighta laid a beating on 'em, and maybe that'd be a reason for why someone might, you know . . ." She nodded her head up and down, not wanting to say the word.

"Murder?" said McCarthy. "Murder him."

"So you're saying that someone who received a beating at the hands of Mr. Browne might have sufficient reason to murder Mr. Browne?" The old detective sergeant had his eyes locked on Maureen again.

Oh, fuck . . . She immediately thought of the five or six times that the people downstairs had called the cops when Bo was going cracked upstairs, the times she'd been down at the station with black eyes, a broken nose, broken ribs, a fat lip, the whole sorry mess of her. She could tell that the old cop definitely thought she did it. She wasn't smart enough for this game. She might as well get it over with and—there was a knock at the door.

The detective sergeant tore his eyes away from Maureen, jumped up and strode toward the door in a fury. "Sorry, sir," the cute young cop said, "but Miss Brennan's lawyer is here, and he said that if you're questioning Miss Brennan, he should be present."

Maureen burst out, "Shure I don't have a lawyer. What would I have a lawyer for? I never even finished Grade 11. I'm working down to Pepperrell at the film-strip library . . ."

George walked into the room.

"Oh," McCarthy said, doing that awful thing with his hands. "You're not just her 'friend'? Now you're her lawyer too?"

George turned politely and stuck out his hand. "George Taylor, graduate of the Dalhousie School of Law, called to the bar four years ago, and you are?"

McCarthy pulled back his hand and wiped it against his shirt as if he were afraid of infection.

"But sure, you're getting a degree in English," Maureen half whispered to him as he sat down.

"I copped to the fact early on I didn't really like the law per se. I just like stories about the law. But I am a bona fide lawyer. Now, where are we? Do you gentlemen mind if I have a few minutes alone with my client, who, by the way, has a right to have counsel present during her interrogation?"

"You've been reading too many story books, buddy boy. She got no right to have a lawyer present during her interrogation. We're not down in da States, Perry Mason."

"So you are conducting an interrogation with my client?"

"That's right," replied McCarthy. "So hop the fuck up out of that seat and out of that door."

"Maureen, did you consent to this 'interrogation'?"

"No! Shure they never even asked me. They just left me in here for hours and then they just started in on asking me questions, like why would I think someone would . . . kill . . ."

"Okay, Maureen, okay. That's enough. You do have a right to silence. As a Canadian citizen, you have a right to not speak." George shot Maureen a quick, knowing look. "Okay, we're leaving. Detective Sergeant, you have no right to compel my client to participate in an interrogation. Miss Brennan has clearly indicated that she does not want to participate in said interrogation."

"No, she never," piped up McCarthy.

"All right. Maureen, do you wish to continue with this interrogation?" asked George.

"No, I'm not that stunned. Why would I want to—"

"That's good," George interrupted. "Thank you . . . Remember your rights, Maureen," George said, tapping his finger against his lips. "There you are, gentlemen. Miss Brennan does not wish to take part, and at this point, she is exercising her right to silence."

Maureen was shocked at this new, direct, to-the-point George—this George who didn't ramble on like an escapee from a Philip Marlowe story. Maureen found this new George much more attractive.

"I didn't know you were a lawyer," she said as they walked out of the police station.

"That's 'cause I'm not."

"You lied?"

George nodded his head.

"To the police?" Maureen was taken aback.

"Yea, I lied to the police. I didn't poison anyone, though."

With a shock, Maureen realized that even George thought she'd murdered Bo.

"I can't believe you think I did it," she said to him as they walked through the door of his apartment.

"Well, you did scream this morning, right here in this very apartment, that you may well have just murdered your violent, abusive boyfriend. I believe you were standing right there when you said it."

"What are you doing, George? Why are you talking so different?"

"I'm speaking in plain English, Maureen, just as you asked me to do this morning, right after you confessed that you might well have murdered your violent boyfriend."

"But how? How could I have done it?"

"Poison?"

"But if he was poisoned—"

"If *you* poisoned him—"

"Yes, but if *I* poisoned him, then how in the name of God did he get in the car while poisoned, get the car up over the Southside Road, up onto The Brow, get out of the car, open the trunk, crawl in the trunk, close down the hatch and then die?"

"We've got to find out what the pathologist's report says," George said.

"They're not gonna have that for at least a week."

George looked askance.

"A little buddy came in and said that everything is all backed up over in Pathology," she explained.

"Yea, because the dead bodies are piling up like seal pelts around here."

"Really?" Maureen said.

"No," said George. "I'm joking. We got a lower murder rate in St. John's than they have in Norway."

"So?"

"Norway has the lowest number of murders of any country in the world. Their . . ."

Maureen stopped listening to George.

"I think I should tell them," Maureen interrupted, just as he was getting to the relative murder rates in the rest of Scandinavia compared to Norway.

"Tell who? What?"

"The cops. Tell them about the chlordane."

"That is a very, very stupid idea."

"Why?"

"Because they'll have to charge you with attempted murder if you confess that you attempted to murder someone."

"Well, they probably will charge me anyway when they find out, but I'd just as soon get it over with now."

"What about if he never drank any of it, and so you didn't kill him? So then who did?"

"I know . . . ," said Maureen.

"You know what?" George asked.

"I mean I know, who did kill him?"

"You know who killed him?"

"No! No, I mean I know, comma, who did kill him, question mark?"

CHAPTER THIRTEEN

THE NEXT NIGHT, MAUREEN PUT ON A TON OF MAKEUP to try to cover her bruises and convinced George to go to a party with her. Roger "Booman" Tate was having his life-ending, soul-crushing annual Christmas party. She hadn't been back there since Bo had given her that awful first beating, but she was going back now because she had a plan. She thought that if she could just get in with one of the DAFT boys and have a snoop, maybe even scout out something at the party, she could find out . . . what? She didn't know, but if she could just screw her courage to the sticking post—or was it stick her courage to the screwing post? She was never sure—and manage to brave that dreadful place again, maybe she could discover something. She knew from experience that if you poked around long enough and deep enough, you would always come up with something, like when she and Carleen first went up to Montreal, to Expo, and were staying at that convent. Maureen went poking through Carleen's stuff and found her diary and Maureen saw her name.

Me and Reenie hitchhiked out to the bar at the Fort Motel. They didn't ask for IDs—they didn't even have anyone on the door. Reenie was afraid to go in, but I just pushed her through. It is so fab in there. They have these groovy phones on the tables and every table has a number and you can just phone over to someone. Like guys can just call you on the phone if they want to buy you a drink or something. Two old gnarly guys called us— Jesus, we got about a million drinks off 'em. I gave Reenie the high sign just as the old fellas were moving in for the kill. We went in the toilet and crawled out the window and ran down the TransCanada laughing so hard we almost pissed ourselves. Three guys in a Pontiac picked us up by the Crossroads, they wanted us to go down to the Kingsbridge Hotel to party but Reenie the Weenie wouldn't go. She is such a drag. She had to be home by 10:30 because she told her old lady that she was down to the Gosling library, studying.

Maureen kept skimming through the diary, looking for her name. She stopped at another entry.

Yesterday morning I came to in a tent in Butter Pot Park, half my clothes off, a big blond dead-eyed guy with a knife was sitting on a sleeping bag next to me. Oh God, I thought I was fucked, but turned out he wasn't going to kill me, he was driving that knife into his own leg—not deep, just a little. But where were Reenie and the Musketeers? I remembered being so loaded I kept falling down. So did they just fuck off and leave

me there? I would never do that to Reenie. She's my friend. If
she was fucked up, I'd look after her.

When Maureen read that, so bald on the page, she felt so bad she tried to immediately justify it to herself, like she was on the stand or something, getting the third degree—justify it because Carleen was being such a pain in the hole that night. She was so embarrassing, Maureen felt ashamed that Dicey and them would think Maureen was like that. They were all drunked up and out camping in Butter Pot Park for the 24th. Maureen was having a great time with the Musketeers, being all loaded and tough, but Carleen kept falling down and crying, and then when Maureen would haul her back up on her feet, she'd start bawling even harder and then down she'd go again. Sam and Sara knew some guys from Mundy Pond, and the girls stumbled into those guys' tent. Maureen was surprised to see the good-looking twin, the nice one from the frat house. Maureen said hi, but he didn't respond, didn't even look up.

"Stoned," Dicey said. "Probably magic mushrooms."

They stayed for a while and then Dicey wanted to leave to go find Trevor, Sara's brother. Trevor and them had a couple of cases of beer in their tent. Sara didn't want to go because it was her brother, but Dicey said it was where the best party was going to be.

Maureen tried to get Carleen up on her feet and out of that tent, but she just couldn't manage it. Each time she got Carleen up, she collapsed to the ground again. The Musketeers had left and Maureen wanted to catch up with them, wanted to keep partying and was more than half in the bag herself. So she left

Carleen there in the tent with those guys and she never even checked back. Maureen came to in the morning with Sara and Sam in their own little pup tent. There was no sign of Dicey or Carleen. It was hard for Maureen, reading that stuff in Carleen's diary, to justify her behaviour. Maureen realized that if she kept reading other people's private stuff, she might be forced to face stuff about herself that she just didn't want to see. Snooping, something Maureen had started in order to soothe herself, to give herself the feeling that she knew what was going on, that she was ahead of the game, that she was on top of it, was now just causing her more trouble.

No one at the Christmas party knew yet that Bo was dead—the police hadn't released the name of the victim, pending contacting the family. *No one*, Maureen thought, looking around warily, *no one except me, George, the police and whoever did it*. Maureen usually hated parties. She figured she hadn't really enjoyed a party since Frances Dearrin's birthday party over at the SUFU Hall on Campbell Avenue back in 1963, when there had been unlimited amounts of Pepsi and egg salad sandwiches and the goody bags were full of great stuff. No, she didn't like parties anymore, and especially not here. She hated this place. She'd felt sick as soon as she got here, but she was determined to do what she came here to do. She walked into Booman's room to put her coat on the bed with everyone else's and was just starting to have a quick poke around when she was interrupted by Jack and Deucey Dunne coming in to drop off their jackets. Maureen hadn't seen Jack since that time at the frat when she was fifteen and Jack had said that awful thing about his forearm. Maureen felt the heat rising in her face just thinking about it.

Deucey was all banged up. He had a fat lip and there were bruises on his face turning yellow, but he looked better than he had that time in Butter Pot Park. His eyes were more alive, more with it. Maureen walked up to Deucey. *Oh my God, is that a bit of his ear gone?* Yes, she could see that the bottom bit of his earlobe was completely missing.

"Maureen Brennan, whaddya at?" Deucey said.

Jack turned toward Maureen and gave her a long, slow look. "Mo-reen."

"Jack." Maureen nodded. She turned to Deucey.

"Not much. How you doin', Deucey? I mean, Dave. Do people still call you Deucey, Dave?"

"No, that's my name. Nobody but Mom calls me Dave anymore. Right, Jacky?" he said to his twin, who was headed out of the bedroom.

"I haven't seen you since that 24th of May up in Butter Pot," said Maureen.

"Oh yea?"

"You probably don't remember."

"Yea, I don't remember much about back then." Deucey looked really uncomfortable. "I got committed right after that, and it was all pretty hazy for about eighteen months or so."

Maureen was taken aback but tried to act as if the fact that he'd been locked up in a mental institution for eighteen months didn't freak her right the fuck out.

"Are you all right now?"

"Yea, I'm good now. It was all the acid, you know? And the shrooms. Turns out thirty hits of purple microdot is too much acid for one Friday night."

Maureen just kept looking at him with a smile pasted on her face.

"It's a joke, Maureen. You know. I didn't do thirty hits of acid in one night—close though."

Maureen was really uncomfortable around mental illness, and even talk of mental illness. She tried to change the subject.

"What happened to your nose?" Maureen asked.

"It was just a really rough game of b-ball. Pickup game with the crowd from Mundy Pond. They play basketball like they're playin' hockey. It's like they always got the gloves off, headin' into the corner."

"They don't wear gloves in basketball, though, do they?" Maureen said, and then quickly laughed, realizing how stupid she sounded. "Just joking. Ha-ha. Yea, Mundy Pond."

"Yea . . . There's a guy from Mundy Pond and a guy from The Brow in a car. Who's drivin'? . . . The cop," Deucey said.

"Yea, Mundy Pond, where they tie on the dogs and let the kids run free," Maureen said.

"What?"

"Oh, I always get things arse-backwards. I mean, jumpins, where they tie on the kids and let the dogs run free. Mundy Pond, heh, right?"

"It was funnier the first way," Deucey said.

"Yea."

"Where's Bo to?"

"Oh, Bo's . . . out in Grand Falls doing a job for his old man," said Maureen as a picture of Bo trussed up in the trunk of his Renault raced across her mind. But that awful picture didn't cause Maureen to miss a beat because, apparently, she'd become so cold and untroubled by conscience, or even by Bo's death and her role in it, that nothing these days could give her pause. Maureen's heart sank, and for a moment she was lost in thought.

"Is he?" said Deucey.

"What?" Maureen said, coming back to the conversation.

"Is he in Grand Falls?"

"Yea, I think. I don't really know. We're broke-up."

"Yea? Now you're broke-up and broke up."

"What?" said Maureen.

"You know," Deucey said, looking straight at the black eye Maureen thought she had so cleverly concealed.

"Bo . . . ," Deucey began, starting to look uncomfortable. "Like, people say that he, you know, gets pretty physical with you, so he broke up your body and now you're broke-up—get it? I—"

"Oh, yea," Maureen interrupted him. "Funny. Where's the bathroom?"

"Whaddya gonna have a bath?" said Deucey.

"No."

"Well, whaddya wanna go to the bathroom for?"

Oh God, for such a good-looking guy, Deucey Dunne was a real pain in the hole sometimes, Maureen thought. But at the same time, she was burning with embarrassment that everyone could see what had happened to her. They could just gawk at her bruises and her disgrace. Sure, Deuce was all beat-up too, but Maureen knew in her heart that it was way different for a fella. And then she had to go and top it off by saying "bathroom" instead of "toilet." She'd rather die than have other people think that she was one of those mealy-mouths who wouldn't say shit even if their mouth was full of it. From now on, she'd call the bathroom "the head" or maybe even "the shitter."

"The toilet, I mean, of course. Toilet. Where's the toilet? Do you know?"

"Yea, just back that way," Deucey said. "There's a bath in there too, if you're feelin' dirty." He moved in on her. "Are you feelin' dirty, Maureen?"

She pushed past him into the bathroom. Jesus, what the fuck was wrong with her? Why would he, out of the blue, come on to her like that? She sat down on the toilet. She was an idiot, nothing but a fucking idiot. She was going to jail and she probably deserved to be locked up. She sat there, her drawers down around her ankle bones, and thought, *I could just keep calling myself down to the lowest, just keep the you're-an-idiot voice going, or I could haul up my drawers, go out there and suck up to Deucey Dunne and see if I can find out anything about what really happened to Bo.*

The door opened. Maureen let out a little scream. George was standing there.

"I've decided, even if you did do it, I'm personally going to find you not guilty, like Holmes and Watson found Captain Croker in 'The Adventure of the Abbey Grange' not guilty."

"I'm using the bathroom . . . ," Maureen said.

"Bo was a brute who constantly abused you in every conceivable way," George continued, uninterrupted, "and so for you to take any action to get yourself free from the power of that madman is justifiable. And so, I pronounce myself judge and jury and find you not guilty: *vox populi, vox Dei*. You are acquitted, Maureen Brennan, and may your future actions justify me and the judgment I have pronounced this night." Just that day, George had started reading a Sherlock Holmes story called "The Adventure of the Abbey Grange."

"Shure I'm not guilty," said Maureen, still on the toilet. "I didn't do it, or I'm pretty sure I didn't do it, anyways. You don't have to pronounce anything, George. Go on! Get out of the bathroom, will ya?"

George walked across the bathroom and hugged Maureen to him. Her face was crushed against his belly while her drawers were still around her ankles. The bathroom door opened again and in walked Deucey Dunne.

"Oh, sorry to interrupt. Geez, b'ys. You don't have to go at it in the toilet; Booman got three or four bedrooms."

"You didn't interrupt anything, except me, desperately trying to have a pee."

"And you need someone to hold on to you so as you can do that? You're a big girl now, Maureen. You should be able to manage that on your own."

"Will you both just get the fuck out?"

"It didn't take you too long to get a new fella on the go," Deucey shot back on his way out the door.

"George is not my fella. He's just a friend!" Maureen yelled.

"I'm not your fella?" George asked, looking all downhearted and droopy as he walked through the door.

"Christ, close the door, will ya . . . Please! . . . I'M ON THE TOILET."

People at the party turned and looked, Maureen was so loud. Finally, George closed the door.

Maureen stayed another minute on the toilet, thinking that if she could get Deucey to take her home with him, maybe she could get a look around his place and . . . Again, she didn't know exactly what she might find or even what she was looking for. *But there's always clues, isn't there?* her mind said. Deucey's bitten ear—that was a clue, a real Bo move. Many times, Bo had been in such a rage and so liquored up and out of it, that he actually bit down on whatever was unlucky enough to be in front of him. Not only had he taken a piece out of Maureen's ear, but when he was younger, before he'd even started drinking, he took a big chomp out of his sister Sara's cheek and it got all infected and pus-y and scabby and looked awful for weeks. Sara said they'd thought she might have to get plastic surgery. The human bite is filthy. "Nothing so dirty as the human mouth," the Sarge always said. Rage-filled biting was Bo's MO and someone had bitten Deucey.

When she came out of the bathroom, George was standing there waiting, still in full sulk. "Stop being such a sook. What is wrong with you?" Maureen asked him under her breath.

"Nothing." George didn't look up.

"Well then, why have you got a face on you like a slapped arse?"

said Maureen, channelling the Sarge. "I need you to get lost. I've got work to do."

George's bottom lip pouted out even further, if that was possible.

Maureen took a deep breath and whispered, "I need to find a way to get to Deucey's so I can have a look around his place, try to find out what happened. You've got to scram, go home. I need you to help me. Remember? That's why we are here," she said, setting her face into what she imagined was a simpering-damsel-in-distress look. "I need you to help me by going home now." She moved in even closer to George. "I'll meet you back there. Later."

Maureen looked away and caught Deucey's eye. She gave George a little push and sailed across the room in Deucey's direction.

"So, you almost got drafted into hockey, did ya. I heard—"

"No. That was Jack."

"Oh, I heard that was you."

"They wanted Jack to play Junior A with the Toronto Oaks, but he wouldn't go."

"Wow! Really? Why not?" Maureen asked, already knowing the answer.

"He didn't want to, I guess. Here, have a toke."

Maureen did and proceeded to drink a lot of whisky and smoke a lot more dope.

As Deucey got drunker, he started talking more about him and Jack and how close they were. Maureen was jealous that anyone would have someone they felt that much connection with and were that close to. It made Maureen feel even more lonely and lost. She was too busy attending her own private pity party and wasn't really paying attention when Deuce said, "We shared a single placenta."

"Well, that would make you close," Maureen said, trying to stop feeling sorry for herself and start getting the job done.

"One egg," Deucey said.

"What?"

"One egg. We are just one egg split in two. Me and Jack. Jack and me. Oh yea, it's all Jack, Jack, Jack with 'em," he muttered drunkenly, "but he wouldn't even be here if it wasn't for me."

Maureen wasn't quite following, but at the end of the night, she went home with him.

CHAPTER FOURTEEN

DEUCEY HAD A NICE PLACE ON NUNNERY HILL. IT WAS just a regular-looking row house on the outside, but inside, it was all opened up and gussied up, with huge windows and a great view of the harbour. Deucey had a loft bed. She had to climb up a ladder and Deucey had to help her up because she was so loaded.

"You got a really nice body with your clothes off, which you can't really tell from lookin' at you dressed," Deucey said as Maureen gracelessly crawled around the water bed, trying to find a place to pitch. Despite the mounting nausea caused by the rocking of the water bed, Deucey's remark made Maureen feel kind of chuffed. No one had ever said anything nice about her body before. She tried to think what Deucey might mean. Bo had scrawled "Tiny Tits" across the inside of her two best bras. Her legs were long and skinny. Her brother Raymond used to say that she had their father's knobby knees. She was 140 pounds and five-foot-eight, well over what the beautiful girls with the perfect bodies weighed. She had a good forty pounds on Twiggy or The Shrimp, but Deucey thought she had a good body. *Oh great, Reenie,* her mind said drunkenly. *A guy who, for all you know, may have been involved in your ex-boyfriend's murder gave you a compliment. Just said something nice to you and you're such a pathetic loser that it's kinda making you feel a little bit better about yourself.*

She pretended to pass out after they did it, just in case he was one of those guys who wanted you to hop the fuck right out of their bed after they screwed you. He did try to wake her up, but she was doing a pretty convincing job of being passed out—so convincing that she actually did fall into a deep, almost comatonic sleep.

The sun was coming up over The Narrows, rising like a big red ball, right up over Cabot Tower, when she finally did come to. Deuce was still snoring. Silently, she threw her clothes over the side of the loft and clambered down the ladder. Tucked underneath the bed loft was what looked like an office: a desk, some metal filing cabinets, stacks of papers and a couple of trophies, one inscribed "Dave Dunne, MVP, 1967," and the larger one read "The Herder Trophy for the Senior Ice Hockey Champions of Newfoundland, The St. John's Capitals, 1969." Despite her deep and abiding contempt for all things sport, Maureen was impressed. Deucey and Jack, they were winners.

Maureen could see bills and receipts, which were probably from the boys' business. There was even a receipt from Bo, but it was just for $225 for one large crate. She could hear Deucey tossing around in the bed above just as she found a copy of a police report filed by Jack, who was the older brother, having come out of the womb a whole five minutes before Deucey. The report said that Deucey had been missing for over forty-eight hours. In fact,

Maureen read, Deucey had been gone for three days, and Jack had searched all the known haunts, had searched everywhere. Maureen figured Jack must have been real worried if he filed a report with the cops, because none of the DAFT boys were what you'd call "cop callers." Next to the report was some medical stuff. Maureen shuffled through and stopped at a file called "Feto-Fetal Transfusion Syndrome," but she couldn't make head nor tail of it. Underneath that was a memorandum of agreement stapled to an original bill of sale for a boat named *The Ikaros*, described as a hundred-foot Norwegian trader, a cargo vessel registered in Liberia and sold to the Dunne, Albert, Furlong, Tate Alliance Group. Why in the name of God were the boys buying a cargo boat? Maureen knew they were dope dealers, but she didn't think they were boat-load-of-dope dealers. They weren't that big.

Just as she found what looked to be a telegram from the Colombia Telegraph Company, Deucey called out, "What're you at down there, Maureen?"

"Oh, just lookin' for the bathroom . . . I mean, toilet." Maureen shoved the papers back into what she thought was the order she'd found them in.

"Yea, we wouldn't want you takin' a shit in the bath."

Maureen got dressed and, without saying another word or even goodbye, got out of there.

CHAPTER FIFTEEN

THE NEXT TIME MAUREEN SAW DEUCEY WAS AT BO'S
funeral service. She was sitting up in the front with Mrs.
Browne, who seemed even more out of it than usual, and Art, who
was sobbing openly. For some odd reason, Sara was sitting in the
pew behind, holding up Dicey Doyle, who looked on the point of
collapsing from grief. Sam Fleming was there too, on Dicey's other
side. Dicey seemed even more devastated than Mr. Browne. Maureen found that strange, but then again, the whole funeral had an
odd, even unreal, feel to it.

Maureen hadn't seen the Three Musketeers in months. Really,
she hadn't seen anybody for months, because she was either too
bruised, too hungover or too drunk, and on top of that, Bo didn't
really want anyone at the house and he didn't want her hanging
out with anybody else. She felt sad seeing them there and missed
having friends—if she could ever really call the Musketeers friends.
Before she got in tack with Bo, they all used to tool around in
Sara's T-Bird, and because Maureen was Dicey's friend, Sam and
Sara let her hang around with them. They all jammed up together

in the front seat, and Maureen sat by herself in the back. They let her know in no uncertain terms that she was not really one of the Three Musketeers. It was "all for one and one for all" but none for Maureen, apparently. She seemed to be the only one who knew that there was actually a fourth Musketeer, the most important Musketeer, the one who actually said "all for one and one for all," the one all the books were written about: d'Artagnan. Maureen would sit, a little bit smug, in the back seat of the T-Bird, thinking she was d'Artagnan, the most interesting Musketeer, but she was careful to keep that thought to herself. The girls—mostly Sam and Sara—had made it clear how boring they found that kind of talk and that she'd better not interrupt them to go on about books and old nonsense, or she might not even manage to make it into the lousy back seat.

Not just Jack and Deucey, but all the DAFT boys were at the funeral. Deucey winked at Maureen as she walked down the aisle behind the coffin. *Dear God, how could he? At a funeral.* Maureen blushed with embarrassment. The cops were in the church too. They gave her a hard look as she passed them.

Maureen knew it was a mortal sin to think ill of the dead, but for all that, she couldn't feel bad that Bo was . . . *gone.* If he hadn't been . . . *done away with,* would she ever have gotten away from him? It struck her that morning that, sooner or later, it probably would have been *her* there in the box. Maybe he wouldn't have done it on purpose, but really, how many flights of stairs can you be thrown down over before your neck finally breaks? How many times had he choked her till she almost passed out? *Oh, never mind goin' there now*, she thought to herself. *For all the crocodile tears I'm going to have to shed here today and for all the bullshit I'm gonna have to spew at the funeral, I will not miss him—not the one little bit.*

The night after the funeral, Maureen told George she was going down to the Black Swan Inn to meet up with someone she knew who was home for Christmas. The Black Swan, tucked in on the side of the War Memorial, was tarted up to look like some kind of English pub or something. It was Friday night, so Wally Brownley and his band were playing. They were all Yanks, Wally and them. They had been stationed at Fort Pepperrell during the war and then stayed on in Newfoundland—probably married Newfoundland girls. They played jazz standards and old favourites, and Frankie, who owned the Black Swan, loved them. As the night wore on and Frankie drank more and more, he would try to make everyone get up to slow dance, and then he'd stand in the middle of the dancers and shake Red Roses talcum powder from the tin so that, he explained, the dancers' feet could move with greater ease. Maureen sat to the bar, and Rita, *Lovely Rita Meter Maid*—bar maid, actually—was standing there in her glory, because Rita had worked down at the base for the Yanks, and listening to Wally's band always brought her back to better times. Rita was in such a good mood, she didn't even bother to ask Maureen for her fake ID; she just asked her what she wanted. Maureen burst into tears.

"I don't know," she said.

Rita looked at her with concern but also with irritation. The band was playing "A Sunday Kind of Love," and buddy on the big xylophone thing was really givin' 'er.

Maureen didn't want to keep irritating Rita, so she ordered a beer. "But I don't really like beer," she said. "Old bellywash, Dad calls it. But I can't start right in on the whisky right off the bat, just like that." She could see she was really getting on Rita's nerves now. "A jockey club, Rita. That's what I'll have, a jockey club."

Maureen took her first sip and, right away, wished she'd ordered the whisky. She loved that burning, the heat that spread through her chest, and that big letting go she felt after she took her first sip of hard liquor. You'd have to drink a dozen beer to get that, and by the time you choked back a dozen, you'd be bloated up like a big pig and vomiting your guts out somewhere, but really, she couldn't afford to let go like that, not tonight, because she had thought it all through lying awake next to George last night, her mind going a mile a minute, making it hard to get to sleep. And when she'd thought it through, she realized she was still no further ahead. Shure she'd seen that bill of sale for the boat at Deucey's—and hadn't Bo said something about a boat and the DAFT crowd that night he'd been in a rage because they wouldn't make him a partner? She felt in her heart and soul that she was right on the edge of seeing it all make sense, but she didn't really have much to go on, did she? She needed to dig deeper. If she could get Deucey to take her home with him again, maybe she could have a better poke around. She'd wait here and if Deucey didn't show up, she'd go down to Dirty Dick's and see if he was down there, or he might be down at the Trot 'n' Pace.

A gaggle of young women came through the door. They were all busy comforting someone in obvious distress. *Oh fuck.* The one being comforted was Fluff Dawe, Bo's old girlfriend. Fluff and Bo had gotten together in Grade 8 and had stayed together all through high school and into university and were supposedly just getting back together when Bo got with Maureen. "Juicy Joyce" Maynard, Carleen's sister, was part of Fluff's crowd, and she shot Maureen a look of such meanness as they passed that Maureen thought, *Jesus, the way she's lookin' at me, you'd think I killed Bo. Oh, that's right,* she thought, her heart sinking, *maybe I did.*

After the girls settled in at their table and ordered drinks and continued to make comforting noises at and around Fluff, Maureen could feel them all looking darts over at her. Fluff's crowd had always been mad at Maureen because Bo had dumped Fluff for a younger model. Not knowing what gave her the guts, Maureen turned around on her bar stool, intending to stare them down. But by the time she did, they were all looking down at their drinks or at each other, except for Joyce. Joyce just stared back at Maureen. Joyce had never known the back-down. Maureen and Carleen had thought Joyce was so cool, they looked up to her. Seeing Joyce made Maureen feel lonely for Carleen. She figured she must still be up in Montreal, being a secretary/piece of tail for that dirtbag club owner/mail-order porn sleezoid, who Maureen now suspected might be face and eyes in tack with the DAFT crowd. Perry had said that night Fox was working with him, and somehow or other, it must all fit together, but Maureen didn't know how.

Maureen, lost in thought, continued to stare right into Joyce's eyes. Joyce owned her own business, a store, Boutique Artistique, the first head shop in St. John's and the hippest place on the whole island. So cool that Maureen didn't like to go in there; she always felt that Joyce and them could see right through her and knew she was still just a greaseball Corner Boy from Princess Street. For all the peace, love and groovy stuff she tried to get on with, at any moment the thin veneer of the Summer of Love could peel off and reveal the real Maureen. She'd never even dropped acid and had only started smoking hash regularly last year, on the same night she'd had her first piece of pizza—both of them burned the mouth off her. By the time the joint got to her, it was tiny. She sucked it in hard like she saw everybody else doing, and then "Jesus, OW!" she dropped the joint and yowled with pain, which just made everybody laugh until tears were streaming down their faces. A pizza parlour, Napoli's Pizza, had just opened up the steps from the Black Swan, and when she took her very first bite of Italian food, she managed to burn her lips again on the nuclearly hot, gooey, delicious, stringy cheese that was hanging off her slice. Bo used to joke that the best Italian food in St. John's was made by people who'd actually heard of Italy.

Joyce had everything in Boutique Artistique: shirts like they wore at Woodstock, those flat leather Jesus shoes, those big coats from Afghanistan with all that curly fur on the inside of the leather that stank of sheep and exotic places in the Middle East—people said that someone had been bitten by a snake hidden in the curly fur, but Maureen didn't care, she wanted one anyway—and those rings that had chains that joined up to a bracelet on your wrist. Going into that store was like travelling to another country, and you could get high on the smell of patchouli, jasmine, dirt, sheep and some kind of poopy smell like that Hare Krishna incense. She'd gone to the store with Bo just after they'd started going out together. Joyce hadn't seemed happy to see them.

"Joyce," Bo said, "how's it goin'?"

"Oh, it's goin'. Have you seen Fluff lately, Bo?" Joyce asked.

"No, I haven't, Joyce. I've been kinda busy lately," Bo said, putting his arm around Maureen and drawing her close.

Joyce leaned across the counter, moving her face in right next to Bo.

"Fellas like you, Bo, fellas like you, they should be neutered." Joyce smiled. "Oh yes, they should just round your kind up, bring you all into the veterinarians and have you all de-balled."

Bo made a menacing move with his chin toward Joyce but she didn't even blink. She just stood her ground, staring right back at him, and he was the one who had to do the back-down.

"Come on, let's get the fuck out of this shithole," he said, pulling Maureen out the door. Just before he left, he turned around, picked up a ceramic Buddha head, teal blue it was, and threw it with force and purpose at the full-length mirror. The head smashed to smithereens and the mirror broke into shards and crashed to the floor.

"Bo!" Maureen gasped. "What'd you do that for? Bo?"

Spittle was flying out of Bo's mouth, and his feet and hands were moving around spasmodically. He was so angry, so agitated, just vicious. He was in a red rage and Maureen felt afraid, very afraid. But at the same time, a part of her believed she would be all right, that she'd be safe. Because, he loved her—didn't he?

☠

In the Black Swan, Joyce was talking to Fluff and nodding in Maureen's direction. Fluff got up from the table and walked toward Maureen. *Oh fuck. What now?*

"Hello, Maureen."

"Hiya, Fluff," Maureen said in a high and fake-y sort of voice.

"I just wanted to come over and say how sorry I am for your loss. I saw you at the wake the other day, but I never got a chance to talk to you."

"Oh, thank you, Fluff. I . . . uh . . . I mean, we were, Bo and me were broken up so . . ."

"Oh, he never told me that."

"Oh, well, it just happened. Tuesday, just before . . . When were you talkin' to Bo?"

"He called on Tuesday afternoon."

"Oh, we broke up Tuesday morning."

"Funny he never said, though I didn't get to talk to him that long. He had to go."

"Where was he goin'?"

"Oh, someone was at the door, it was a meeting, or he was meeting someone. I'm not sure now. I didn't know then that it was the last time I'd ever get to talk to Trevor."

Fluff called Bo Trevor. She was the only one. Now here she was, standing in front of Maureen, dissolving into tears again. Maureen didn't know what to do. She half-heartedly patted Fluff on the shoulder.

"You're so strong, Maureen. How d'you do it?" Fluff said.

"Do it?"

"Keep going, I mean."

"Oh, well, I think it's what Bo would have wanted." Was there a phrase book of bullshit remarks that she'd inadvertently swallowed since Bo's death? Where did all this empty nonsense come from? She stood up, put her arm around Fluff and walked her back to her table of friends and comforters. Joyce thanked Maureen in that off-putting, direct way of hers.

"You seem to be holding up pretty good, Maureen."

"Yea, well, Joyce, what else can you do?"

Maureen felt rather than heard the door open and Jack and Deucey Dunne come in. With a sense of relief, she turned away from Joyce and them and walked over to Deucey.

"Whaddya at, Deuce?"

"Not much, Maureen. Whadda you at?"

"Lookin' for you."

"Oh, yea?"

"Yea."

Jack stepped up to Maureen, leaned in and said through gritted teeth, "Yea, and the cops came lookin' for us too, right after the funeral yesterday."

"Did they?"

"Did they?" Jack mocked her. "Yes, they did, Maureen." He took a step in closer. "And why do you think the coppers came lookin' for us?"

"I don't know," Maureen practically whispered.

"What? Speak up, Maureen. You don't have no trouble speakin' up when you're talkin' to the cops, have ya, rat?"

Suddenly, the club was quiet, the band having gone on break, and everybody heard Jack call out Maureen.

"I never said anything—"

"That's not what the pigs were sayin'."

"I just said that Bo had problems with lots of people, and like he had a problem, like, with Deucey."

Deucey was standing back, just looking on. He looked deeply uncomfortable with the way the conversation was going. His eyes were darting back and forth like he was looking for a way to escape. He raised his hands in a this-got-nothing-to-do-with-me kind of gesture.

Jack moved even closer to Maureen. "Next time you're talking to your piggy pals, Mo-reen"—he poked his short, stubby finger into Maureen's chest with enough force to drive her back a step—"you leave me and Deucey out of it."

Joyce was suddenly standing between Maureen and Jack.

"Back off, Jack. Leave her alone."

"None of your business, Juice. This is between me and her."

"Well," said Juicy Joyce, "now it's between you and her and *me*."

The club was so quiet, Maureen could hear her heart beat. Jack gave Joyce one long look, grabbed Deucey by the arm, gave Maureen a final poke in the chest and walked out the door.

"Are you all right?" asked Joyce.

"Yea, yea," said Maureen. She turned half pleadingly to Joyce. "I don't know why I can't keep my big mouth shut. It's like as soon as I think it, I gotta say it." Joyce caught Maureen's eye. "All I said to the cops, Joyce, was that Bo was mad at—"

"Maureen, Maureen, you're doin' it again. Don't be tellin' every-body everything, okay?"

"All right, all right," Maureen said and, with great effort, stopped talking. She stood there for an awkward moment and finally said, "How's Carleen? Do you guys ever hear from her?"

Joyce's face darkened.

"Is she still up in Montreal with that fella, Joyce?"

"No, no she's not."

"Oh, is she home?"

"She's not home." Joyce turned away.

Maureen just barely stopped herself from saying, "Well, where is she then?" Some word that Maureen could never remember was supposed to be the better part of valour. *But you're so far away from being whatever that word is*, Maureen's brain said to her, *that you don't even know that word.*

"Discretion," Maureen said. Out loud, she realized.

"What?" Joyce turned.

"Nothing, just a word."

Joyce looked like she was going to say something, but instead started back to the table.

"Well, say hi to Carleen when you talk to her."

Joyce didn't answer. Maureen turned and sat back down at the bar. *Well, I'm just gonna sit to myself here at the bar and not talk to anyone.*

"Rita, can I have a whisky please? Oh, no, no, no, Rita, I won't have a whisky. I'll have a Glenfiddich."

"Which is a whisky," Rita said.

"Yea, but it's a special whisky. And that's what I want: a special whisky . . . a special double whisky."

As soon as Maureen had a mouthful, she felt that wonderful I-don't-give-a-fuck-about-anything-or-anyone feeling spread right through her, and with a thud, finally her heart fell out of her throat and back into the spot where it was supposed to be.

CHAPTER SIXTEEN

As Maureen sat at the bar of the Black Swan, she thought that maybe she wouldn't finish her second double whisky. Maybe she'd go back to the apartment and have a look around. Of course, the cops had probably gone over every bit of the apartment by now with a fine-tooth comb and would have it all roped off, too. But maybe she'd be able to spot something that they couldn't. *Yea, right. Because you're so smart . . .*

"Okay, okay, shut up!" Maureen said to her mind. Even if she *was* an idiot, she still wanted to go back to the apartment and have a poke. The cops must have Bo's bank book and would have noticed the big deposits he'd made over the last couple of months. Why hadn't the cops already known about DAFT? Were the boys paying them off? Oh Christ, paying off the cops. That probably only happened in the movies. She finished off the double whisky.

The apartment wasn't roped off and the key still worked. Maureen crept in. It was pitch-black. The curtains were closed. She'd tie-dyed some cotton for the curtains and Bo's mother had run them up on her machine when they'd first moved in together. Bo had made a rough table that folded back out of the way in the tiny kitchen, as well as a number of other improvements, and he pointed out that she'd done nothing. He seemed hurt by that, by her lack of involvement. So she made the curtains and he was pleased, and then he had his mother line them so they would block out all the light. With the curtains closed, the apartment was like a cave. There were no windows in the bedroom or the kitchen, and there was just one small frosted window in the bathroom. She could see now with hindsight that she did nothing with the apartment because she didn't want to be in that apartment, but at the time, she didn't know it. She couldn't remember one good time they had there. Most of the time, she'd been angry—angry when she was drunk, depressed when she wasn't.

Even at the very beginning, Maureen was already living like a person in a dream. Events moved on, and without thought, Maureen moved on with them. Sometimes when she didn't get out of bed for days on end, time would disappear on her. Right in the middle of whatever she was doing, just putting on her boots say, she'd be staring down at her feet when she'd realize that she'd been staring at them for a long time, because every tiny detail of the boots was so familiar to her: the green laces, the gold stitching, the slewed toe.

Maureen took a chance and turned on the desk lamp, figuring that if she couldn't see the street light, then the street probably couldn't see her. She poked through the desk Bo had built, a little rough secretary made out of plywood, but found nothing new since the last time she'd gone searching. She tried not to look at the big brown bottle of chlordane in the corner of the living room or the Flit gun right next to it. She snapped on the light in the bedroom. It was covered in green and gold wallpaper—not just the walls, but also the ceiling. It looked like wrapping paper. The bedroom was like a big awful present that she and Bo had been trapped inside all that time. Gathering her courage, she stepped into the room and started searching through the wardrobe. There was Bo's grey suit on a hanger, still shredded. The tiny manicure scissors she'd used wouldn't cut through the shoulders, so the suit still hung. It frightened her to remember herself standing there at the closet, blankly cutting away at whatever piece of grey fabric would give in to the scissors. She remembered now how she'd stood there in that awful bedroom for hours destroying that suit. When she had done as much damage as she could, she had closed the wardrobe door, walked over to the bed and gotten quietly under the covers. It was after that, she supposed, that Bo had scrawled "Tiny Tits" across her two best bras.

Jesus, being back in the apartment was getting her nowhere and just making her feel even worse. The jockey club and the two double whiskies were giving her that too-much-but-not-enough-alcohol feeling: the headache, dry mouth. Maybe she'd go back to George's and see if he had anything to drink, or maybe she'd just lie down right here. It was still half her apartment; she'd paid half the rent till the end of December. No, she wouldn't get in that bed, the bed that Bo built. Maybe Bo had made her bed, but she didn't have to keep lying in it. She'd just lie down on the floor—she was used to that anyway. Whenever he was mad at her, he wouldn't let her lie in the bed. She would just put her head down here on the floor and rest her eyes.

SHE WOKE TO A NOISE AT THE APARTMENT DOOR. SHE COULD hear the door open very slowly. *Fuck, I forgot to lock the door*, Maureen thought. She heard footsteps. She held her breath. Maybe she could get in under the bed—no, it was a platform bed. She crept around to the other side, away from the bedroom door. She heard a big thump and a voice that sounded like Jack Dunne's.

"Ow! Fuck!" the voice that sounded like Jack's said.

"Shut up, Jacky," said a voice she'd recognize anywhere: Fox Albert. "What are we looking for here?"

"I don't know, b'y. Something, anything—receipts, invoices— anything that could compromise the business."

"Jesus, Jacky. The cops got all of that by now, and please tell me that you are not stupid enough to have given out invoices and receipts pertaining to our other businesses, are you?"

"No, b'y. I just thought that prick mighta had something, or . . . Just shine the flashlight around the floor. Jesus, what a state of dirt. What—do Maureen never clean up?"

"Something tells me that Maureen is not exactly a star in the whole housekeeping department," said Fox.

"Well, what department do she star in?" said Jacky, snickering.

"I wouldn't say Maureen would shine in any department."

You prick. Maureen thought back to the night in Montreal. *You weren't exactly a star yourself.* She felt like sticking her fingers in her ears; she wasn't sure she could bear hearing any more bad shit about herself right now.

"Except the Useless, Loaded Drunk, Falling Down and Startin' Rackets Department," Jack said. "Or the Sookin' and Bawlin' All Night Department," he added.

"Nice legs, though. And tits."

"Tiny, though."

"Yea, nice though for all that," said Fox.

"Jesus," said Jacky. "Look at that! There it is: my chip. That's where I lost it."

"What?"

"My twenty-four-hour chip."

"What are you talking about?"

"My Desire Chip, b'y, from AA. You get it for twenty-four hours of sobriety—the hardest twenty-four hours I ever fuckin' put in."

"What are you doin'?" Fox asked.

"I'm picking it up. I'm takin' it. I must've dropped it on Tuesday."

"You were here on Tuesday? The day Bo disappeared?"

"Yea. Just for a minute, though."

"What were you doing?"

"I just needed to talk to him, after what happened with Deuce. I wanted to put the frightners on him. But just talk. But you know Bo . . . We had a few shoves at each other—he started it—and that's when I lost my chip, I guess."

"Jack?"

"Cool it, Fox. He was fine when I left him, b'y; hungover like a bastard but definitely breathing."

"Jack, if you're lying—are you crazy? Put that back right where you got it. The cops probably know exactly where that is, and if it's gone, they'll go lookin' for it."

"Jesus, my twenty-four-hour chip. It's my lucky chip. I've been going cracked looking for it since Wednesday. I don't even know if I can stay sober without it."

"Don't be stupid, Jacky. I didn't even know that you were an alchy."

"Oh, yea. Sober alchy. Sober almost four and a half years."

"And you never told the rest of the boys?"

"Why should I?" said Jack.

"No secrets in the DAFT brotherhood—that whole thing. Remember that, Jack?"

"Bullshit. It's an anonymous program, Fox."

"Yea, and what other secrets are you keepin', Jacky?"

"Me to know and you to find out." Jack laughed.

"Yes," said Fox. "And make no mistake about it, I will find out. You made me come back here for that? All the receipts and stuff, that was just bullshit?"

"I had to find it, b'y."

"Well, now you're going to have to put it back on the floor where you found it, and we're gonna have to get the fuck out of here. Who knows you're in AA?"

Maureen heard their footsteps heading back toward the door.

"Nobody."

"Nobody?"

"No-body. Nobody but the crowd in AA."

"Oh, well then. We're fucked."

"Anonymity is the whole fucking foundation of the entire fucking organization, Fox."

"Yea, right. Does Deucey know?"

"Yea, Deuce knows," Jack said as he closed the door quietly after himself. Then he said something about Deucey not drinking because of the meds or something, but his voice was muffled. Maureen wasn't sure.

She didn't move for another few minutes. So that's what they thought of her: that she was useless and a troublemaker to boot. Thinking about it made her feel sick to her stomach. She got up from behind the bed and dusted herself off. It was true: the floor was rotten with mildew and dust bunnies and general dirt and stuff.

What had Jacky been doing here on Tuesday, the day the cops figured Bo had disappeared—the last time, as far as Maureen knew, anybody had talked to Bo? Fluff said there had been a knock at the door and Bo had hung up, and now Maureen figured that must've been Jack coming to see Bo. But then what happened?

The whole thing was starting to seem like math to Maureen, and her mind was doing the exact same thing it did whenever it was presented with a math problem: *A man gets on a train at Philadelphia. The train is travelling at 60 miles per hour. On a parallel track, another man gets on a train* . . . Where that train was coming from, Maureen didn't even know, because every time she got to that part, her brain would check out. It would just fill up with white noise and start screaming at Maureen, *You're an idiot! You're a fucking idiot!* Maybe if she just lay down for a few minutes more, she could figure it all out. Or maybe the answers would come to her in a dream like they came to Carlos Castaneda or Don Juan. She had never read those books, but Bo and them talked about the books all the time, so she had pretended she'd read them too—so much so that sometimes now she forgot and thought she had read them.

Of course, nothing had ever come to Maureen in a dream, except the Old Hag. Sometimes when she was sleeping, Maureen couldn't get her breath because an old and terrifying woman was lying on top of her, crushing her chest, and no matter how hard Maureen tried, she couldn't get the old woman off because Maureen's arms would suddenly have no strength, and if she struck the old woman, her blows had no impact. Maureen would get weaker and weaker, but just before she died from not being able to breathe, she'd wake up screaming.

The Sarge said that back when she was young, the Old Hag was so common, and people were so crucified with her riding them every night, that they actually made Hag boards—pieces of lumber with the pointy bits of nails sticking up out of them, which you'd strap onto your chest every night before you lay down to go to sleep, to keep the Old Hag off. By the time Maureen got to thinking about Hag boards, her head was back down on the floor and she was drifting off.

CHAPTER SEVENTEEN

THE NEXT TIME MAUREEN WOKE UP, THE POLICE WERE in the apartment. She could hear McCarthy and Kent.

"Was he in AA?" Maureen heard one of them say.

"Well, not according to anyone who knows him," said the detective sergeant.

"But it is just a twenty-four-hour chip," McCarthy said. "He coulda just joined."

"Well, let's talk to the girlfriend. See if she knows anything."

Maureen made only the tiniest of sounds as she tried to make herself as small as possible, but McCarthy was standing in the doorway of the bedroom like a shot. *His mind might be dull*, Maureen thought, *but he's got ears on him like a fucking hoot owl.*

"Who's here? It's the police. Come out with your hands up!"

"It's me," Maureen said.

"Me? Who me?"

"Me: Maureen Brennan." She felt stupid walking into her own living room with her hands up over her head. The constab didn't even have guns—what were they going to do to her if she didn't have her hands up? Hit her with their nightsticks, she guessed.

"Miss Brennan," said Kent, "this is serious business. This apartment is a crime scene. The site of a possible murder."

"What? He was murdered here? There's no blood or anything. Why do you think he was murdered here?"

"Miss Brennan, *we* are asking the questions," he said, losing his temper. "Now, what are you doing here?"

"It's still my apartment, isn't it? 'Cause I'm paid up till the end of the month, so I was just gonna sleep here for a night or so, just till, you know, I figure stuff out."

"You can't just sleep here. Didn't you see the notice on the door, maid?" McCarthy said.

"No. I never seen a sign or nothing, and nobody told me I couldn't sleep here."

The detective sergeant sighed.

"McCarthy, open those curtains."

When McCarthy opened the curtains, the grey morning light poured in and there was snow swirling around outside. Maureen realized she'd slept through the night.

"While we've got you here, Miss Brennan, was Mr. Browne a member of Alcoholics Anonymous?"

"No! Jumpins! Bo always said he'd rather be dead than not drink. Oh, Jesus, and now he is." Maureen tried to look suitably sad about that fact. "He always hated people who wouldn't take a drink. He didn't trust 'em, he said."

"Are you?" asked the detective sergeant.

"Am I what?"

"A member of Alcoholics Anonymous?"

"No, no, gosh no. I maybe should be, 'cause, you know, it's not like every time I drink I get in trouble, but every time I'm in trouble I was always drinking, you know?" Maureen laughed half-heartedly. "What do you think? Do you think I should join?" While Maureen waited for Kent's answer, McCarthy shoved a little brown coin the size of a silver dollar in Maureen's face.

"Well, where did this come from then, missy?"

"I don't know. I never laid eyes on it till you showed it to me now." Maureen felt relieved. It was so much better when you could tell the actual truth.

"Have you got friends who are members of AA?"

"Have I got *any* friends, really, is more the question," Maureen said, but seeing the detective sergeant's look, she quickly added, "Not that I know of. Like I told ya: anyone too weak to be able to take a drink, Bo never trusted 'em."

"What about your friend Mr. Taylor?"

"Uh, George? Oh, no, sure George was never here in this apartment." Yes, that's all she would have needed, for George to have shown up here when she was with Bo. Bo flipped if a guy even looked at her. She was never allowed to talk to anyone when they went out, and he never wanted anyone else in the apartment either. She guessed she should tell the cops about what she'd overheard last night. That's what a good girl would do. But the way things were going, a good girl could very easily find herself dead, trussed up in the trunk of a car, up on the South Side Hills.

"We've spoken to Mr. Dunne," said the detective sergeant.

"Which one?" said Maureen.

"To both of them, actually."

"I already know that," said Maureen, "because both of them 'actually' spoke to me. Thanks a lot for ratting me out to the boys, 'cause that's really gonna make my life a whole lot easier."

"Yes, that is one of our major concerns, Miss Brennan, making your life easier," said Kent as McCarthy used his handkerchief to pick up the brown gallon bottle of chlordane.

Maureen blanched. She tottered to the left. Whenever Maureen got a fright, her equilibrium just went off and she kind of drifted to the left. Kent put out his hand to steady her.

"Are you okay?"

"Yea," Maureen said, "yea. It's just that I didn't eat, and you know, Mom got diabetes and so I got blood sugar, and so unless I get something to eat, I just get weak."

McCarthy opened the fridge door and used the same handkerchief to pick up the glass decanter of orange juice.

"Here, I'll pour you a glass of this and you can knock that back in ya."

It was the glass decanter, the one that cheap Canadian whisky comes in, the one that Maureen and Bo used to mix up frozen orange juice—the poisoned one.

"No, no." Maureen instinctively took a step back while fighting hard to keep her face in neutral.

"Go ahead, it's not gonna kill ya," McCarthy said.

Yea, that's what you think, Maureen thought. Her mind, totally out of her control, was deciding to crack jokes.

"No, no," she said out loud. "I hate that orange juice. It's not even real orange juice. It's just old Tang, and it will make me all hyperglycemic. I'll just go down to George's and get something, some breakfast, some cornflakes or something."

"There's a piece of pizza here," McCarthy said, his head still in the fridge. "You scarf that down."

"No, no thanks."

Kent finally intervened. "McCarthy, that's all evidence. This is a closed crime scene."

Maureen was somewhat relieved that Bo hadn't eaten the piece of pepperoni pizza, and she could still see the tomato, the deli turkey and the piece of cheese, so he hadn't eaten those either, but had he drunk some of the orange juice? She thought she remembered the decanter being about half full after she'd poured in the chlordane on Tuesday morning, and it still looked about half full. But she didn't have a real clear picture of how full it had been. He could have downed a couple of gulps. If only the cops weren't there, she could maybe think better and get a grasp on exactly how much orange juice there'd been.

Kent picked up the chlordane bottle. "Where did this come from, Miss Brennan? This is 100 per cent chlordane. It's not the kind of thing people usually have in their apartments."

"Yea," said Maureen. "See, the landlord sent in the exterminators to get rid of the earwigs, and I did see a cockroach too one time, and buddy went off and left that, and that Flit gun too. We called him right away. He was supposed to come back and get it

Wednesday morning. And by Wednesday, I was gone, and I guess . . . so was Bo."

Gone, gone, thought Maureen's crazy mind. *Gone in a big way. Real, real gone, man.*

"Miss Brennan, you're smiling. Is there something funny?" Kent said.

"Oh, no. That's just what ya call, what ya call it . . . I got that . . . George calls it . . . uh . . . inappropriate laughter response, and the more I get upset, the more I smile. If things get much worse, I'll be laughing like crazy all the time. Yea, I got that," she said again, lamely. "That inappropriate laughter response thing."

"You were the last person to see our victim alive."

"But Fluff was talking to him later on that same day."

"Fluff?"

"Yea, Bo's ex." Maureen paused. "Fluff. Florence, I guess, is her name. Florence Dawe."

"And she was still in communication with Mr. Browne?"

"Oh, yea. They were close. She talked to him all the time. And I never really talked to him where I left Tuesday morning. The last time I saw him was, you know, four o'clock that morning."

"And what was Mr. Browne doing at that time?"

"He was going in to go to bed."

"And you?"

"I was staying out here, on the couch . . . floor, really. Yea . . ." She didn't know how much to tell them about the events of late Monday night and early Tuesday morning, how Bo had finally worn himself out hauling her around the living room by her hair, how she had stopped screaming and just lay there, like nothing, like empty clothes on the painted wooden floor, how she guessed he'd just got sick of kicking away at a dead thing, like they say that people do get sick of eating lobster, drinking champagne and kicking dead bodies. She wanted to tell them everything but feared that would put her in an even worse light.

"We were, you know, not getting along that good," Maureen said finally.

"You were often not getting along 'that good,' were you, Maureen?" The detective sergeant made air quotation marks around "that good."

"Yea, I s'pose," Maureen muttered.

"Mr. Browne was often violent toward you, Miss Brennan, and you told us earlier, you said yourself, that being the recipient of Mr. Browne's violence could well cause someone to retaliate, and that retaliation might get out of hand." Detective Sergeant Kent's eyes had Maureen locked in the eye hold again.

"Are you interrogating me?" Maureen tried to break eye contact with the detective sergeant. She was aware that she was shifting around from foot to foot and generally acting like someone who had something to hide.

"You have a long history of domestic disputes involving Mr. Browne, and you were often at the receiving end of Mr. Browne's blows. Did you do anything to provoke this violence, Miss Brennan?"

"Breathed."

"What?"

"Well, sometimes that's all I'd have to do: breathe. Just the sound of my breathing, he said, would send him into a red rage and then . . ." Now it was Maureen who tried to hold Kent's gaze, but he looked away.

"Why didn't you bring charges against him?"

"Right," said Maureen. "Why didn't *you?*"

"Well, we can't, by law, bring charges in that instance," Kent said. "The theory being that couples involved in domestic disputes are in a 'special relationship,' and the police and the courts and other people should not interfere in that 'special relationship' unless called upon to do so by one of the parties involved in that 'special relationship' . . ." His voice trailed off.

"I was afraid to charge him—afraid of what he might do to me if I did," Maureen said.

McCarthy burst in, "Did you kill him, Miss Brennan?"

Maybe I did. Maybe I didn't. I don't know. Maureen's crazy mind was racing, pushing her to say everything it was thinking.

"Why would anyone do something like that?" Maureen said aloud. McCarthy pointed at her and then at Kent.

"See that, Sergeant Kent? See that? That's classic. She's evading the question, plus she's trying to disassociate herself from the event by taking the 'I' out of the sentence. She's opting out. She's a text-book case of a Deceptive Individual."

"Okay, McCarthy, you read the Behaviour Systems Analysis Review section of the police manual. Good for you. As you can imagine, I've read it too, and I can see where you paid special attention to the profile of the Deceptive Individual, but I wonder how you managed to miss the part in the Reid Nine Steps of Interrogation Method that states, categorically, that the interrogator must allow the subject to go through their *entire story*, so that the suspect can give the 'pure' version of the events. Do you remember that part of the training, McCarthy? Do you?"

"I'm a suspect?" Maureen said.

McCarthy kept his head down and looked suitably abashed.

"Shure Bo used to murder me—I mean, he brutalized me. How could I get someone the size of him all trussed up and into the trunk of his car?"

"How do you know the victim was trussed up inside the trunk of his car?" McCarthy shot back.

Maureen looked at him. "'Cause you said he was? Remember? The first time I was talking to you."

"Oh yea," McCarthy mumbled.

The look Kent gave McCarthy seemed to put a hole right through the young cop's know-it-all facade, and Maureen could see all his cockiness leaking out through it.

Maureen wanted to tell them that Jacky Dunne was in AA. She could just say that she'd heard a rumour and that she didn't know for sure, but Christ, with blabbermouth McCarthy, she couldn't afford to be caught with her mouth going and get in any more trouble with the Dunnes.

The officers detained her at the apartment for a couple of hours. McCarthy mostly kept his mouth shut, but Kent really gave Maureen the gears. He asked, "Could you tell me in more exact detail about the events of the night of December 7, morning of

December 8 . . ." And when she described them, he asked her to go even further into the details, followed by "Miss Brennan, what made you decide to . . ." and "When and why didn't you . . ." Then he started in all about her emotions and how she was feeling then and how she was feeling now. What was her reaction when she'd first heard the news? How did she feel after that Monday night beating? Those were really hard questions for Maureen to answer because she was never quite sure how she felt at any given moment. It usually took her a couple of months to figure out how she felt. Plus, by the time the cops had gotten to the feelings and emotions part, Maureen was already worn down to a thread, and so she just shut up out of it. She had a right, she remembered, to remain silent, and that's exactly what she was going to do, even though remaining silent was against the very nature of her being. She was going to remain silent and, unless they were going to arrest her, walk out the door.

"Maureen, even though you would never go through with it, would you ever think of murdering Trevor 'Bo' Browne?"

A silent Maureen was almost to the door when she turned.

"No. Why would I think about that?"

"You never thought about it? Not once? Not even when he beat you so badly that"—the detective sergeant reached into a folder and took out a page and read—"you were 'detained overnight at the Grace General Hospital with a broken rib and a fractured collarbone,' and the admitting doctor was concerned about a concussion and a possible brain bleed?"

"Yea, not even then," Maureen lied. But was she really lying? Because she had had no intention of killing Bo. But if she hadn't meant to kill him, then what in the name of God had she meant to do? And how much chlordane would it take to kill a person? Maureen didn't have a clue.

The detective sergeant told her to come down to the station first thing tomorrow morning.

CHAPTER EIGHTEEN

MAUREEN WAS RELIEVED TO FINALLY BE OUT OF THE apartment and free and on the street—*Oh God! George!* She'd forgotten all about him. He was probably worried sick about her. She'd been gone all night. Well, good. Let him worry, because the more you were nice to them, the more you considered their feelings (Ha! Like they even had any feelings. They only had the one feeling: stick it in and go at it) and the better you were to them, the worse they treated you. But she knew she should go down to George's. But first she was going to the library, the Gosling Memorial Library on Duckworth Street.

Maureen had always loved the library, despite having been in the stacks when some guy had hauled it out and waved it at her. Another time, a fella standing in Biography was pulling away at himself. Jesus, why did they always have to find her? It was like she had a sign on her that said, "Abuse me. I'm no fucking good anyway. If you require someone to waggle your dick at, here I am." *I'm like a walking buffet for the pervert crowd.* She was getting worked up.

To calm herself down, she went straight to the card catalogue.

She loved the card catalogue: everything there was numbered and in its place. Good old Melvil Dewey. She looked under the 500s, for Science, maybe 540, she supposed for Chemistry. Oh, it was glorious. All the books on one subject all together on the shelves, all numbered, no chaos, three numbers to the left of the decimal point and a limitless amount of numbers after the decimal to indicate what each book was and where it was, and the cutter number to tell you the author of the book.

She found *Poisons and Pesticides of the Modern Age* by G. Botkin. Chlordane was even listed on the typed-up part of the card. She wrote out the number 542.580973B8261956COP2. She knew she didn't have to write it all down, but she wanted to—she wanted to head into the stacks fully armed.

Maureen looked for chaos and instability and loved the unpredictable. But there was a part of her that longed for the comfort of order, a part that felt so much better inside structure. She loved the soothing certainty of a place for everything and everything in its place. She loved that 542.580973 was right there in the stacks after 542.580972. It brought her a real moment of joy that there were two copies, just like it said on the card. Yes, she loved the library and all the glorious organization that the library contained. But she had never let on to anyone that she felt that way. She was ashamed of the dweeby person who loved all that order. She didn't want anyone to think that she was one of those foolish, pasty-faced, overweight, drippy dorks going around being joyous about books, lurking about in the stacks, burying their heads in texts, with food stains on the front of their blouses from always reading while trying to eat. Who she wanted to be was someone more like Faye Dunaway in *Bonnie and Clyde*, or Julie Christie in *McCabe & Mrs. Miller*, beautiful and hungry and living wild and free and ... She wasn't really sure what the words were to describe who it was that she longed to be, but she longed to be that other person so badly, she could practically taste it. It wasn't just that she wanted to be someone else; she physically *needed* to be someone else.

Maureen sat down with *Poisons and Pesticides of the Modern Age* and opened it up to the section on chlordane. "Chlordane: a man-made mixture of chemicals widely used as an insecticide ... Chlordane is moderately to highly toxic. Symptoms usually start within 45 minutes to several hours after exposure to a toxic dose." Okay, but what was a toxic dose? How much straight chlordane had she poured in the orange juice that morning, and was it enough to be a toxic dose?

"Convulsions may be the first sign of poisoning," she read. *Oh! Convulsions? Oh dear Jesus!* "May be preceded by nausea, vomiting and gut pain." Of course, if Bo had those symptoms, he'd assume that it was because of the almost full bottle of whisky he'd baled back into him the night before. "Initially, poison victims appear agitated." Well, Bo was always up on bust agitated-wise. "But later, they become depressed, uncoordinated, tired and confused."

Except for the convulsions, it sounded like a real bad hangover, the kind where you wake up still drunk, and then as you start to sober up, you feel worse and worse. She kept reading and finally found what a toxic dose would be. The amount of chlordane that was lethal orally was called LD-50, meaning that 50 per cent of the subjects died. The dose that would kill 50 per cent of study subjects was 50–500 milligrams of pure chlordane per kilogram of body weight. *So, how many kilograms was Bo? And how many the fuck was 50–500 milligrams? How much did that mean? What was it in ounces or pounds, or whatever the fuck?*

All she wanted to know was would the amount of chlordane she put in the orange juice be enough to kill Bo. God, she was drowning in her own ignorance. She had to look up everything. She knew fuck all about fuck all, just like Bo always said. According to the librarian, the slash in "mgs/kgs" meant "per," so it meant "milligrams per kilograms." But, Jesus, she was still no further ahead, since they'd only just brought in the metric and Maureen still thought in the old ounces and gallons. She got out the *Encyclopedia Britannica*, which had weights and measures conversion tables. *Oh God, why don't I just kill myself?* Math had the opposite effect that the Dewey Decimal System had on her, though she knew it was all numbers. Some numbers gave you comfort and some numbers— like conversion tables—just fucked with your head and made you angry and hopeless all at the same time.

Okay. She could do this, but she'd need a piece of paper. So grams. Okay, how many grams are there in a cup? Turns out there are 340 grams in a cup. And it would only take six grams to kill a 210-pound man. So it was starting to look like it would only take a very tiny amount of chlordane in the orange juice to kill at least 50 per cent of the people who were given chlordane-laced orange juice. The thing that was becoming clear to Maureen was that she'd probably really overdone it on the chlordane—she'd always had a heavy hand. The Sarge told her that's why she was no good at making cakes.

So, she had poured a lethal amount—actually probably a thousand times the lethal amount—into Bo's orange juice. She'd tipped up the bottle of chlordane and poured *glug glug*, and maybe even a third glug, into the decanter. But where did all that fancy number fuckery get her? It was now clear that she could have killed him, according to what she could understand from the book. It seemed like she had definitely put enough poison in the orange juice to kill him, but the question was did he even *drink* the orange juice?

The person across the table from her got up and walked away, leaving behind a pile of books. Maureen looked at them, desperate for a distraction. One was called *Alcoholics Anonymous*. On the cover it read, "This is the Third Edition of the Big Book, the Basic Text for Alcoholics Anonymous." Geez, everywhere Maureen looked these days, there it was. It was like AA was haunting her.

CHAPTER NINETEEN

GEORGE WAS AT THE UNIVERSITY WHEN MAUREEN GOT to his place, so she just walked in. He never locked the apartment. He said that if people were determined to come in and rob him blind, there was no lock he knew of that was going to keep them out, and they would just end up doing a whole lot more damage if they had to kick down the door to get at his stuff. Maureen sat down and called Fluff. Whoever answered the phone said that Fluff was down at the boutique, giving Joyce a hand.

"Boutique Artistique—cool threads for kind heads," Fluff answered the phone.

"Fluff, it's me, Maureen."

"Maureen." Fluff's voice registered a little coldness, and then she gave that apologetic little laugh of hers and said, "Joyce is just making me try out a new slogan for the shop." Another little apologetic laugh. "What's going on?"

"Yea, yea, I just wanted to ask you, Fluff, on that Tuesday, the last time you were talking to Bo"—Maureen could hear a little catch in Fluff's breathing when she said Bo's name, so she hurried on—"how did he sound?"

"Regular, you know . . . a bit pissed off, but then that was Trevor."

"Did he sound agitated or excited at all?" Maureen asked, looking at the notes she'd taken at the library.

"No more than usual, you know. He was fed up with the job and he wanted to get away from the boys at DAFT, and he had a bad hangover, you know."

"Really?"

"Yea. He just said he was sick as a dog with a hangover and he was gonna have to start taking it easy."

"Did he sound"—what was it they said in the book?—"you know, down in the dumps, desperate or confused at all?"

"No, someone came to the door and he had to go."

"What time was that, Fluff?"

"What, are you suddenly the Riddler, Maureen? Why are you asking all these questions?"

"Well, Fluff, I just want to know what exactly happened that day that Bo went missing."

"Why? What good will that do? That won't bring Trevor back."

The thought that Bo could come back sent Maureen into a spin. Her thoughts went right off the rails for a second.

"Maureen? . . . Maureen? Are you still there?"

Maureen couldn't answer. She was lost in a violent reverie, seeing herself on the floor that night, trying to shield her face from Bo's kicking.

"Maureen, look I gotta go. Someone just came in the shop. Maureen? . . . "

Finally, Maureen croaked out, "Okay, Fluff. See ya. See ya later on."

Maureen hung up, still shaken from the thought of Bo being resurrected. She had to sit—her knees felt buckly. She fell back into the beanbag chair and felt a hardcover book under her. The page the book was open to said, "Section 23, The Offences Against the Person Act." Maureen continued to read: ". . . whosoever shall unlawfully and maliciously administer to or cause to be adminis-tered to or taken by any other person any poison or other destruc-tive or noxious thing, so as thereby to endanger the life of such person, shall be guilty of an offence. The maximum penalty for an offence under Section 23," Maureen read with mounting horror, "is ten years' imprisonment." She closed the book, *Martin's Annual Criminal Code, 1969.* According to the back cover, George had bor-rowed it from The Law Society of Newfoundland Library.

George thinks I'm guilty . . . Maybe I am guilty? She could hear the big iron bars slamming shut all around her. Just then, George came in through the door. Maureen screamed and jumped up. George fell back, at first alarmed and then defensive. Maureen rushed to apologize.

"I was so lost in thought. I was in another world . . ."

"I don't know what you're getting so hinky about. You're putting the Chinese angle on me, and all I'm doing is trying to come into my own joint. No need to throw another ing-bing."

"I don't even know what you're saying. I'm sorry. I was just startled."

"I could bounce, if you like."

"What?"

"I could leave. What have you got there?" George asked, nodding toward the book.

"Oh, this was . . . I was . . . this was just . . ."

"Oh, *Martin's Annual Criminal Code*," George said, taking the book from her hands. All of a sudden, he was full of false jollity. "I guess I should have cheesed that."

"George, I don't know what you're saying. Please, just talk to me like you're a normal human being and not someone from one of those stupid Mickey Spillane books."

"Not Mickey Spillane; it's Raymond Chandler."

"You think I'm guilty, don't you?"

"Maybe. Maybe not. But I gotta couple of Cs that says you will never see the inside of the calaboose."

Maureen gave him a hard look.

"I'm just saying, whether you're guilty or not, I don't think you'll ever do any jail time."

"Why?"

"'Cause there's too many people who'd like to see that booze hound in a Chicago overcoat."

"George!"

"You know he—Bo—coulda been trying to put the Chinese squeeze on that crowd of dope dealers. You know, chisel 'em outta their drug fortune."

"George, I found out today at the library that chlordane has an LD-50."

George looked at her blankly.

"It kills 50 per cent of the people that it's administered to, and I put a huge amount of chlordane into his orange juice."

"But when did you find out that chlordane kills people?"

"Today."

"Right. So, according to English law," George said, flipping through *Martin's Annual Criminal Code*, "an act doesn't make a person guilty, unless that person's mind is also guilty."

"I don't get it—what?"

"See, unless you had malice of forethought, *mens rea*, the guilty mind—did you mean to kill Bo with the chlordane?"

"No, I don't think so. It was like I wasn't the one who did it, like I was standing beside myself the morning when I did it." As Maureen spoke, she could see herself pouring in the poison and spraying the food with the Flit gun, but it was like she was remembering a movie or like someone else had done the deed and she just happened to be there to witness it. Oh, now her head was really pounding, just on one side—her eye, the side of her nose, all the way to the back of her neck. "But according to what I read there, even if I didn't kill him, I'm still a criminal. It says right in that book that if anybody pours any poison that endangers the life of a person, they'd be guilty of what they call in there 'a heinous crime.' I don't know what to do. Maybe I just need to take off."

"Yea, good thinking. Be a bim with a bindle. I mean, go on the lam . . . just run away. Look, it's as easy as duck soup. All you gotta do is drop a dime on them."

"Them who?"

"The boys, the DAFT boys. Put the finger on 'em."

"Oh, George," Maureen said in exasperation. "It'd be all right if you had a dust of sense, even two clicks to call a clue."

"Now I don't know what *you're* talking about."

"I'm already in trouble with the boys and with the cops, and now you want me to be a—"

"Snitch. A stoolie."

"Yea, and tell the cops about something I don't know that much about anyway. I'm just not smart enough for any of this."

She could see herself getting up on the stand, not like Marlene Dietrich, a woman of mystery with a jaunty hat and all that composure, giving nothing away, remaining a fascinating question mark. No, she'd be up on the stand all red-faced and burbling, spilling her guts to all comers. Sometimes Maureen despaired of herself: she really was deeply shallow. Here she was, guilty of what was called cold-blooded murder in books, and she was worrying about how she was going to look on the stand.

CHAPTER TWENTY

WHAT THE FUCK ARE YOU DOIN' HERE, RAT?"

Maureen had just walked up over the stairs and into the DAFT offices, which were right over the DAFT storefront on Duckworth Street. The storefront, presumably, was there to make the purchase of DAFT wooden shipping boxes more available to the general public, but the few times Maureen had actually been in there and all the times she'd passed by, she'd never seen an actual customer—just one of the boys' girlfriends or some fawning hanger-oner standing behind the counter, overseeing an empty store dotted with wood crates that were, according to the sign on the wall behind the counter, "heat-treated and stamped for export shipment."

Jack Dunne was sitting on the edge of his desk, and Maureen was surprised to see Joyce Maynard sitting on a chair in front of him. Joyce was not looking that happy.

"I need to talk to you," Maureen said to Jack. "What're you doin' here, Joyce?"

"Doing some business. Why?" said Joyce sharply.

"Oh, nothing. No reason. Just nosy, I guess," Maureen mumbled.

"Well, I'm just leaving. Remember what I said, Jack . . . Here, take my seat." Joyce gestured to Maureen.

Jack walked Joyce out of the office. Maureen sat down.

Would you take her grave as fast? Maureen's mind said.

Oh, come on, let us please just stay focused, Maureen said to her mind.

Focused on what? her mind asked.

I don't know . . . Focused on what happened to Bo.

You poisoned him! Maureen's mind shot back.

Maureen knew she had to stop having this internal dialogue because Maureen's mind was definitely not her friend. It was always calling her names, making fun of her, calling her down to the lowest, and that was probably the best of it, because otherwise it was just wandering around lost or making jokes at the worst possible times.

While Maureen was engaged with her mind, her hands and eyes were not idle. Her hands were shuffling through the papers that were right in front of her on the desk, turning them toward her so she could read them more easily. Her eyes rested on a document with the Canadian High Commission of Jamaica letterhead. It was a letter addressed to the Maynard family concerning one Carleen Maynard.

What! Holy fuck-a-moley, Carleen! . . . See, Maureen, you should never have left Carleen in Montreal.

Shut up! Maureen said to her mind.

She read: ". . . Carleen Maynard . . . held in custody, awaiting trial on charges of drug smuggling with intent to traffic, presently in remand at the St. Jago Women's Prison in Kingston." The document further said that Carleen Maynard was being provided "the most basic of meals, no bedding, the conditions were well below minimum standards . . . hole in the ground toilet . . ."

Maureen dropped the document and sat back in shock.

"So, like I said, rat, what are you doing here?"

"AA," she said in a whisper. "I heard you had something to do with it."

"Go on," said Jack. His expression did not ease up—not one little bit.

"Well, I wanna, you know, maybe not quit drinking altogether, but I'd like to drink more like other people drink, you know? I'd like to learn how to do that, and I thought maybe AA could help, and maybe you could tell me how to join up and maybe even give me a hand."

"AA is in the phone book, Maureen. Look it up."

"'Whenever someone reaches out for help, I want the hand of AA always to be there, and for that I am responsible,'" Maureen read from a scrap of paper she pulled out of her pocket. "I was reading some literature on AA at the library and that's what it said: that your main purpose, if you're a member of AA, is to stay sober *and* to help other alcoholics to achieve sobriety." Her stomach was churning, but she just kept staring at Jack.

"You've got a nerve on you like a toothache, Maureen, coming here, asking me for help, after you set the cops on us."

"First off, Jacky, promise soul to God, I never set the cops on ya. I just said Bo was mad at you and Deucey," Maureen said with a little bit of a tremor in her voice. "And second off, I didn't know where else to go."

The door opened and a jubilant Fox burst in, his flaming red hair shoulder-length now. "Okay, Jacky. We're all ready to peel out. We've got our last million. A doctor down the southwest coast has a hunk of cash and—Oh . . . hello . . . Maureen, I didn't know you were here." His look to Jack fairly screamed, *What the fuck is she doing here?* There was an awkward pause.

"Oh, hey, Fox," Maureen said. Suddenly, she was in her hospital room in Carbonear, seeing a flash of red hair as a baby, her baby, was being taken away from her. Did she dream that little scene? With that cocktail of drugs—the Miltowns, the epidural, the novocaine—she really couldn't be sure of her memories from that day. She caught herself gawking right at Fox's bright red head and blurted out the first thing on her mind: "Fox, ever hear anything from Carleen? You know, my friend Carleen, who started living with that guy Perry? You know, the fella you knew who owns The Rainbow Steps? Remember you were working for him or something?"

Fox shot Jack a worried look. There was another awkward pause.

"You know, Joyce's sister, Carleen? God, I never hear anything from Carleen anymore." Maureen was hoping one of them would say something about Carleen. Neither of them said anything; they just stared at her blankly. Finally, after a long, almost endless silence, Maureen stood up and said, "Well, I'd better not keep you guys, where you're so busy . . . getting ready for that big job." Maureen laughed hollowly. She was afraid she would just keep on saying the wrong things, one after another, and nobody else was saying anything, and so she feared that she was going to keep talking until there'd be nothing left of her; she'd just be talked out.

"Yea," Fox said, holding Maureen's gaze till she had to look away. He turned to Jack. "I'll see you later." He walked out of the room. Another long silence.

"Maybe you're not as stunned as you look, Maureen," Jack said.

Maureen tried to smile. "Yea, and that's lucky, isn't it? Because if I was that stunned, I'd probably be dead, like all those turkeys. You know turkeys: they're so stunned, they're always going around looking up at the sky when it's raining with their mouths open, so they end up drowning."

Jack's look was putting Maureen further off than she already felt. He didn't say anything.

"Like, that's really stunned, right?" Maureen said, wishing that the nuclear warheads they had in Cuba would fly over right now and land at the DAFT office here on Duckworth Street and obliterate everything. Why couldn't she just shut the fuck up?

"How'd you know I'm in AA?" Jack said.

Maureen didn't have an answer. She couldn't very well say, "I overheard you at the apartment."

"I don't know—it's just around. People know, that's all," she said.

"You seem to know a good bit about a lot of stuff, Maureen."

"I'll tell you the God's truth, Jack: I don't. I wish I was a person like that, but I'm not. Bo was right. He always said, 'Maureen,' he used to say, 'you know fuck all about fuck all.'"

Jack's eyes narrowed at the mention of Bo's name.

"Jesus, Maureen . . . All right, I'll take you to one meeting, but then you're on your own. Now, get out of the office. I got work to do." He sat back in his chair and put his feet up on the desk. "I'll pick you up at seven-thirty. Where will I pick you up?"

"I don't know." Maureen's mind raced to all of the places she didn't live anymore. "I'll meet you here, I guess. I'll be here for seven-thirty."

Boy, that was gutsy, Maureen thought to herself.

Or stupid, her mind said.

Well, I had to do something. I could end up in jail.

Or dead, her mind said. *If you keep bothering the Dunne boys, you won't have to worry about jail.*

Yea, keep a good thought, Maureen said to her mind.

Maybe if she spent time with Jack, she could find out what happened at Bo's apartment on Tuesday and she could—

Oh yea, right, Linc Hayes. Maureen's mind turned on her. *You're the real Mod Squad, you are. Oh, you'll find out who did it. Right. Of course, you will, where you have a hard time even finding out where your arse is using both hands.*

Maureen tried not to listen.

When she went downstairs, into the shop, Joyce was waiting for her. She grabbed Maureen by the arm and spat out, "What are you doing here?"

Maureen was taken aback and Joyce's anger frightened her, so of course, she came back at Joyce twice as angry.

"I could ask you the same thing, Joyce. And by the way, I saw the letter from the Canadian High Commission in Jamaica."

"Keep your voice down." Joyce practically hauled Maureen out into the street. "What are you doing poking around where you're not wanted? Do you think all this is a game or something?" Joyce was shaking, she was so upset. "It's not. Some big players got some big money in all this . . ." She gestured vaguely toward the DAFT premises. "And you can't fuck around with these people." She tried to calm down. "Listen to me, Maureen: we've got to do everything we can to keep the heat away from the boys. The boys are the only thing keeping Carleen alive right now because"—Joyce grabbed Maureen's arm again and tightened her grip until it really hurt; Maureen didn't make a peep, though—"Carleen got arrested at the airport in Montego Bay with three pounds of cocaine strapped to her legs."

Maureen gasped. She couldn't help herself.

"She'd already gotten through customs and everything," Joyce said. "She was just getting on the plane when it happened. The wind blew up her skirt and they saw it and stopped her and arrested her on the spot. That bastard she was with—"

"Perry," Maureen chimed in.

"Yea, Johns, the one she was living with, the one she was muling for, he had nothing on him, so he got on the plane, went back to Montreal and left her there. Even water costs money in jail in Jamaica. All they give Carleen is rice and sugar water twice a day. She could die if no one from the outside brings her any food. She's in constant danger and so are other people." She looked pointedly at Maureen. "Just think for a second, Maureen," Joyce said in a warning voice, pulling Maureen even closer. "For once in your life, try to listen. Even if you don't give a shit about yourself, my little sister is sleeping on concrete in front of a hole-in-the-floor toilet. One person in her cell was already murdered just since Carleen got there. The only reason—the *only* reason—that Carleen is alive today is because Jack and the boys got the word out that she's got to be looked after, and they're paying one of their 'friends' down in Jamaica to go in there once a day and visit her and bring her in food. So face it: I am going to do everything in my power to not upset or bother the boys, and so will you if you care about Carleen. What do you think you're doing poking around here, making trouble about Bo?"

"Joyce, there's something big going on. I know there is—and it's got something to do with Bo and Carleen."

"Look, shut up. You don't know what you're talking about. It's got nothing to do with Carleen. Except the people who make it possible for Carleen to stay alive could, if you keep poking around and fucking around, find themselves in jail—or worse . . ."

Joyce looked straight in Maureen's eyes, then turned sharply on her heel and walked away.

Maureen was left there feeling like she'd been hit in the back of the head with a piece of two by four, and all of a sudden, the words she'd read in Carleen's diary appeared: "I would never do that to Reenie. She's my friend. If she was fucked up, I'd look after her." Maureen knew that was true, but she didn't know what she was supposed to do about it or even where she was supposed to go. She knew she had to be at the cop shop in the morning, but if she tried to save herself from being arrested and charged, would that mean she'd be condemning Carleen and abandoning her all over again, for the third time? She was feeling like Simon Peter. She could almost hear the cock crowing in the distance, but she moved along the street, lost in fear and panic, and found herself blindly heading down to work, down to the film-strip library, even though she hadn't been there in days.

CHAPTER TWENTY-ONE

W ELL, THE DEAD AROSE AND APPEARED TO MANY," Gerry said when he saw her. He looked even smaller and older than he had the last time she'd clapped eyes on him. He looked thinner too; he was almost see-through.

Gerry was surprised to see her. Her work attendance had been nothing if not erratic. But there had never been much of a job to her job, and nothing for her to do there all day long. She'd just sit, all by herself, surrounded by useless strips of film that were trapped in dusty plastic canisters waiting for borrowers who never came— unless, of course, George came in and managed to get right up on her last nerve by going through the incredibly lengthy exercise of telling her every single solitary detail of the 1946 version of *The Big Sleep*, or all about Orson Welles in *Touch of Evil*, or about *The Big Heat*, and on and on and on and on, each telling of the film taking as long as it would to watch the actual movie. George would talk about "frails" and "stacks of wheats" and "throwing a Joe" and "spondulix" until Maureen thought her head would explode from the toxic mix of confusion and boredom.

But this time, of course, there was no George to be seen, only Gerry. Maureen had never understood why, but for some reason, Gerry liked her—not like that, not her parts, but her altogether—something about the her-ness of her Gerry liked, and that's why the whole job charade had been allowed to go on as long as it had and why every week Maureen got a small pay packet from the provincial Department of Education. It was all thanks to Gerry.

"Gerry, I just came in to tell you that I'm quittin'."

"Oh yes, I was wondering when the stress of your high-powered position was going to catch up with you."

Maureen didn't laugh. "Don't be mocking me, Gerry. I know I haven't been showing up that much lately and I'm still drawing down a salary, and it's wrong, I think. It's not right anyway, and I'm here to officially quit my job . . . Really, to tell you the truth, I just came in because I had nowhere else to go."

Gerry looked at her with real concern.

"And I'm trying to put things right in my life before I get—" Maureen almost said "arrested." She hadn't known before she came down but she realized now that she was longing to get some stuff in her life straightened out. She wanted to get right with whatever part of her world she could get right with, although she couldn't really do anything about Carleen, and she was no closer to finding out what really happened to Bo, and the baby . . . well . . . and the cops thought she was a suspect because of all the domestic abuse calls they'd received—but Maureen knew that the cops weren't retarded and must know that she couldn't truss up someone the size of Bo and get him into the trunk of his car, but

MARY WALSH

maybe they thought she'd had help or something, and let's face it, the chlordane—

"Before you get what?" Gerry said.

"Before I go away for a while, maybe. It could be a long while, I don't know. I'm just trying to tie up some loose ends. Well, this is the only loose end really, other than saying goodbye to Kathleen."

"Goodbye?" Gerry asked, looking really concerned now.

"Not goodbye 'forever' goodbye. Just like, you know, goodbye for now."

Gerry, somewhat mollified by that answer, asked, "How are you planning to get by without even the job?" He paused. "I know it's none of my business, but if you are going to put things right in your life, you're going to have to get rid of Brutus . . . Are you listening to me, Olive Oyl?" Gerry always called Maureen Olive Oyl because of her skinny legs and said Bo was a real Brutus—and not just the comic book one either.

"I already did get rid of him," Maureen said. *Oh God, what was she saying?* "No, I, I, I didn't, but somebody did . . . Did you hear about that buddy that they found up on The Brow in the trunk of his car? That was Bo."

Maureen tried to look as she imagined someone might look if they'd lost someone they lived with, lost them in a sudden and violent way. She wasn't sure about a lot of the looks she was putting on lately; she didn't have much to base them on. Mostly, she copied her more tragic, heartbroken, shattered expressions from TV, but really there wasn't a whole wealth of looks on TV for a young woman to copy. You couldn't very well stand around wailing and bawling clownishly like Lucille Ball all day, not that much happened to Kitten on *Father Knows Best*, and Mrs. Cleaver's expression on *Leave It to Beaver* never changed anyway and who else was there? Most of the faces she put on lately were based loosely on Miss Kitty, the barmaid/working girl from *Gunsmoke*.

"Well, it couldn't happen to a nicer guy," said Gerry, and then he caught himself and quickly made the sign of the cross. "God forgive me. He was somebody's son. But the way he brutalized you, my dear. Now, now, no crocodile tears, you are well out of that."

"I'm just crying 'cause I'll miss you, Gerry."

"Oh, my dear," Gerry said, putting his arm around her, "you didn't see that much of me at the best of times. With your work attendance the way it was, I doubt if you'll even notice a difference now that you're officially quit. Maybe we'll actually see more of you. I'm always here if you need something."

Maureen turned to go, feeling like she was leaving her last safe place, maybe her only safe place.

"Have you seen George?" Gerry asked her.

"What? He's not here?" Maureen said innocently.

"No, he didn't come in today. Taking a page out of your book, seems like."

CHAPTER TWENTY-TWO

MAUREEN HAD MEANT IT TO BE A KIND OF LOVING goodbye scene—like the one between Anne and Diana when Anne leaves to go to college in *Anne of Green Gables*—because, despite the fact that Kathleen drove Maureen right around the bend, Maureen knew that she did love Kathleen.

But she also knew that she did not want her right up on top of her all the time.

"Gosh, Kathleen, two pieces of matter cannot occupy the same space at the same time. It's a basic law of physics or something," Maureen said as she pushed Kathleen off her lap. Kathleen looked crestfallen as she fell, but she had a determined look on her face at the same time and started inching her way back toward Maureen's lap right away.

"Where's Dad?" Maureen asked her mother.

"No boats in today, so he's down to the Ritz Tavern. Where is he ever at if he's not down to the wharf? Make yourself useful and go down with Raymond and haul him home out of it," the Sarge said.

"Jesus. No way, Mom," Raymond said. "Let him rot down there if he wants to."

"Aw, come on, Raymond," said Maureen. "We'll go down and get the old man." Maureen was longing to do something, anything really except just sit there, sweating bullets, worrying about the cops and trying to find a way to say goodbye.

"I got better things to be at with my time," Raymond shot back as he went out the door.

"Yea, better things like B and E's and breaking into the Humpty Dumpty warehouse and stealing bags of chips. You big bastard, if you're going to be breaking in somewhere, get something worth robbing, you big stupid gom," said the Sarge.

Raymond sailed through the door and didn't give her a second look.

"Mom, don't be encouraging him."

"Oh, shut up your foolishness, Maureen. What in the fuck do you know about it? We haven't seen hide nor hair of you this six months, and now suddenly you knows all to do about everything around here. Don't make me laugh, my dear. He's in with a bad crowd, Sylvie Farrell and them—big, dangerous *and stupid*. And if that's the way he's going, if he's getting ready for the pen, he better get in with a smarter crowd . . . What are you doing here today?"

"Actually, I just stopped in for a minute. I got to go down to the cop shop in the morning."

"Jesus, Mary and Joseph, what are you going down there for?"

"They're questioning me about Bo's murder."

"You?" The Sarge fell back, staggered but not knocked down, and she was immediately on the offensive. "Murder? Murder? . . . What in the name of God have you done now? Murder?"

"Mom, I never murdered him."

"Well, the police have got to have something on ya, Maureen. They don't go around accusing people of murder out of the blue."

"They never accused me of murder, Mom. They just said I was of interest and I had to come down to the police station to be questioned."

"See, I said that, see, as soon as ever I clapped eyes on that bastard . . . Oh, he's up at the university, you said, his father got his own business, Miss All-the-time-trying-to-be-what-you're-not. Now, fuckmentions, now look where that's after landing ya. You got to stick with your own kind, Maureen. Going around putting on airs. Oh, 'I'm the film-strip librarian for the Department of Education.'" Edna minced around the kitchen and screwed up her face in a cruel mockery of Maureen.

"I quit that," said Maureen.

"What?" the Sarge snapped. "Have you got another job?"

"No."

"Jesus. You were lucky to get that job. You can't just go quitting jobs before you got another one to go to. You haven't got a fucking dust of sense. Kathleen got more sense than you do."

"Well, if . . . you know . . . the police do charge me, then what odds?"

"Well, foolish arse, that is the most foolish thing that ever came out of that foolish mouth of yours ever. And that's saying something. 'Cause you have made a vocation of spitting out foolishness."

"Mom, get off my case, will ya?"

Kathleen had worked her way back into Maureen's lap. She said,

"Get off Maureen's case, Mom, get off her case, 'cause Maureen never comes over here, and here she is over here, so we got to all not get up on her case." She looked back at Maureen and smiled. "Get off Maureen's case, get off her case—"

The Sarge turned like a savage. "You keep your mouth shut. Now, what did I tell you about having your big mouth goin'? None of your business. I'll put you up over those stairs and into bed for a week."

"I'm twenty-eight. I'm not going to bed. I'm not a baby. I'm not going. I'm not going to bed. I'm not a baby, I'm a big girl, big girls don't go to bed in the afternoon."

The Sarge came barrelling at Kathleen, hauled her up off Maureen's lap and started manhandling her up over the stairs. Kathleen was desperately holding on to the banister and fighting every step of the way. Maureen didn't know what to do and she didn't know where to go. Bringing her troubles to Princess Street had proved to be no help to anyone. She was on the street before she realized that she hadn't even managed to say goodbye to Kathleen, the whole reason she'd gone down there in the first place.

CHAPTER TWENTY-THREE

At a quarter past seven, Maureen was on the second floor at DAFT, walking toward Jack's office, when a voice from what she thought was an empty room said, "What, are you here all day every day now, are you, Maureen?"

Maureen jumped and then was relieved to see Fox. She was kind of hoping that she might run into him and thought that because of their "incident" in Montreal, he might be a bit more sympathetic.

"No, I'm not here all day every day, Fox, but . . . " Maureen paused as she stepped over the threshold of his office, and she felt her resolve slip and her courage fail just a little. "But where I gotta go see the cops tomorrow, it just occurred to me that maybe I should talk to you first." She looked him right in the eye. "Talk to you, you know . . . before I go . . . to the cops."

"Oh yea, why do you want to talk to me, Maureen?" Fox looked at her with a totally flat, but at the same time hard, gaze.

"Well, see," Maureen said, talking fast now, "I'm supposed to meet Jack here, but before he gets here, I wanted to tell you, before I told the cops, that I heard you and Jack at the apartment that night when you were looking for Jack's AA chip."

"Did ya?" Fox said, never taking his eyes off Maureen.

"Yea, and where Jack was the last person to see Bo alive . . ."

"Was he?" Fox said.

"And now, see, where the cops are looking at me 'cause Bo . . . well he . . ."

"Beat the shit out of you."

"Yea, but when I talked to the cops, I never told them anything about you guys bein' in the apartment that night. They asked me all about you guys, about DAFT, if Bo worked for you and all that, and all I said was that he built boxes." She was still facing that same flat, hard look.

"Yea," she went on, "I heard Jack say to you Bo was still alive when he left him there at the apartment that day, but . . . Jack was the last person to see him alive, and I don't wanna say anything to the cops, but . . . I don't know."

"Yea, that's kinda funny, Maureen, 'cause you weren't with Bo on Tuesday, were ya? You left Bo and the apartment late Monday night or early Tuesday morning and went down to"—he hesitated and looked down at a paper on his desk—"George Taylor's house on King's Road, where you spent Tuesday and Wednesday night and where the police found you on Thursday morning."

"Well, so what? That got nothing to do with anything." Maureen was rattled, really rattled. How did Fox know she was down to George's? Were they following her? They must be. Jesus in the Garden of Gethsemane. Was she just being paranoid? But like they said on those psychedelic buttons, "Just because you're paranoid doesn't mean they aren't after you." Hardly anyone knew that she'd gone down to George's—only the police and George. Had George sold her out? Or were the police in with DAFT?

"Look," Maureen said, "I'm just here 'cause I don't want to cause any trouble."

"Bit late for that," Fox said, not looking up.

"I don't think I'm threatening you or anything—"

"You'd better not be." Fox, again, didn't look up, but something about how totally still he was frightened Maureen.

"Look, Fox, they're going to be asking me questions and they might even arrest me, and I can't very well lie to them when they ask me what I know."

"Why not, Maureen? You already did."

"But I can't keep lying to them, can I? I gotta tell 'em about Jack being the last person to see Bo alive. And if that means they come sniffing around DAFT, well . . . I mean . . . you can't very well let Jack bring down the whole organization, can you?" Maureen looked at Fox mournfully but had to quickly avert her eyes when she saw the look he was giving back. She knew she was playing a very dangerous game. On her way down here, Maureen had worked it out in her mind that if she could get them to turn against each other, if she could convince Fox, or one of them, that it would be better for DAFT and their "big operation" to turn Jack in to the cops, then she'd be safe, and if DAFT kept going, they'd continue to take care of Carleen. But what if the police were in with the boys? Maureen couldn't let her mind go there. It would mean that there was nothing solid, nothing left in the whole world to count on at all.

Maureen started talking even faster. "If they start lookin' into Jack and Bo and Tuesday afternoon . . . well, how long is it going to be before they figure out"—she shot Fox a look and managed to stammer out—"everything?"

Fox rose from behind his desk and parked himself on the corner, right in Maureen's face.

"Everything like what, Maureen?"

"Well, I don't know, do I? You know." Maureen was nervously trying to move back in her chair and making little sounds almost like laughs, hyperventilating, trying to get as far away from Fox as she could.

"No, I don't know," said Fox, as he moved in even closer. "Why don't you tell me?"

He was so close that for one mad moment, Maureen thought she was going to kiss him, like she'd kissed him in Montreal, but she didn't. Her throat felt like it was closing over, and she could barely squeak out, "Well, I don't know anything, so how am I gonna tell you anything?"

"You are fucking A right you don't know anything to tell me. And you don't know anything to tell the cops, either, do you, Maureen?"

"Well, what about . . ." But nothing else came out of Maureen's mouth. All her energy was engaged in shoving her chair back and trying to stand up. At the door, she bumped right into Jack, who had been standing there, she didn't know how long.

"Jack! . . . Jack, you said to meet you at seven-thirty."

"Yea," Jack said, grabbing her roughly by the arm and leading her out of Fox's office. She saw Jack shoot Fox a look that she couldn't quite read, but that look made her feel even more frightened.

CHAPTER TWENTY-FOUR

LET US NOW HAVE A MOMENT OF SILENCE TO CONTEMPLATE our reason for being here. And those who wish, please join me in the Serenity Prayer," said the woman at the head of the table at the AA meeting. The moment of silence stretched into an eternity. Maureen looked across the table at Jack, who, like everybody else at the meeting, had his head bowed.

"God grant me the serenity to accept the things I cannot change . . . ," everybody began. Maureen pretended to say the words; it was like pantomiming with the choir. When they finished the prayer, the missus in charge asked if there were any newcomers. A fella, dirty, raggedy—you could almost smell how bad he looked—put up a shaky hand.

"Joseph. Alcoholic," he said.

"Hi, Joseph," everybody in the room chimed in together. "Welcome."

It was like being on *Romper Room* or something, Maureen thought. She could feel Jack looking at her. When she looked up, he gave her the nod, so she tentatively put up her hand.

"Maureen," she muttered.

"Hi, Maureen. Welcome."

Jesus, you'd need a drink after spending a few minutes with these phony bastards and their bullshit smiles and hi's. The missus in charge asked for topics. Someone smiled in that sickly sweet bogus way at Maureen and said, "Since there's newcomers, how about staying around the first step and the third tradition."

"And what about rigorous honesty," a small voice said. "My name is Verna, an alcoholic, and I'd like to hear people share about rigorous honesty."

Jack Dunne, or Jack D as he was called at the meeting, was asked to speak first. Maureen could see he didn't want to—probably because she was there—but he went ahead and spoke anyway.

"I was gonna pass," Jack said, "but this is my home group, and you know, you never know, maybe I'll say something that'll help somebody else or, like what usually happens, maybe I'll say something that'll help me."

"Hi, Jack," the room chimed in.

"Oh right." Jack laughed uncomfortably. "Sorry. Sorry. My name is Jack and I am an alcoholic."

"Hi, Jack," everyone chimed in again.

Jesus, it *was* like being in kindergarten. Maureen doubted if she would be able to stand a whole hour of this crap.

"I knew I was an alcoholic, but I never wanted to admit that I was powerless over it. I thought I could control it. I thought I was a tough guy. But the truth is, I wasn't tough at all. I thought I didn't need anybody's help, but I've always needed the help of somebody.

In fact, I wouldn't even have made it into this world if it wasn't for my brother."

Maureen's ears pricked up when he mentioned Deucey. How weird. Because Deucey had said basically the same thing the night she'd gone home with him.

"I thought I could beat the liquor by myself. I've been in lots of rackets over the years, and, sure, I came out of them in pretty bad shape, but I could always say, 'You should see the other fella.' So I figured I could pound the piss out of alcohol too. But it was always me that got the shit-knocking. After every beating, I'd just pick myself up and crawl right back in the ring with the liquor. I was doing the same thing over and over and over again, but I was always expecting different results."

Boy, thought Maureen, that's the way she'd always felt about Bo. No matter how many times he beat her down—*beat you up*, Maureen's mind added—part of her always thought that if she just kept at it, she could get the better of him, change him, make him see how wrong he was to be doing that to her. If only she could have been nicer, or tougher, or quieter, or louder . . .

"But finally," Jack was saying, "I had to admit defeat. I had to get out of the ring, walk away and stop fighting it. And about the rigorous honesty thing . . ." Jack darted a quick look over at Maureen.

What in the name of God is he going to say now? Maureen thought. *Is it all gonna come out? Just like that?*

"Well, I got nothing to say about that right now. I want to wish everyone a good twenty-four hours, and I'll take one for myself."

Yea, thought Maureen, *I bet you got nothing to say about rigorous honesty, 'cause you wouldn't know rigorous honesty if it kicked your head off.*

Yes, there was that piece of shit, jarred up here with people saying, "Thank you, Jack," every time he opened his piece-of-shit mouth. Maureen thought of Carleen, about how sweet she was and good, and how she was rotting away in some stink-hole cell in Jamaica right now. Maureen looked up and saw that everyone was staring at her. *Oh, Jesus in the breadbox, she hadn't said that out loud, had she?* God, they might as well just lock her away in jail because she wasn't fit to be out in public.

But it was just that missus who was running the meeting asking her for the second time, apparently, "Would you like to share?"

"Me? Oh no, no, no. I don't have anything to share really. I just . . . no."

"You can just pass if you want to," the missus said, giving Maureen a kind look.

"Yea, yea, that's what I'll do, I'll pass."

Maureen spent the rest of the meeting burning with shame, thinking that everybody else must be thinking what a moron she was, how stupid she was to not know what to say. She looked around, but no one was looking at her or paying any attention to her at all.

Verna, the "rigorous honesty" woman, was saying, ". . . I was always caught up in what everybody else thought, what they thought of me, how I could make them think better of me. After I got sober, I realized mostly people weren't thinking about me at all. Mostly they were too busy thinking about themselves."

How trippy is that? Maureen thought. *That missus is saying exactly the same thing that I'm thinking.*

"So, I had to start first getting honest with myself. It's still a struggle," Verna said, and she wished everyone another twenty-four.

Then some guy said he wanted to "talk about principles before personalities, the part of the tradition that, with anonymity, was the spiritual foundation of all our traditions."

Anonymity? Maureen thought. *God, who wants to be anonymous? I want everyone to know me. I want to be famous or something. I want to. . .* Maureen was never quite sure what she wanted, but she knew she wanted something, anything really, that announced to the world that she was a necessary part of it. That because she could do . . . whatever that thing was, that special talent—which was, please God, bound to become apparent any time soon—she would be allowed on the lifeboat and "they" would let her live. Principles before personalities? Who were they trying to kid? Maureen hated those holier-than-thou smug arseholes going around, stuffed up with their own goodness, filled up to the eyeballs, gone rigid with principles. Maureen would always pick personality over principle any day—and so would everybody else, really, if they were telling the truth.

Before Maureen knew it, everyone was on their feet and getting in a circle. Oh my God, she couldn't believe it: now they were holding hands and saying the Proddy version of the Our Father, the long one: ". . . for Thine is the Kingdom, the power and the glory, world without end, Amen." Why'd the Prods have to add that on? Made no sense to Maureen, but she didn't have time to think about that now. She moved quickly and stood in front of Jack, stopping him from getting out the door.

"Thanks for bringing me."

"Yea, that's okay."

"But that whole rigorous honesty thing, that really meant a lot to me. It really got me thinking, so I thought I should tell you."

Jack was looking uncomfortable. Suddenly, Verna was at Maureen's shoulder, putting a piece of paper in her hand, saying, "If you feel like picking up a drink, call me. My number's right there. Call me anyway and we can have a cup of tea or something. I could come over or we could go down to Marty's—"

"Oh, thank you," Maureen cut her off. She could see Jack getting away from her. "Thank you, thank you, I just got to . . ." She took off after Jack.

"Jack, Jack!" She stopped him just outside the front door. He was talking to an older guy. They seemed to be caught up in something, but Maureen was desperate. She interrupted. "Jack, when you have a minute, I got something I gotta tell ya."

"So, who is this, Jacky?" the older fella said, turning toward Maureen. "Aren't you going to introduce me?"

"Oh yea, yea, right. Maureen, this is my sponsor, Ed, Ed H."

Ed took Maureen's hand in one of his enormous paws and shook it, saying, "Welcome aboard, Maureen. Come back to another meeting." Maureen didn't want to take her hand back, because it felt so safe wrapped up in his big one.

"I'll wait for you over there," Maureen said, finally letting go of Ed's hand. She walked out toward King's Bridge Road.

"You go on, Jacky," Ed said. "It's not nice to keep a young lady waiting. But you got to start being rigorous. If not, you're putting your sobriety at risk, and what have you got if you haven't got that?"

"Yea, thanks, Ed," Jack said, shaking Ed's hand. "Thanks. I'll see you Thursday night down at the Harbour Light." He walked over to Maureen.

"Jesus, Maureen, what do you want now?"

"Sorry," she said, "but it's just that with everybody talking about rigorous honesty, I started to feel bad, real bad. I've only been telling the cops the half-truth. I never told them . . ." She paused and couldn't look at Jack for a moment. "I never told them about how I heard you guys in the apartment when you came lookin' for your chip that time."

Jack was taken aback.

"And how I heard you say you were there in the apartment Tuesday with Bo—the last day that Bo was alive. But I got to go down to the cop shop in the morning and, Jack, they think I did it."

"Well, did ya?" Jack said. He seemed to be honestly asking her.

Weird, said Maureen's mind, *since you did it, Jack, you big bastard.*

But Maureen quickly answered, "No, of course I never did it. But like I said to Fox there today"—she shot Jack a look to see if that was having any effect on him—"if I tell the cops how you were the last person to see Bo alive—which I definitely would never do, Jack, you can count on that—but Fox said to me that if the police found that out . . . you know . . . you were the last person to see—"

"Yea, I got it." Jack stopped Maureen.

"That bit of information could, you know, threaten the whole 'operation,' 'cause if the cops came around DAFT and started asking questions about you and Bo, and then asked questions"— she kept her eyes clapped right on Jack—"well, one question, you know, could lead to another, and the next thing you know. . . " Maureen's voice was getting very thin. "Well, the whole, you know, Jamaica, Montreal, Colombia . . . connection, well . . ." Maureen knew she was shooting in the dark, but she could tell by the look of rising rage on Jack's face that she was hitting some targets.

"Get the fuck away from me, Maureen, and stay the fuck away from me. Do you hear me?"

Maureen was terrified, but she wasn't finished yet. If she could get the DAFT boys to turn on each other, then Jack would surely go down, and the cops would probably never even bother to test Bo for chlordane or any other poison, and she'd be safe, and so would the rest of DAFT. And if the rest of DAFT was safe, Carleen would be safe. She could just sit back then and laugh like Mouse Daley used to do up at Power's Court at the dances. Mouse would start a racket, hit some buddy from Mundy Pond, and then act like it had been the other buddy from The Brow who'd done it, and then the Mundy Pond buddy would turn on The Brow buddy, and then everyone would join in, and the racket would rise. Mouse would sit back and watch them knock the shit out of each other, and he'd just laugh.

"I just wanted you to know that if, God forbid, the cops ever did come after you, remember it's not my fault, 'cause the boys, the rest of the boys, they don't want the cops in sniffing around DAFT, and they might just throw you—and maybe even Deucey—like a bone to the—"

"Shut up, Maureen." Jack moved closer and said in a quiet voice, "You know, some people, some people are the type, Maureen, that they deserve a beating. It's just too bad that Bo's still not here to give you one."

God, no one had ever actually said that out loud to her before, but that was exactly what Maureen always thought: she was the type that deserved a beating. Hearing it out loud like that made it even more true. She guessed that's what everyone thought. Her heart was up in her throat and she couldn't quite catch her breath. Then Jack was gone, getting into his sporty little blue car.

Maureen walked back to George's, feeling as low as she'd ever felt, as low as she felt when she realized that they had taken her baby. Was this what life was going to be? Just bad and shitty and low, every new day worse than the last, every day further proof that the Sarge had been right all along and that Maureen was "no good for nothing"? She'd been knocked up, beat up, fucked up, and all that was left was to be locked up. And that was coming, Maureen knew it. She walked back to George's and, though it wasn't that far, it seemed to take forever.

Despite how she was feeling, she kept her head up and looked straight in front of her. She knew from experience that if you looked down and trudged, just the physical fact of your head hanging down made you even more low-minded than you already were. But she felt like there were weights on her chin, pulling it into her chest, and her feet were like lead. She thought how useless the whole thing was and how very useless she was, and how she couldn't even get one thing right. She just stumbled from one giant life-destroying mistake into the next, and down and down and down it went.

"You did what!" George exploded.

"Well, I told Jack that I—"

"It was a rhetorical question, Maureen."

"Oh."

"I just can't believe you would be naive enough to bait criminals."

"They're not criminals!"

"They are in every way criminal. They engage in organized crime."

"Oh, come on, George, you're the one who told me to rat the boys out to the cops, and it's only the boys! They're more like— what do you call it—counterculture hippies than criminals."

"Yes, just countercultural hippies who happen to run a criminal organization importing illegal drugs."

"It's marijuana, George. I mean, it shouldn't even be illegal."

"And cocaine. And possibly killing people."

"Yea, but that's what people think about me," she said.

"That you import illegal drugs?"

"No—that I possibly kill people . . . And if we are going to be rigorously honest about it, I did, in fact, try to kill people—well, one person anyway."

She told him about the small cargo boat the boys had bought.

"Whew," George said, "they're taking it up a notch. They're moving it into the big time."

"What do you mean?" Maureen said.

"Well, a small cargo boat . . . They'll sail it into Colombia, fill it up with drugs, come back, land in some small, isolated place, off-load in the dead of night and move the drugs out of here and into the North American market. International drug smuggling, it's called."

"You don't know that for a fact."

"But it makes sense, Maureen. They're not going to go back to selling dime bags at the Thompson Student Centre. They're gonna get bigger. And the bigger they get, the more they have to lose, the more dangerous they become. Boy, Bo . . . he got you in with a nasty crowd."

There was a long pause, and then George said, in the quietest voice possible, "Why didn't you just leave him, Maureen?"

"George, why are you asking me that question now?"

He didn't answer.

So many, many times, Maureen had asked herself the same question. The reason wasn't financial, because money-wise, she could take care of herself, and they'd had no youngsters, so why hadn't she just walked out the door? Well, for one thing, of course, she thought she deserved it. And then, because she was so beaten down, so crumbled into pieces, so beaten into bits that she didn't know how to gather up all the crumbs of herself to do anything. Plus, she'd been afraid. Bo had never directly threatened her that if she left him, he'd kill her. In fact, there was a small part of Maureen that felt Bo would be relieved and glad if she just one day up and disappeared completely. But the bigger part of her knew he was just never going to let her go of her own accord. He was never going to let her act as if she had the power to make decisions for herself.

"I was afraid," she told George. "I was just afraid. And now I'm afraid again, afraid of having to go to the cops tomorrow."

"But now," George said, "after what you did, you have even more reason to be afraid. Because no matter what you say to the cops, if the cops, by happenstance, start nosing around DAFT, Jack and the rest of them will think it's your fault, because you threatened them."

"I was trying to get them to turn on each other."

George looked puzzled.

Maureen explained the whole Mouse Daley scheme. When she had finished, George asked, in that irritating, detached, scholarly way he sometimes had, "And Mouse's reason for this behaviour?"

"I don't know. He just did it for laughs, I guess."

"Are you having a laugh, Maureen?"

"I did it, George, because I thought Fox and them might turn in Jack just to stop the cops from . . . you know . . ."

"Breaking up their criminal organization? That is really—"

"Dumb?"

"Well, it wasn't smart, was it Moe?"

"Gee, nobody except Carleen ever called me Moe before. And why are you suddenly talking like a normal human being?" She looked down at the beanbag chair and saw the book George was reading: *The Reid Technique: A Police Training Manual of Interrogation Tactics.*

"Maureen, please," he begged, "just try to keep your mind on one thing for two minutes. You're like some kind of flibberty-gibbet."

"Flibberty-gibbet? Is that what they say in Lethbridge?"

"Coaldale, actually. Eleven miles south of Lethbridge."

"Sorry, but you know what's driving me nuts, George? It's the way your mind just plods along its boring, boring way. Always on the same subject until you've worn the fuck right out of that subject and then it's on to another subject with the intent to stay on that till it's worn down, beat out and destroyed."

"Maureen, why are you attacking me right now?"

"Why? I was just defending myself. You were, you know, saying I was . . ."

"A flibberty-gibbet. I know, it was unconscionable of me."

"It wasn't just that, George. It was the way you . . . oh . . . I'm . . ." Maureen paused. She didn't want to start down the "I'm sorry" road, because when you said you were sorry, fellas always used that against you the next time there was an argument.

"George, please, I need you to help me get ready for tomorrow with the cops. What'll I do? What'll I say about Bo and Jack and Deucey and all that?"

"Don't say a word. Avoid all topics. Because once they get you to start talking about any topic whatsoever, it's easier for them to get you to start talking about other topics."

"I know, I'm a blabbermouth. I'm an idiot—"

"No, Moe, you're just the same as everybody else. It's just human nature. Everybody's the same. So don't answer any of their questions—none of them."

"Well, I mean—"

"No. Don't even answer 'How are you?' 'Did you have breakfast?' 'How do you feel?'"

"Why?"

"Because the cops are trying to establish a baseline. They're trying to see how you normally respond when you're answering questions that are no big deal. They'll be watching your facial expressions, your body language, when you answer those innocent questions, and it'll give the cops an idea how you look and behave when you are answering a question truthfully."

"Well, that's not fair," Maureen said, thinking, *Wow, the new straight-talking George, he's kind of, if not exactly dead attractive, kind of . . .*

George gave her a baleful look. "Then, when they start asking about Bo and what happened, they'll have some idea if you are telling the truth."

"That's bullshit."

"No, it isn't bullshit. It's based on solid evidence, and sometimes, according to what I've been reading, they even try something called the 'neuro-linguistic interviewing technique.'"

"Oh Jesus, I don't even know what any of that means, so I guess I'm fucked."

"Not necessarily. As long as you don't answer anything, you'll be fine. Because if they ask you something you have to remember, like what you had for dinner last night, they'll watch where your eyes go as you try to remember. Then they might turn around and ask you something that you have to think through, like two times five equals—"

"Jesus, George, they're not going to ask me that."

"Yes, they might, because if you have to think through something, your eyes will probably go to the right, and if you're just remembering something that actually happened, your eyes naturally go to the left—everybody's eyes do. So, depending on where your eyes go when they ask about Tuesday night, they'll have an indication of whether you're really remembering what actually happened or whether you're just making up your answer in order to hide the truth. You've got to remember to invoke your right to keep silent."

"But that'll just make them think that I'm guilty."

"Let 'em think what they want. If you start talking, they'll know."

"That I'm guilty?"

"That you're hiding something."

The phone rang. George bawled out, "Maureen, it's Joyce."

"Joyce?" She took the receiver. "Hi. Hi, Joyce. What time is it?" Why was Joyce calling her this late?

"I don't know what time it is, Maureen. I need you to meet me."

"What?"

"I need you to meet me."

"When?"

"Right now."

"Jesus, Joyce, it's almost twelve o'clock."

"Meet me down to Mrs. Duff's."

"Where?"

"It's the bar on the other side of the War Memorial from the Black Swan."

"But—"

"Meet me there in half an hour. It's important. Don't be late."

"But Joyce—"

Joyce had already hung up.

Maureen turned to George. "I've got to go."

"Where?"

"Out."

"Out where?"

"Out, out."

"Maureen, I'm not just letting you go out without knowing where you are going. You are at risk. You have knowingly placed yourself at risk."

"George, I don't have time to talk right now. I gotta meet someone in half an hour, but just for your information, I have been at risk since that first night Bo threw me down over the stairs. So really, how much more 'at risk' am I right now?"

"You've threatened criminals. Your life could possibly be in danger."

"My life has been in danger now for . . . Jesus, I don't know how long, so really, nothing is any different."

George stood in front of the door.

"I'm not letting you leave."

CHAPTER TWENTY-FIVE

OVER HERE, MAUREEN." JOYCE WAS SITTING IN THE dingiest, darkest corner of a dark and dingy bar. "Do you want a beer or something?"

"No. Not right now."

Sometimes Maureen could go days without having a beer or even thinking about having a beer, but once she started, there was no guarantee when she was going to stop. She knew she would be in much better shape to go down to the cop shop in the morning if she wasn't suffering from a vicious hangover. Joyce looked at her watch, looked at Maureen and didn't say anything. *What the fuck?* Maureen's mind thought. But Maureen's voice said, "Well, Joyce, what do you want?"

"Nothing," Joyce said.

"Nothing? You got me down here at—what is it now—midnight?"

"Ten to," Joyce said.

"Okay. Ten to midnight. For nothing?"

"I got something to tell you, Maureen, but I can't tell you yet."

"Jesus in the breadbox, Joyce, what?"

Joyce looked quizzically at Maureen.

"You know, Mom says it all the time, 'Jesus in the breadbox, eatin' all the cheese, didn't leave none for the poor Chinese,'" Maureen said.

"That's fox."

"What?"

"That's fox."

"Fox Albert?" said Maureen.

"No. You know, it's fox in the breadbox, eating all the cheese."

"I don't think the Chinese even eat cheese, do they? Anyway, look, Joyce, I got things I got to be at."

"Like what?"

"Well, like getting ready to talk to the cops tomorrow, for one thing."

Joyce's eyes opened really, really wide but she didn't say a word.

"Okay, fuck it, Joyce. I'm going." Maureen got up.

Joyce leaned across the table and grabbed Maureen's arm with that surprisingly strong grip of hers. "Please, Maureen, just wait; it's only another five minutes or so."

Maureen sat down. Joyce looked at her watch again. It was a big watch with big numbers on it, just like a man's watch.

"Nice watch," Maureen said. *For a fella*, her mind said in that irritatingly relentless way it had.

"Yea, it's Dad's. He gave it to Carleen for a good luck charm when she went up to Expo. The boys had them send it back with some of her other stuff from the jail. Dad won't wear it anymore, can't stand the sight of it now, he says."

Maureen remembered the watch now, sitting huge on Carleen's pencil-thin wrist. She remembered feeling jealous that Carleen had a father who even had a watch, let alone would give it to her as a good luck charm when she was going away.

But Carleen's mother is an awful old bag and a drunk on top of that, Maureen's mind interjected.

But Carleen had her dad, Maureen argued with her mind, and he loved her even though he was always at work 'cause they lived in on the back of town on one of those expensive tree streets, those *Father Knows Best* kind of streets, where the *Leave It to Beaver* crowd lived. Maureen could feel herself getting angry at the thought of all that snooty crowd going around with their noses stuck up in the air, that crowd who thought they were so much better than her—

Joyce interrupted Maureen's rising resentment: "Okay, now it's time. We got to go across the street to the DAFT office."

"No way, José. I'm not going over there, Joyce."

"I've got something I want to show you, Maureen, but it's over there. So you've got to come."

"What something?"

"Something to do with Bo and all that, something important."

Joyce looked at her watch again, then grabbed Maureen by the arm.

"Come on, we don't have much time."

She ran Maureen across an almost empty Duckworth Street and opened the door to the DAFT shop with a key.

"Why do you have a key, Joyce?"

"I just borrowed it."

"Borrowed it from who?"

"Oh, shut up, Maureen. Come on." Joyce locked the door behind them.

"I really, really don't want to be here, Joyce, and I'm not going up over those stairs until you tell me what this is all about."

Joyce, already halfway up over the stairs, came back down.

"All right. Upstairs in Deucey's office, there is proof of what happened to Bo." She grabbed Maureen again and practically hauled her up over the stairs. It was dark up there except for a dim light leaking out from under Jack's door. Joyce opened it and pushed Maureen through, almost into the arms of Jack Dunne.

"Oh, what a pleasant surprise. Look, it's our new little AA first-timer. Well, we meet again," Jack said, holding on to Maureen.

Maureen turned to Joyce. "But Joyce, you said—"

"I'm sorry, Maureen. But Carleen . . . she could be down there . . . I—"

"Get the fuck out, Joyce," Jack said. "And lock the door after you."

Maureen's mind couldn't quite grasp what was going on, but her feet seemed to understand, because they started moving backwards, fast. But Jack had her, and as he was bolting the door, he said, "Now, Maureen, what in the fuck are we going to do with you?" He pulled her deeper into the room and sat her down in a chair, hard.

Maureen was speechless. She couldn't believe that Joyce would . . . Well, she couldn't believe any of it; it all seemed like a story. She could see herself in the room, in the chair, listening to Jack, and she could feel her legs shake with terror, but at the same time, a big part of her could not believe that this was actually happening to her. Stuff like this didn't go on in St. John's. Your best friend's big sister didn't trick you and leave you in a room in danger of . . .

Oh, come on, Maureen's brain kicked in, *normal up. It's hanging around with George and all that Mickey Spillane murder book stuff. The reason this doesn't seem real is because it's not real. Jack's just gonna tell you what really happened to Bo and then . . .*

Maureen decided to get up and get the fuck out of there, but Jack, with just one hand, kept her on the chair. She struggled, but he had so much strength in just that one hand. Then he grabbed Maureen's wrists and hauled them behind her. He tied them together with a rope and fastened her hands to the back of the chair. Then he used the same rope to tie her feet. Maureen kicked as hard as she could, but Jack was determined. He tied one foot to each chair leg, way too tight, and the rope was itchy and sharp.

So this is what being tied up is like, Maureen's mind said. *And where in the fuck did that rope come from?*

"Jack, come on. What are you doing? I mean, you can't just—"

"What I can't just do, Maureen, is let you go to the cops tomorrow morning. So I'm just going to make you disappear."

Her mouth opened up without her knowing it and just started screaming, loud, ear-shattering screams that were louder and higher than Maureen thought she was capable of producing.

"Not disappear for good," Jack said. "Jesus, Maureen, shut up. Shut up! Just disappear for a couple of days."

She was not reassured and the high, piercing sounds kept

coming. Jack clapped a hand over her mouth. She kept screaming and bit down hard on his hand.

"Owww! Jesus, Maureen, shut up!" In desperation, he kicked off his shoe, hauled off his sock and shoved this dirty sock into Maureen's mouth and halfway down her throat.

Oh my God, oh my God, I got Jack Dunne's dirty sock in my mouth.

Maureen started to gag but then she stopped the reflex. She knew it could be deadly; she could choke and die on a dirty sock and her own vomit. Big, hot tears rolled down her face. She felt so sorry for herself. She had thought that getting the piss pounded out of her every other day by someone she was supposed to be in love with but who, in fact, turned her stomach had been the low point of her entire life, and that once she got away from Bo, then maybe she'd piece her life, her shitty, shitty, shitty life, back together again. But apparently, her shitty life, unlike shitty lives in books and movies, her shitty life just kept getting shittier, 'cause now here she was, tied to a chair on the second floor of a building on Duckworth Street, choking on a dirty, big sweat sock. The big tears kept rolling down her cheeks, and she thought, *Maybe I'll cry so much, I'll just drown here in my own tears.* That thought made the tears come even faster and harder.

She heard a key in the lock, the door opened and an overhead light came on. It was Fox. He looked around the room and said, "What the fuck are you doing, Jack?"

"What the fuck does it look like I'm doing, Fox?"

"What? Are you just going to go ahead and murder her too?"

Maureen's eyes widened. She was so alarmed, her tears dried up immediately. If she could have gasped, she would have.

MARY WALSH

"Jesus, Fox, I told ya—I never murdered Bo. When I left him in the apartment, he was still alive. Like I told ya a hundred times, I just went over there to put the fear of God in him for what he did to Deuce. You know Deuce, he's not up for that kind of stuff; he can't take that. I couldn't let Bo just get away with it."

Fox looked over at Maureen as Jack was busy reassuring him that he wasn't a ruthless killer, just somebody's big brother doing what any decent big brother would do. Maureen tried to beg with her eyes, beg Fox to get her out of there.

"Jesus, what's that you got stuck in her mouth?"

"My . . . a sock."

Fox moved toward Maureen like he was going to haul the sock out.

"No, Fox. Don't, for fuck sake, take that out of her mouth. She'll just start in screaming and screeching, and I . . . I can't take it."

"Then what's this all about," Fox said, pointing to Maureen, "if you didn't murder Bo?"

"I got my reasons."

Fox was getting angrier. "Oh yea, reasons like you are a lying cocksucker and you did murder Bo?"

"No. Just reasons. That's all. Leave it at that."

Fox looked hard at Jack. "No, Jack—"

"Just leave it, Fox."

"You're not going to throw everything away again just—"

"Shut up, will you, Fox."

Maureen could see on Fox's face that something had just dawned on him, and he did shut up and just stared at her for a moment.

"So what's your plan for her? You do have a plan, don't you, Jack?"

"I just wanted to stop her. She's supposed to go down to the cop shop tomorrow. She's going to tell them about overhearing us in the apartment that night . . . I just wanted to stop her from talking to the cops tomorrow, that's all, so I can get a chance to think, to figure something out."

"And then what? Then you're just going to let her go? 'Cause what's going to stop her from talking to the cops on, say, Wednesday?"

"Fuck off, Fox. Stop being a patronizing prick. I was just going to keep her for a couple of days up in the old man's shack in Hogan's Pond, 'cause maybe by that time, we'll have it all figured out. Maybe we'll fly the fuck out of here. *The Ikaros* is set to sail for Colum—" Jack shot a look over at Maureen. "Down south early next week. We've got friends down there. Who knows? Maybe I could run part of the business outta there?"

"Yea, sure. What are you, fuckin' retarded? Our 'friends' down south, it's not their hospitality and welcoming nature that they're known for.

"Well, maybe I'll just keep her up to the old man's shack until the heat dies down."

"The heat doesn't die down when one of the suspects in a suspicious death disappears. The heat turns up then, way up, and everyone around the heat gets burnt. Get me?"

"I get ya," Jack said. "But what the fuck am I *s'posed* to do, then?"

There was a knock on the door, and then the handle started to rattle and the knocking got louder.

"Jack, Jack, it's me, Joyce. I know you're still in there . . . Listen, Jack, let me in, will ya? Jack? Jack?" She was getting louder. "Jack!"

Fox stomped over and hauled open the door, and just like in a movie, Joyce came flying in. She must have been taking a run at the door when it opened. She fell down hard on the battleship linoleum. Fox burst out laughing, even though you could see he didn't want to, and even Jack was fighting back a guffaw. Joyce stood up fast.

"What is this?" she said, staring at Maureen. "You told me you only wanted to talk to her, to explain a few things to her."

"Yea, and that's what I'm doing: explaining a few things."

"Well Jesus, Jack," Joyce said, "you can't do this. You can't just kidnap and tie up everyone who gets in your way."

Jack looked at Fox and said, "What the fuck?" Then, to Joyce, "What do you think you're talking about, Joyce?"

"Oh, fuck off, Jack." She turned on her heel and headed for the door.

Maureen felt her heart sink. Jack took a step toward Joyce. Fox stepped in between them and put the flat of his hand on Jack's chest to push him back, not hard but definite.

"I'm calling the cops," Joyce said from the door. "And I'm telling them everything. Everything," she said, looking right at Fox. "The boat, the connections in Colombia, the names of all the 'solid men of business' guys who invested—"

"That won't be necessary, Joyce," Fox said, "because Jack is going to let Maureen go, apologize to her for his rough handling, and tomorrow morning, he's going to walk right into the cop shop and tell them his whole story." Fox looked over at Jack. "Or tell 'em the truth—whichever he decides."

"Yea, right," Jack scoffed.

"Yea, it is right, Jack. It's right, because we all got big money, capital *B* Big money invested in—fuck, why couldn't you have stuffed a couple of socks in her ears?" Fox said, nodding toward Maureen. "Millions of bucks. And our business can't bear the scrutiny of a police investigation. Do you see what I'm getting at here, Jack? We got people invested in the success of our latest operation, and if the heat moves in and the pigs start bearing down, well there goes our latest operation, and millions of bucks up in smoke—and not the kind of smoke we were planning on."

"Yea, fuck that and fuck you, Fox. Who died and made you the boss?"

"We had a meeting."

"I wasn't at a meeting."

"No, we couldn't find ya. I guess you were busy making a bad situation"—he looked over at Maureen—"a hundred times worse . . . Listen, Jack, don't worry. We'll get you the best lawyers in the whole country. If it was an accident, the evidence will show it was an accident. Fuck it, we'll get Clarence Darrow or one of them, or whatever the fuck his name is, and he'll make sure that you won't even have to do any federal time, if you even have to do any time at all."

"Time? Time for what?" Jack was furious. "Time for doing back to that crazy fucker exactly what he did to Deuce?"

"Let me explain it to you, Jack, as simply as I can." Joyce was practically spitting. "You would be doing time for kidnapping and forceful confinement causing death." Joyce's expression grew more sympathetic. "Everybody knows, Jacky, that you were out of your mind because of what Bo did to Deuce that day."

"Yea," Fox said. "That day after Deuce had to explain to Bo that he was too volatile to become a partner, that he got angry too fast, that he was too much of a greaseball to get the job he wanted crewin' on *The Ikaros*, going down south to pick up the"—he shot a look at Maureen—"goods. Yea, ironic," Fox said almost to himself. "We could have avoided all this. Too bad Bo was always so fuckin' out of control. Nothing we could do. We couldn't just let him jeopardize our whole operation . . . Now the bastard is doing it from the grave."

"We know it wasn't right, Jacky," Joyce continued, trying to bring him round with understanding. "Everybody knows it wasn't right what Bo did, giving Deucey a beating, tying him up, putting him in the trunk of his car, driving around with him for the weekend. It was a bad thing to do to anyone, but to do it to Deucey . . ."

Maureen, again, would have gasped if she could. The truth was slowly dawning on her. She had a sudden flashback to the afternoon that Bo had told her about Jack looking for Deucey:

"What the fuck are you at?" Bo said.

"I'm just trying to get into the trunk."

Maureen was going to have a snoop around the trunk of the car, seeing what she could see while waiting for Bo, who'd gone back into the apartment to get something he'd forgotten. Why was the trunk locked? Of course, she was supposed to be sitting in the car now like a good girl, waiting, waiting for her man, and keeping her mouth shut—and all the time holding her pee, she guessed, like a good dog. Three of the many things Maureen just wasn't very good at. Oh, fuck . . . he didn't like her not doing what he told her to do.

"I think I got my old sweater in the trunk, and I need it, I'm froze. Remember when we went down to Motion that time and it was so hot and we went for a swim, but I didn't want to just leave my purse and that in the car, so I put it and my old sweater in the trunk and then—"

"Jesus!" Bo said. "It's not in the trunk."

"Then where is it?" Maureen said, proud of herself for being so bold.

"How the fuck would I know?" He took a menacing step toward her. "I thought I told you to wait in the car."

"Yea, it must be in the house somewhere." Maureen tried to smile.

"Yea, it must be," Bo said.

Maureen stood there, frozen, with her hands on the trunk, unable, for some reason, to get the message to her legs to get in the car.

"Come on back inside. I'm not going now," Bo said.

"But your mother—" Maureen started to protest.

"Fuck it. Get your hands off the fuckin' car, Maureen." Bo moved toward her and Maureen, despite her best effort, cringed.

That's why he'd been so vicious that day: because Deucey was probably already in the trunk. And that's why Jack put a beating on him and why Bo ended up in the back of his own car, tied up and dead, up on The Brow.

"I'm not doing it," Jack said. "I'm not taking the fall."

"Well, Jack, someone's gonna have to take the fall. What's your decision?" Fox paused for a moment, staring hard at Jack. "You don't have to fuck up your life again—"

"Shut up, Fox. You don't know what the fuck you're talking about."

"All right then. I don't care who it is, it's not going to be her, but somebody's got to go to the cops. Because if someone doesn't step up and take responsibility, well, the company is going to have to step off. And then that's it for us, Jack. We cut off all ties with you and Deuce, and we wipe the slate clean. And within a half-hour, one of the DAFT executive goes to the police, horrified to have learned that one of his former business partners was caught up in what looks to be a murder, or at the very least, manslaughter. DAFT had no idea, but as soon as it had an inkling, we came right to the cops, etc., etc. You see what our approach will be, do ya, Jack? We put a shitload of distance between you and DAFT, you go down and down hard and we finish our latest operation. But if you turn yourself in, if you confess to tying him up, say you put him in the trunk of his own car and left him there, and you tell them you acted out of brotherly outrage, you had no idea that what happened could even happen, because Bo had done the same thing to Deuce, and Deuce had come out of it all right. And tell 'em about how even though your brother had continuing issues with mental illness and will probably never be the same again as a result of the kidnapping, he did come out of the trunk very much alive. When you left Bo in the trunk of his car, he was yelling and definitely breathing, and when you came back . . ." He gave Jack a pointed look. "If you do that, whatever money and resources the company has, we'll pour into finding you the best defence. We will buy expert witnesses, we will put up your bail, all the things that without us, you'll have a hard time taking care of."

Jack put his hand up to silence Fox.

"What about her?" he said, pointing at Maureen. "What about her going to the cops in the morning?"

"Well, you go to the cops tonight. Tell 'em the whole, sorry story, and then what'll she have to tell 'em?"

"About all this. She'll tell 'em about all this!"

Fox had hauled the filthy sock out of Maureen's mouth by this time, and between gagging, coughing and gasping, Maureen was saying, "No, no, promise soul to God, Fox, I won't say a word . . . I'll never . . . I'll just, I was never here tonight."

"Yea, well, maybe, maybe . . . ," Jack was saying. "But she can't shut up, Fox. She's all mouth and she can't keep it shut about any-thing."

Fox squat down next to Maureen, who was still tied to the chair. "What is it that *you* want, Maureen? What is it you want that DAFT can help you get?"

All eyes were on Maureen, expectant, waiting for her to have an answer, but she just sat there because she didn't know what she wanted. She never did know what she wanted. In fact, she was half afraid to ever want anything for fear she'd never get it. Maybe all she wanted was everything, to be someone else, to have a whole other life. Then, without even thinking about it, Maureen blurted out, "I want to find my baby."

CHAPTER TWENTY-SIX

Fox, Jack and Joyce looked horrified. There was total silence for a minute.

"You and Bo had a baby?" Jack said. "And you somehow or other lost it? Though I wouldn't put it past ye two booze bags—"

"No, not me and Bo," Maureen said. "I had a baby when I was sixteen." She purposely avoided looking at Fox. "Mom gave it up for adoption and I don't know where and she won't ever even talk about it."

Again, no one spoke for a moment.

Then Joyce said, "Are you sure you want to find your baby, Maureen? You know the old 'more tears shed in heaven over answered prayers than unanswered ones.' I mean, a baby? . . ."

Quietly, Maureen said, "I want to find my baby and then, if I can, I want to get my baby back. And then . . . well . . . we'll see what happens then."

Joyce reached down and untied Maureen, but when she stood, she immediately fell back down in the chair again. The ropes had cut off her circulation. She looked up at Fox and said, "But I don't know what the fuck you guys can do to help me find my baby."

"Well, we'll put a lawyer on it, for one thing. There's got to be a birth certificate somewhere."

"Mom burned it and she destroyed all physical evidence."

"Yea, but Maureen, she couldn't burn the official government records." Seeing the look on Maureen's face, Fox said, "Oh Maureen, come on, she's not that all-powerful."

"You don't know the Sarge," Maureen said, praying she was wrong and that Fox was on to something.

"And we'll get a private detective on it. Where did she take the baby?"

"I don't know," Maureen said.

"Well, you're gonna have to find that out."

"How?"

Fox glared at Maureen. "Ask her."

"Oh yea, right. I'm not even allowed to mention the baby."

"Oh, grow up, Maureen. Find out where your mother took your baby, and we'll do the rest. Now, Jack." Fox put an arm around Jack and, in an almost caring, respectful way, said, "Do you want to go down to the cop shop now or do you want to go home first? They'll no doubt want to arrest you on the spot. I'll send down Alistair Cramm. We got him on a retainer. Alistair'll go in with you . . ."

Maureen stopped listening. *Oh yea, right,* her mind was saying, *you're gonna march right up to the Sarge and ask her about what she warned you to never speak of again? Good plan. I can't see any problem with that except for the fact that the Sarge will annihilate you.*

The thought of facing down her mother terrified Maureen, and once again, her stupid mind wasn't helping. It kept telling her exactly what her mother was going to do to her: *The Sarge is going to kill you. She is going to make you sorry you were ever born. She's going to blind you. She is going to crucify you upside down like Mussolini . . .* But for the first time in her life Maureen magically turned off her mind and recognized that sure, the Sarge might hit her, but that wasn't such a big deal for someone who'd been beaten up by Bo. And, so what if the Sarge yelled and threatened? Fuck it. What could her mother really do to her? Maybe it wasn't the Sarge who was holding Maureen back; maybe it was *herself* who firmly believed all the bad stuff her mother said about her. Every name the Sarge had called her, every time her mother called Maureen down to the lowest, all that had lodged in Maureen's heart and she believed she was an idiot, that she was no good and on top of that, she was a fool, a gormless, clumsy, lazy, good-for-nothing fool, and all she'd ever known how to do was to beat up and destroy and, oh God, it was such an endless list. Well, if she was all those bad things, then that's who she was. So be it. She was just going to have to accept it. Nothing the Sarge could say was going to make one iota of dif-ference. *Oh shit, I am in charge.* And the thought of being in charge made her feel lost and found all at the same time. She wanted to run away, have a drink maybe. Yes, she definitely wanted a drink. No, no. She wouldn't have a drink. Not right now. She'd just hold on to that little shred of insight or whatever it was, just hang on to it like her life depended on it.

CHAPTER TWENTY-SEVEN

MAUREEN WENT DOWN TO PRINCESS STREET AND managed to get in the house without waking the Sarge. That was another first for Maureen. But of course, the Sarge was not expecting her that night. Maureen sat on the couch. She didn't think she'd be able to strike a wink of sleep. Not with everything that had just happened to her. Not with everything she'd just found out. Maureen felt the world shifting under her feet. Nothing was like she had thought it was. No one was who she had thought they were. She lay down, planning the words she'd use to get the Sarge to tell her where her baby was. *Mom, Mommy, you know Dr. Young?* No. That was stupid. But before she could get any further, her eyes shut and she fell almost immediately into a deep and dreamless sleep.

"REENIE, REENIE, REENS, REENS! REENS! ARE YOU AWAKE, Reens?"

Kathleen was shaking her by the shoulder, but Maureen kept her eyes closed. She didn't want to face the day or her family—not yet. But Kathleen was insistent and physically pried Maureen's eyes open.

"Mo-Mo-Reen, Reenie . . . Mom, Mom don't know you're here yet. Get up, get up, Reens—"

Maureen exploded off the couch. "What do you think you're doing, for Christ's sakes, Kathleen?"

Kathleen fell back on her bum, frightened. Maureen bent down to help her up and said she was sorry, but then Kathleen pulled Maureen down and started tickling her. Maureen was helpless against tickling. She started screaming, "No! NO! I can't—stop it, stop! . . . I can't—ahhh—I can't stand it! Oh no! No, stop . . ."

"Oh, now I got ya, Reenie!" Kathleen wouldn't stop.

They were both screaming and squealing when the Sarge walked into the room and said, "Get up off the floor, you foolish arses!"

She reached down and hauled Kathleen to her feet by the front of her shirt.

"Jesus, Maureen, it's all right for Kathleen—she's simple—but what's your excuse? Rolling around on the floor like a retard? . . . What are you doing here anyway? Shouldn't you be over shacked up with your fancy new fella from the university?"

"Mom," Maureen said from the floor. "Mom, I've got something I got to ask you."

"Jesus Christ, Maureen," the Sarge said as she headed for a mostly empty bottle of Canadian Club lying on its side next to the chesterfield. "I'm changing all the beds and trying to shovel out upstairs." She tipped the bottle up and drained what was left in it. "Trying to give myself a bit of ambition," she said by way of explaining the bottle of C.C. She headed for the living room door.

"Mom," Maureen said, standing up to her full height, "I gotta ask you something."

"Well, go ahead then and ask what you gotta ask me, fuckmentions. Hurry up. I got work to do."

Fixed in the Sarge's sights, Maureen could feel every bit of courage drain right out of her, but she managed to spit out, "What did you do with my baby? What did you do with my ba—" Before she got out the second "baby," Maureen felt herself flying back into the chesterfield from the force of the smack the Sarge had given her.

Kathleen was bawling, "Mom, Mom, no, Mom!" She went over and sat next to Maureen, plucking at her sleeve. "Reenie, don't cry. No, no, Reenie, don't cry, Reenie."

The Sarge turned on her heel and headed up over the stairs. Maureen's face was burning from the slap and tears were pouring out of her eyes, but she wasn't crying. She propelled herself out of the chesterfield and up over the stairs, running after the Sarge. She caught up to her at the last few steps past the landing and reached out and grabbed her mother's housecoat. Her mother kicked back and got her square in the guts. Maureen lost her balance and started to tumble backwards, but she was still holding on to the housecoat and dragged the Sarge back with her. They tumbled arse over teakettle until they came to a stop on the landing. Kathleen was hysterical. Maureen had ended up on top of the Sarge, and the thought came to Maureen that she could not remember a time when she had been this physically close to her mother, or even if she had ever been this close to her mother, and her next thought was to get away as fast as she could. She was so . . . close. She could feel her mother's breath on her face. The Sarge was pushing her.

"Get off me, you bitch's bastard! Get off me, you big bastard! Kathleen, get her off me!"

Maureen thought better of getting off her and, instead, put her knees on her mother's shoulders. The Sarge pushed back, but she'd twisted something in the fall and winced with pain. Maureen held her down. "Where is my baby?"

The Sarge made a mighty effort but still couldn't dislodge Maureen, who felt suddenly that she had the strength of ten because her heart was pure, or at least purely determined to get the answer to her question.

"Where is my baby?" she said again.

"The little bastard went back where it came from. Back to where it belonged."

"The baby is up in Montreal?" Maureen looked straight down into her mother's face.

The Sarge nodded, barely, and said, "Get off me," and then pushed Maureen, who didn't resist. "And don't you ever dare to lay a hand on me again, or I'll have the cops down on you so fast . . ."

Maureen was no longer listening to her mother. As she lay there on the landing, she thought, *Montreal. The baby's up in Montreal.* At last, she knew where her baby was, and now that she knew, everything was going to have to change. She was going to have to go back to Montreal and find the baby. With the baby in her arms, she would finally be able to fill in that hole that had been gaping in the middle of her for so long. That thought, which Maureen knew should have made her happy, instead frightened her to death. Her wish to find her baby had always kept her going, but if she found the baby, then what?

"Get up, Reenie, get up!" Kathleen was trying to pull Maureen to her feet. "I'm always gonna be the baby. Right, Maureen? I'm the baby! I'm the baby! Mom said I'm always going to be the baby 'cause I'm retarded."

PART III

CHAPTER TWENTY-EIGHT

MAUREEN, STILL SHAKING FROM HER CONFRONTATION with the Sarge but feeling a bit heady because she had all that new information, arrived at the cop shop before nine o'clock. It was almost empty, so she went up to the registration window to say she was here to see Kent and McCarthy. The young cop at the desk, the duty sergeant, gave Maureen the once-over, stopping right at her breasts, and seemed to be addressing her breasts when he asked, "What's it about?"

"They asked me to come down," Maureen said, trying to get him to look up at her face.

"Why?" he said, still staring at Maureen's chest, making a simple question sound like some kind of leering accusation.

"I don't know," she said, coopying down so that she was looking right in his eyes. "You're going to have to ask *them* that."

"Yea?" he said. "Well, take a seat over there. Someone will get ya when they're ready to talk with ya."

Maureen could feel his eyes boring a hole right through her backside as she walked to the bench. She turned around and caught him eyeing her, but he just looked boldly back at her like she was a common streetwalker or something. She wanted to scream at him, "I'm a murder suspect, fuckmentions! Not a prostitute!" But another part of her thought, *I guess I do look like a ditch pig streel.* She had on a pair of old bell-bottom jeans, a ribbed turtleneck sweater that she'd been wearing for three days now, George's Burke House residence jacket and a pair of workboots. Well, they weren't really workboots; they were just made to look like workboots, only they were dainty and Maureen had loved them as soon as she'd seen them at Dalmy's. Bo had called her a phony and told her to go out and get the real things and stop pretending to be something she wasn't all the fucking time. Yes, she definitely looked like a bit of a streel, but jumpins, she didn't think she looked like a slut. Maybe after you'd slept with enough fellas, people could just feel the slutdom coming off you in waves, a torrent of that ol' prossy vibe. Maureen had never, of course, done it for money, but she'd certainly done it for other things: she'd done it because she didn't know she was allowed to say no, she'd done it for a place to stay and she'd done it for affection and because she wanted to be wanted. She'd done it for many reasons, but she'd never, as far as she could remember, ever done it simply because she wanted to.

"Maureen—Miss Brennan?" Sergeant McCarthy was calling her name, pulling her back to the present. Maureen stepped forward, wondering if McCarthy and Kent had already talked to Jack and the lawyer and figuring she would be out of this meeting in jig-quick time.

An hour later, Maureen was still in the interrogation room, and

McCarthy was raging away at her about what she'd heard about the trouble between Bo and the Dunne brothers and when she'd become aware of all that.

"I wasn't aware of it."

"But sure, girl, you told us about it, the first time we talked to you."

"Yea. Then . . . after Bo was . . . dead. But, before . . . I knew he was pissed off like, with them . . . but jumpins, I mean, I didn't know there was . . ." Maureen paused, gathered her thoughts and said, "Was anyone in here this morning?" Oops, Maureen just remembered that George had warned her not to say anything—too late now, she figured, and what odds everything was different now.

"You're going to have to be a little more specific, Miss Brennan, because, as you can imagine, there have been quite a few people in here this morning," Kent said, giving Maureen that look—the one that felt like he was staring straight into the middle of her.

"Yea," Maureen said. "Right, I know . . . but was anyone from DAFT or anyone like that in here this morning?"

Kent kept staring at her.

"You know . . . like any of the b'ys, like Bo's crowd . . . Were any of them in here this morning?"

"Why do you ask, Maureen? Were you expecting anyone from DAFT to be here?"

"No, no, no . . . I wasn't expecting anything . . . I was just . . . asking."

"Oh." Kent nodded, still looking hard at Maureen.

"We've got the coroner's report, you know," McCarthy said.

"Oh ye-a?" Maureen's voice broke on the "yea," her throat actually closing in desperation, as she tried not to seem too interested.

"Yea," said McCarthy. "Asphyxia."

"Asphyxia?" Maureen said, alarmed. Were they looking at her in a new way? Was that why she was still here? "That's not poison, is it? Is that what killed him?"

She'd just gone ahead and said it: *poison*. It was all over for her now. Her mind raced and a scene played out: Kathleen was crying and reaching out to her as Maureen sat in the dock while a judge from an old black and white movie, with a big, ridiculous wig, said, "And you shall be taken from this place to another place, and there you will be hung . . ."

". . . can't get enough oxygen," McCarthy was saying as Kent continued to study her face. "Either because of some kind of obstruction to your airway, like say asthma or something like that, or there's not enough oxygen available to ya 'cause you're in a low oxygen area, like say you're in the trunk of a car or something."

Suddenly, Maureen was right there with them, out of the prisoner's dock and back in the room.

"Bo had asthma," she said hopefully. "He always had to have his puffer with him. Sometimes, he had to go over to the hospital and get a mask—"

"The cause of death, according to this," McCarthy read from the coroner's report, "was positional asphyxia. The victim was restrained, left prone, his hands were bound, his ankles tied up, a sock stuffed in his mouth to gag him."

Maureen's eyes widened despite her best effort to maintain an expressionless fish face. Just the mention of a sock was enough to bring a little bit of sick right up to the front of her mouth, and she tasted again the stinky cheese tang of Jack's filthy sock. Maureen swallowed and tried to look like someone who was just told that her boyfriend died under terrible circumstances. In truth, Maureen didn't feel anything beyond wanting to vomit from thinking about Jack's sock.

There's something really wrong with you, Maureen's mind said to her. *I mean, for Christ sakes, he was a human being.*

Yea, a human being who put the boots to me every other day, Maureen argued with her mind. Maybe she was heartless.

And empty, her mind said. *There's just a big sucking hole right in the middle of you, Maureen, right where your heart and your guts are supposed to be.*

Maureen didn't bother arguing with her mind any further because she knew it was true and that it was the baby. That's what the hole was, and she was doing everything in her power to get that hole filled, wasn't she? If she could just get out of here and let Fox know the baby was up in Montreal, he could get the whole process started with detectives and the lawyers or whatever, and then she could get her baby back and everything would be okay— wouldn't it?

McCarthy continued reading from the coroner's report, ". . . and in his exertion to free himself, he compressed his chest and that, coupled with his pre-existing asthma"—McCarthy nodded to Maureen—"increased his oxygen demand and decreased the oxygen delivery; he inhibited his chest wall and diaphragmatic movement by struggling against the restraints, plus his alcohol toxicity level was—"

"That's enough, McCarthy," Kent said.

"Oh!" Maureen said, trying not to seem too relieved. "It was an accident . . . Bo, he died by accident."

"Oh no, this is a murder," McCarthy said. "Murder for sure."

Maureen's heart came right up in her throat.

"But you said he did it himself by struggling against the restraints and his asthma and being drunk and all like that."

"But someone put him in those restraints, didn't they, missy? And someone put him in the trunk of that car, where there was insufficient oxygen available."

"But the asthma, and he was drunk—"

"Was he drunk, Maureen?"

"Well, he was drinking heavy the night before, I know. I know that much."

"Well, all that doesn't matter because, by law, we have to take the victim as we find him. The eggshell skull law." McCarthy was warming to his subject and seemed glad to have an opportunity to show off his knowledge of the law.

"What?" Maureen asked, thinking she'd heard wrong.

"In common law, if buddy was born with a thin skull and you beat him over the head and, because his skull is so thin, you end up killing him, it doesn't matter that he has an eggshell skull." He looked directly at Maureen. "It's still you . . . murdered him."

Maureen blanched but tried to keep her face in neutral.

Kent said, "And so, Miss Brennan, what do you know regarding the person or persons who placed Mr. Browne in those restraints, put a sock in the victim's mouth and put him in that environment of oxygen insufficiency?" He had the look of a man who was asking a question to which he already knew the answer.

"No, no, I don't know anything about any of that. I mean, I don't know fuck all about fuck all—that's what Bo used to say about me."

Maureen had almost been fooled last night when Jack insisted he didn't kill Bo, but the sock. The sock was proof positive that Jack Dunne was the murdering bastard that Maureen thought he was. She looked at the two cops with what she hoped was a wide-eyed, butter-wouldn't-melt-in-her-mouth, wouldn't-say-shit-if-her-mouth-was-full-of-it look and hoped that they believed she was as stupid as she looked.

"You mentioned poison earlier, Maureen."

"Did I?"

"Yes, yes, you did. And oddly enough, trace elements of the poison chlordane were found in the victim's stomach."

"Trace elements?" Maureen asked.

"Yes, a minute amount of the poison was found in Mr. Browne's stomach—an almost insignificant amount."

"An *insignificant* amount?" a wide-eyed Maureen asked.

"Yes. And how do you think that insignificant amount got there?"

"How would I know?" newly naive and stunned Maureen said.

Bo must have tipped up the orange juice and drank straight from the decanter, just like you figured he would, her mind said. *Tasted the chlordane and just spit it out again.*

Yes, Maureen agreed with her mind. Because if Bo had taken a big swig of the orange juice, they would have found much more than an *insignificant* amount. According to what she'd read at the library, she'd put enough poison in that orange juice to . . . kill him.

Out loud, Maureen said, "I mean, I know there was a big gallon of the stuff the exterminator left. He could have just . . . I suppose, breathed it in. Did he?"

"No. It was in his stomach, so that means he would have had to ingest it," Kent said.

"Why would he do that?" Maureen laughed, but even to her ears, it sounded hollow.

"Exactly. I don't think he would do that, Maureen. We're in the process of testing all the food in the fridge to see if any of it contains chlordane."

For the second time that hour, Maureen's heart leapt up into her throat and tried to choke her. Test the food? If they did, they'd find straight chlordane in the orange juice, and the diluted poison on the pizza, on the cut-open tomato, on all of it. If only she'd thought to eat it when McCarthy offered it to her back at the apartment. It would have been just as well if she had died. Better to be dead than endlessly waiting for the other shoe to drop, for everyone to find out what she was, a poisoner, and they'd charge her with attempted murder, and she'd rot away in jail and she'd never see her baby. Oh jail. Oh Jesus. In jail, the prisoners, the other women, they'd see right through her tough girl act just like the girls down at The Agora had. She'd never survive it. She might as well just kill herself right now.

"Miss Brennan." Kent's voice, once again, brought her back to the present. "If you do know anything at all about the people who might have been involved in kidnapping and detaining Mr. Trevor 'Bo' Browne against his will, the people who ultimately murdered Mr. Browne, I would suggest that now would be the time to—" Kent suddenly stopped talking, looked up, said, "What are you doing here?"

Maureen's eyes followed his, and she saw, standing in the doorway, a small, thin-faced, blond-haired man.

"What the fuck are you doing here, Cramm?" McCarthy said.

"Oh, I've been standing here quietly for quite some time. Very interesting. Alistair Cramm, counsel for Miss Brennan," he announced and closed the door behind him.

McCarthy made that disgusting sign again, driving the fingers of his left hand through the circle he'd made with his right, and said, "Another *friend*, Maureen?"

"No!" Maureen was outraged. "I don't even know who he is. I've never even seen him before."

"I'm your lawyer, Miss Brennan. I've been retained by friends of yours to assist you in your . . ."

Maureen shot a warning look at McCarthy when she heard the word "friends," but he just threw both his hands up in the air in disgust.

CHAPTER TWENTY-NINE

OUTSIDE THE COP SHOP, ALISTAIR CRAMM ASKED MAUREEN if she wouldn't mind going down to Marty's Snack Bar with him for a quick cup of coffee. He just had a few things to go over with her and it wouldn't take long.

Maureen kept trying to say that she didn't want to go into Marty's, that she didn't want a cup of coffee, but he just kept talking at her and nudging her along Water Street, and she could tell that even to get a word in edgewise with this guy would take an enormous amount of energy, and she didn't have that energy. So she sat in one of the back booths at Marty's and faced the lawyer who DAFT had on retainer, saying no, she didn't want a coffee or a Coke or anything. She was desperate for an opportunity, an opening, to say what she really wanted to say, which was: Why didn't Jack go into the cop shop this morning and confess, and why was I being questioned again by the cops? But Cramm wouldn't shut up long enough for Maureen to get her questions out. He just kept talking. Talking in broad terms about his clients, talking about his need to protect his clients, and how now, of course, she was his client, not his major client, but a very important client, make no mistake about it . . . and on and on and on and on and on and on and on . . .

Finally, Maureen just put her head down on the table and gave up. She should have just gone ahead and told the cops the truth at the beginning, and the truth was she was guilty, if not of Bo's actual murder, then certainly of trying to murder him, and you could do life for that—she'd looked it up—and what difference would it make if she did do life, because she had no life now anyway. Jack hadn't shown up and confessed, so the boys weren't going to keep their promise. How was she ever going to find her baby on her own, let alone get her baby back? What would she do? Move back to Princess Street and spend all those long, long years, years that stretched out in front of her now like a big empty void fighting with the Sarge? Even though the thought of prison terrified her, she felt in her heart of hearts that she would probably do easier time in a federal pen than living down with the Sarge; plus, in the pen, she'd probably learn French or something.

"Look," she said, picking her head up off the table, "I don't know why they sent you down—"

"That's not important right now." Cramm cut her off.

"Yes, it is important. To me, it's important."

"That's what you think. But you see, I don't care what you think. Nobody really cares what you think, Miss Brennan. As far as you're concerned, the only thing that anybody really cares about right now is what you told those two police officers before I arrived."

"Nothing! That's what I told them: nothing. I was just waiting for them to tell me that Jack—"

Cramm's eyes darted around the restaurant and then gave Maureen a warning.

"All right, that *someone* was in to the police station this morning and confessed. I never said anything. So . . ."

"So?"

"Well, I kept my part of the bargain."

"Bargain?"

"Yes, bargain. I was going to shut up and *someone*," Maureen said pointedly, "*someone* was going to confess, and the boys were going to help me find my baby."

Cramm, silenced for the first time since he'd walked into the interrogation room, seemed to be taking Maureen's measure. "I'm afraid that bargain may no longer be possible, not under the present circumstances. The boys, you see, who are so good at certain things—really, they seem to have a genius for turning small investments into huge profits—the boys really don't have a solid grip on the law of the land. Now . . . Now finish up, Maureen." Cramm stood.

Maureen looked down: she had nothing to finish up because they hadn't ordered anything. Cramm was already at the door, holding it open for her.

"We'll just scoot up over the hill to my office, where we will have more privacy, and then we can discuss your case."

"My *case*?" Now Maureen's flabber was well and truly ghasted. Everything used to ghast Carleen's flabber back in Grade 9, and it used to slay Maureen every time she said it, like that cartoon "Cain Slayed Abel," where Abel was lying on the ground, holding on to his sides for dear life because he was laughing so hard.

"And don't you worry about costs, because they have already been covered. You are in good hands, young lady. And as long as you keep your wits about you and your mouth shut and do the right thing . . ."

Maureen's mind wandered. She tried to interrupt him a couple of times, but she finally gave up and accepted that it was true: he wasn't the least bit interested in anything she had to say.

Finally, they arrived at his office. It was right below Booman Tate's loft. She couldn't believe she was back there again for the second time, back where Bo had first hit her and thrown her down the stairs a lifetime ago, back before the permanent fog, before the half-life between being awake and asleep, between being drunk and sober and just about to get drunk again, before the dark dream world that Maureen had been stumbling through ever since. Of course, Maureen could have walked away that night and gone back to Princess Street with her black eye and her broken rib. But it hadn't seemed possible then. Now, she could walk away and she turned to do just that, but Cramm had her by the arm and in through the door and sat down in a chair before she'd had time to tell her feet to get going.

"As the officers just informed you, they found trace amounts of chlordane in the body of your lover, the deceased."

"You were in the room then?"

"I was in the room for quite a while. What will they find, Maureen, when they test the food?"

"How should I know, and what difference does it make? He

was murdered. That's what the cops said. Jack murdered him."

"Uh, no. No, Miss Brennan. My client Mr. Dunne may be—and I say *may be*—guilty of the crime of manslaughter but certainly not of murder. If and when the alleged incident took place, presumably my client was in the heat of passion, provoked—"

"Provoked?" Maureen said.

"Yes, provoked. As I'm sure you're aware, Miss Brennan, your lover, Mr. Trevor 'Bo' Browne, assaulted, kidnapped and held Mr. Dunne's younger twin, Deucey, against his will in the trunk of that very same red Renault where Mr. Browne's body was later found."

"Yea. Someone told me about it. I didn't know about it, like, when it was going on or anything."

"My client Mr. Jack Dunne has always been fiercely protective of his younger brother—younger by five minutes. As you know, Mr. Dunne and his brother are identical twins, and what you probably wouldn't know is that meant they shared the same placenta. But, tragically, in the case of the Dunne twins, it was shared unequally. Jack Dunne had a share that was too small to provide the necessary nutrients for him to develop normally or even survive. And that's when David, in the womb, sacrificed himself and started sharing his blood supply with Jack, thus saving his brother's life. Twin-to-twin transfusion syndrome is what it's called. And because of that, the donor twin, David, was smaller than his twin brother at birth, anemic, fragile and unstable. The recipient twin, Jack, was born, thanks to his brother, larger, healthier and stronger. So you can understand, can you not, Miss Brennan, why this wrongful act against his twin, his saviour, this horrendous insult against his younger brother's body and spirit was—and I know we can prove it based on the medical evidence—was sufficient to deprive any ordinary person of the power of self-control, let alone a person whose life had been selflessly saved by his brother in utero. The proof is there that Mr. Dunne's retaliation is certainly proportional to the provocation, as he merely did to Mr. Browne exactly what Mr. Browne had done to Mr. Dunne's brother. So there we have it, because of the irrefutable medical condition, it is eminently possible for us to prove provocation and thereby get the charges set at manslaughter." Cramm's smile was somewhat disturbing, and his pointy tongue darted out and actually licked his lips when he said the word "manslaughter." "In R. v. LeFrancon 1965, '. . . if provocation does exist the verdict must be manslaughter and in—'"

"You know, I'm not really following you," Maureen said.

"Provocation, Miss Brennan. In law, the act of provocation consists of three elements." Cramm held up his hand and counted each on his fingers. "One, the act of provocation. Two, the loss of self-control both actual and reasonable, and three, retaliation proportionate to the provocation, all of which I believe we can prove. And if we go further and convince a jury that Trevor 'Bo' Browne was an individual who often provoked both friends and strangers to where they were deprived of the power of self-control and that Mr. Browne was indeed a man who made a meal of provocation and a vocation of vexation and torment."

Maureen started to say something in Bo's defence and then thought better of it.

"Did he not often provoke you, Miss Brennan, past reasonable thought, past thought altogether, past caring, provoke you to the point where you purposefully caused your lover to ingest the poison chlordane?"

Maureen wished he'd stop calling Bo her lover and tried to keep her face impassive around the whole poison thing.

"Isn't that so, Miss Brennan? Wouldn't you agree?"

"It's like you're putting Bo on trial."

"Exactly. What a smart little bit of fluff you turned out to be, Miss Brennan, because that is precisely what I will be doing. And that's why I, or rather we, need you as the star witness."

"What?" Maureen squeaked. "No, Jesus, I said nothing to the cops. I already did what I was supposed to do. I said nothing. I found out from Mom where she brought the baby, and Fox said that I could go . . . and if you're my lawyer—"

"Well, technically, I am not your lawyer yet. Not yet, at any rate. I could easily become your lawyer, but as of this moment, I am not legally engaged as your lawyer."

"But you told McCarthy and Kent—"

"A little legal sleight of hand, Miss Brennan." He raised his hand. "Now of course, if we can come to an agreement, then I will become your lawyer, and then we can prove that said Trevor Browne was a bad bit of business, a man who could provoke even those who loved him"—he looked at Maureen meaningfully—"provoke them to the point of"—he leaned across the table and lowered his voice to a stage whisper—"murder. Murder most foul."

He sat back and looked well pleased with himself. Maureen was speechless.

Cramm continued, "You'll appear in court, say you tried to poison him, tell the whole sordid little story of the relationship, the drunkenness, the violence, the constant brutality against your person—"

"I don't want to," Maureen finally got out, after trying to interrupt him a number of times.

"Of course, it will be humiliating. They, the prosecution, the Crown, they'll try to prove, oh, that perhaps you deserved the beatings, that maybe you brought them on yourself, perhaps even welcomed them. Knowing the Crown and the good Catholic St. Bon's boy that he is, he probably won't go so far as to suggest that there was anything more depraved involved, anything of a sado-masochistic nature." He looked at Maureen's appalled and questioning face, and said, "Sado-masochism: mutually consensual sexual acts involving violence, one partner being the brute or sadist, the other a willing victim or masochist—very common, really, but not, I'm thinking"—he paused and gave Maureen a sardonic smile—"by the look on your face, among the downtown shopgirl set."

"I am not a shopgirl!"

Cramm continued as if she hadn't spoken. "You will tearfully inform them that in a moment of deep desperation, fearing for your life, in a passion of fear, in fact, you blindly reached for the deadly poison and dot dot dot."

"No, no, I'm not saying that. I'm not doing it. Jesus, they'll charge me with attempted murder!"

"No, they won't. Simply because Section C5 of the Canada Evidence Protection Act states that with respect to any question that a witness is compelled to answer, if that answer could tend to incriminate him, the answer given shall not be used and shall not be admissible in evidence against the witness in any criminal trial or in any other criminal proceeding against such witness. Except, Maureen, if they prosecuted you for perjury if you lied on the stand, that's the only thing for which you could be prosecuted. So you can see, Miss Brennan, how necessary it is for you to tell the truth, the whole truth and nothing but the truth, and so on, and so forth."

By this point, Maureen was so completely rattled by him, how he never shut up, how he just kept going on. No wonder they said he was a good lawyer; he was so confusing, he could trip up a church, for Christ sakes.

"No, no, I'm not doing it! I'm not sayin' that I tried to poison Bo. I'll never get another boyfriend. Besides, you can't pin anything on me. I didn't do anything. You have no proof."

"But if the police find poison in the food in the refrigerator—"

"So what does that prove?"

"Reasonable doubt, and I'll convince a jury that Mr. Browne provoked you to the point of attempted murder in the same way he provoked my clients."

"Yea, well, I'd like to see ya try," Maureen said in desperation. Whenever she was really afraid, she got as saucy as a shitfly. "Come ahead, 'cause if you do, I'll tell everyone about . . . I'll tell them all about DAFT, the boys and what they're up to, all the big investors and the big catch they've got planned off the coast of Colombia, plus I'll tell them where Jack kidnapped me and tied me up in the DAFT office and stuck a dirty sock down my throat just like he did with Bo, so that will pretty well blow your whole defence of 'he was provoked and driven cracked in a passion of anger.'" She looked him straight in the eye. "Is that important enough for you?"

"What big catch off the coast of Colombia?"

"I don't know. It's just something I saw in a telegram down to Deucey's."

"And the big investors?"

"Fox said it to Jack, said they couldn't afford to have the cops sniffing around now that they got the big investors."

"And who are they?"

"How should I know?"

"Well, you seem to know a good deal, don't you, for someone who 'knows fuck all about fuck all'?" He paused. "Were you threatening me, Miss Brennan?"

"No. Yes. I don't know. I just know we had a deal."

"Did we?" Cramm asked, his eyebrows flying up.

"Not me and you—me and the boys. And I kept my part of the bargain. I never said not the one word to the cops. I risked life and limb to find out where Mom brought my baby to, and now all I'm saying is why should I keep my part if yer not gonna do yer part?"

"Hmm, yes, a compelling argument. We seem to have reached a classic standoff here. To my mind though, Miss Brennan, you would be much better served to do exactly as I have asked."

"Well, of course, that's what you think. You think I should do just what you want, but I don't think that."

"Look at it this way: either way, you will be exposing yourself to public humiliation, cross-examination on the witness stand—"

"Yea, but at least I won't be getting up down to the courthouse and saying that I tried to murder my boyfriend, which I never by the way—that's just you suppositioning or whatnot. All I'll be saying is that someone, Jack Dunne, kidnapped me, tied me to a chair and shoved a dirty sock down my throat just like he did to my boyfriend. And I'll be saying that DAFT is not just a plain old above-board business, and that will put a big spotlight on all their investors, just when, according to what Fox said anyway, they can't afford to have anyone looking at 'em because some of the investors are—whatcha call it?—a bit skittish. I don't know what word Fox said, but that's what it meant."

"Well, like I said, it's a bit of a standoff, isn't it? But I would ask you, Miss Brennan, to remember your lover, Mr. Browne, and what happened to Mr. Browne when he attempted to do harm to one of my clients."

"Now it's you threatening me." Maureen stood up. "I think you are anyway, but I'm that confused now I don't know what to be at. I'm just going to go home and think about it."

"Well, don't take too long. None of us have any guarantees."

"You are, you are threatening me."

"It's just today; that's all we've got, Miss Brennan."

"Oh, are you one too?"

"One—one what?"

"You know."

"No, I'm afraid I don't."

"An alcoholic."

"No, I am not."

"Oh, 'cause they're always talking about just having the one day."

"I'm merely suggesting that Mr. Browne would probably not have been aware when he woke up that fateful morning that the end of that seemingly ordinary day would find him bound and gagged and dead in the trunk of his own car. If he only knew that was his last day on this earth, who knows what he might have done differently."

"Yea, I'm going." Maureen was moving fast toward the door.

"Well, be my guest," Cramm said, standing up and going to open the door for her. "I will contact you in the morning."

"How do you know where I'm going to be?"

"Oh, I'll know. Don't you worry your fluffy little head about that."

CHAPTER THIRTY

MAUREEN, HOLD ON . . ."

It was Deucey, calling out to her from across Duckworth Street just as she stepped out of Cramm's office. Maureen's first instinct was to run. Deucey was one of them, after all. But as her eyes darted back and forth along the street, she realized that unless she wanted to duck back into the office she'd just escaped, she'd have to face the Deuce.

"Hey, Deuce," Maureen threw out as casually as she could muster. "Whaddya at?"

Deuce was deking in and out between traffic as he crossed the street to her.

"What are *you* at, Mo-Reen?" Deuce said when he got close to her.

The way he stood so close to her and said her name made Maureen wonder if he was being sexual or threatening or a bit of both.

Probably both, Maureen's mind started in. *Sex, always a threat, always highly dangerous, pregnancy, shame, violence, finding yourself in the thrall of some rotten, vicious fella who'd just as soon pound the piss out of ya as look at ya.*

Okay, okay, I get it, Maureen told her mind to quiet it, but her mind was set on going through all the possible threats that sex could hold for a young Catholic girl in St. John's, Newfoundland, in the year of our Lord, Anno Domini nineteen hundred and seventy.

All this time, Deuce had been talking. ". . . I'm worried about Jack. Poor Jack is just unlucky, like you, Maureen. He got no luck. He starts something, then things go all to hell on him, and he always ends up in a mess."

"Like me?" Maureen said, horrified. "I'm not unlucky." She couldn't believe that Deucey thought she was unlucky. Oh God, the idea that people thought she was unlucky filled Maureen with the deepest feelings of anxiety and despair. If people went around saying out loud she was unlucky, jumpins, that pretty well proved that she was unlucky. And not just unlucky, but too stunned to even know she *was* unlucky.

She had to get Deucey to take it back, to say that he was wrong about the whole unlucky remark.

"And what mess, Deuce? I'm not in a mess."

"Jesus, Maureen, get a grip, girl. You're drowning in mess."

"Hmm, nothing I can't handle. I mean to say, Deuce"—Maureen was frantic now to make him take back what he said—"I'm good at mess. I've always been good at mess. It's when things are tidy, that's what kills me. When things are just going along all good like, that's when it all falls abroad for me. I'm not unlucky; I'm making a choice. I just choose . . . chaos. It's a choice I'm making. It's just how I am." Maureen was trying with every fibre of her being to get Deucey to go along with her and take back the terrible curse of unluckiness he'd placed on her head by saying it out loud. But no matter what she said, she couldn't get Deucey to reverse that horrible judgment of unluckiness. Maureen's mind cut in with, *The best you can hope for now is to stop him from saying anything else, anything worse.* Maureen knew that if Deucey said anything else bad about her, like she was doomed or born under a bad star or any of that other shit, it would probably kill her. Deucey's voice pulled Maureen out of her head.

"Look, Jack, he's a bit—"

"Nuts," Maureen said.

"Yea, well, not nuts exactly, but you know, he gets carried away sometimes and—"

"Yea, he's a fuckin' murderer and a kidnapper and nuts."

"He's not," Deucey said. "He's a real good guy, Maureen. He'd do anything for ya. And he didn't kill Bo." Deuce corrected himself quickly: "I mean, he didn't mean to kill Bo. I mean, if he did kill Bo—which we really got no proof that he did—he was just doing to Bo what Bo did to me. He had me in the back of that Renault for almost two days. Tied up like a pig. And every now and then, he'd open up the trunk and give me a drink of water and tell me he'd let me out of there as soon as I agreed to tell the boys that we had to take him on as a full partner. And if I didn't, I could stay there in that trunk until I rotted. And if I ever told anyone what happened to me, he would destroy DAFT, tear down the entire organization, bit by fuckin' bit. And he had enough information to do that, too."

Maureen hadn't really thought it through before, Deucey being tied up in the dark in that airless trunk. Poor Deucey. When he was talking about what had happened, his eyes looked like they had that time in Butter Pot Park. "How'd you get out?" Maureen asked quietly.

"I finally told him I'd do what he wanted. I'd tell the boys to make him a partner. To tell you the truth, Maureen, I probably would've said anything at that point just to get out of that goddamn trunk."

Maureen and Deucey stood silently looking at each other. Maureen felt herself swept under by a wave of pity for Deucey and herself—but she couldn't afford to go there.

"But you went ahead and told anyway?"

"What?" Deucey said.

"You went ahead and told Jack what happened to you."

"Yea." Deucey looked at her blankly. "Yea, yea, that's right. I told Jack, and Jack had wanted to pay him back—but not kill him. Geez, anybody'd do the same thing. And realistically, Maureen, if you look at it, we—Jack saved your life."

Maureen's mouth fell open. She didn't know what to say to that. Deucey, of course, took her silence for agreement and started to hold forth on his ridiculous theory.

"I'm not saying you owe Jack your life or anything like that, but in ancient cultures, say the Chinese or Native cultures, well if someone saves your life, then you owe them your life."

"Deuce, normal up. That's just something you heard on *The Lone Ranger* or somethin' when you were a youngster . . . Anyway, he didn't save my life; he took Bo's."

"Fuck Bo," Deucey said. Maureen was surprised at the hatred in his voice. "He was a prick. I know that and you certainly know that, and Maureen"—Deucey looked directly in Maureen's eyes with what she assumed he thought passed for sincerity—"all we need you to do is get up on the stand and say that, say the truth."

"Yea, I know. Your lawyer already threatened me about it. And I'm telling you what I already told him: I'm not doing it." Maureen could see that standing up for herself and saying that she wasn't going to get up on the stand and talk about all the beatings and the misery of her life with Bo was just hardening Deucey's resolve. His face was setting against her.

What Maureen really felt like doing was bursting into tears. Because it wasn't fair. When was everyone going to get off her back and stop pushing her around? The more she felt like bursting into tears, the more she was determined not to, and the more she resolved not to do what Deucey and Cramm had asked of her. No, she wouldn't do it. She wouldn't go on the stand and say that she tried to poison Bo. Nobody had any proof. Nobody knew, except her and George—and Bo. But Bo was dead, and if George was a problem, well . . . Maureen stopped herself from going down that ridiculous road. She just wasn't going to do it, and she didn't care what they did to her. She couldn't trust them anyway. They had a deal in place, and she had kept her part of the bargain, but they reneged on theirs. They were just going to fuck her over, but one thing was certain: she was definitely not going to cry. She hated girls who always cried, cried to get their own way, cried to get out of trouble, cried to make everyone feel sorry for them. She felt nothing but contempt for them. It was so easy, it was so cheap . . . But then, before she could do anything to stop it, there she was, standing on Duckworth Street, dissolving into tears, sniffling and bawling.

"It's not that I don't want to, Deuce," she said, "but see, it's just that I'm afraid." She thought she'd try appealing to his own self-interest. "Not for myself, but for your crowd. I mean"—sniffle, sniffle—"you know what I'm like, Deuce. If I get on the stand and start telling the truth, the whole truth and all that"—she was really crying now—"well, once I start, I don't, honest to God, know where I'm going to be able to stop. Shure I'll start off telling 'em all about Bo and all the shit knockings he gave me and how I was in a daze half the time and didn't know what I was doing. But then before I know what I'm saying, I'm telling them everything. All about all the makeup I stole all the time down to Woolworths, about the time I cut Mom out of all the family pictures and swore that it must've been Kathleen, my retarded sister, doing it, about how Jack kidnapped me and tried to make me disappear and shoved a sock in my mouth just exactly like he did to Bo . . ." She was crying so hard now that she was hiccuping. People on the street were glancing over at them to see what was going on. Deucey noticed the attention and kept trying to make her stop crying but she couldn't. She gasped for breath and hauled her sleeve across the bottom of her nose. She knew she must look some state, tears running from her eyes, snot running from her nose, and even some kind of stuff running from the corner of her mouth. ". . . And about those Colombian telegrams I saw down to your place, and the bill of sale for that big boat."

Deucey actually looked shocked.

Maureen said in her defence, "They were just right there on your desk . . ." She sobbed. "And I might tell them all about what Bo did to you. And it'll all pour out in one big, awful ball of truth. But I mean to say, not so much for me, but for you and the boys, I'm just worried." She hawked back a bunch of phlegm, wiped her eyes and kept going. "I just don't think I'd be a very good witness. It's not that I wouldn't tell the truth; it's that I'd tell too much truth—see what I mean?"

She was holding on to Deucey's arm now. She could see he was desperate to get away from her.

"I'm not threatening you or anything like that, Deucey, promise soul to God I'm not, but I'm just so freaked out about everything that's going on. I'm just so bugged out, I—"

"Yea, bummer," Deucey said, finally managing to haul his arm out of her grip. "Real bummer, Maureen."

"You know, Deuce, I don't want to burn you guys, but I'm just . . . I don't feel I . . ." She started in bawling and snotting again.

Deucey looked down, helpless. He was freaked right out and wanted to get away from her, but at the same time, her tears were having that magical effect on him that all those other girls' tears had on everyone else. He looked at her with such pity and terror. He seemed willing to do anything to make her stop crying. It surprised Maureen to see that Deucey was so frightened and so moved by her crying. She always tried so hard not to cry; she'd been taught that it was weak and gutless. On Princess Street, you had to go around being a man, like the Sarge. Now she wondered if that "be a man about it" thing wasn't just some more Princess Street bullshit.

She was a girl, for God's sake. Why did she have to go around being a man about anything? All her threats and rough talk had never made anyone look as scared as Deucey looked right now.

"I'll do it," Maureen said, grabbing hold to Deucey's arm again. "I'll get on the stand, but will I be able to control what I'm saying?"

Deucey hauled his arm free, stood there for a moment, unsure of what to do, and then took off like a scalded cat.

"I'll talk to the boys, Maureen," he yelled over his shoulder. "Don't worry. We can work something out."

"No, I'll go to court, Deuce . . . if you really want me to."

Deucey was practically running down Duckworth Street toward the DAFT offices. Maureen blew her nose and headed up Church Hill. She was worn out, as tired as she'd ever been. It was really hard work, this full-on crying business. She just wanted to get in out of it somewhere and get a bit of quiet and not have to answer any questions from anyone—least of all from George or the Sarge or the cops—and maybe then she could think.

When she walked past St. Thomas's church, past the parish hall, she saw a bunch of people standing around outside. She knew there was an AA meeting going on inside and felt in her bones that she should go in. It was a nooner, and she was early. She sat down, relieved to be in out of it. She closed her eyes and felt almost safe, and as she was sitting there, for some reason, her exhausted mind started running through the seven Corporal Acts of Mercy. She found them comforting. Harbour the Harbourless—that one had always been Maureen's favourite because it seemed to be about them, about St. John's; they had a harbour. Ransom the Captive,

Bury the Dead—but Bo was already buried . . . but would he ever really be dead? Dead to her so that she wouldn't still have to worry about him all day, every day?

I might as well have just gone ahead and killed him anyway, she thought. I wouldn't feel any worse.

Well, it was no fault of yours that you didn't, was it? her mind said.

She tried to think about something else, but she was too tired. She opened her eyes and looked around her. Everyone there was so old, so not groovy. A feeling crept in that she didn't want to be there. What if she knew any of these losers? It was all bad enough; she didn't want anyone thinking she couldn't hold her liquor. Being a lightweight in the boozebag department was almost as low as being cheap, and as far as Maureen's family was concerned, all those people were below contempt. It was okay to be a slut, battered woman, liar, poisoner—okay, but alcoholic? Oh gentle German Jesus. First, she'd been reduced to snotting and bawling and getting on like a girl, and now everyone was going to think she was an alcoholic. Just how low was she going to let herself go?

She could feel the blood rushing into her face as she got up and hurried toward the door. Then she spotted Dicey Doyle. She hadn't seen Dice since the day of Bo's funeral. Maureen put her head down and rushed for the exit, hoping Dicey hadn't seen her. She was almost out the door when she felt a hand on her shoulder and Dicey said, "Hey, Reenie, whaddya at?"

"Not much, Dice. What are you at?" Maureen said back, trying to look relaxed.

"Is this your first meeting?" Dicey asked.

"Yea . . . I . . ."

At that moment, Verna from the last meeting passed by and said, "Hey, Maureen, good to see you back. One day at a time."

"Yea." Maureen turned back to Dicey, embarrassed. "See, I was here . . . before, but you know, but I'm not . . . like an alcoholic or anything. I was, you know, trying to find out what happened to Bo." Maureen's voice got flatter and quieter with each word. She could tell from the look on Dicey's face that she didn't believe her.

"Let me get you a cup of coffee. Do you want a cancer stick?" Dicey was smoking the green Export "A"s. Maureen gratefully took one of the stubby smokes out of the package, lit up and sat down in the back row. Dicey came back with the coffee, trapping Maureen before she could make her escape.

"Dice, look I know probably everybody says this, but I'm not an . . . an . . ."

"Don't." Dicey put up her hand. "It's okay." She handed Maureen a cup.

Maureen took a big gulp of the hot liquid and almost spat it right out again.

"Geez, it's some sweet—how many sugars did you put in there?"

"Five sugars and almost half a can of Carnation. Since I've been getting off the booze, I've been craving sugar really bad, 'cause I guess there's so much sugar in the liquor."

"Oh . . . I'm not craving sugar," Maureen said. "I don't—"

As Maureen was about to go into a long explanation of how she didn't drink, not like that anyway, the meeting started. For the first fifteen minutes, Maureen paid no attention to what was going on around her. She couldn't really hear anything; she just sat there going over and over again in her mind everything that had happened that morning. She knew that even if she did get on the stand and do what they wanted, there was no guarantee that they'd help her find her baby. They'd already welshed on their promise of Jack going down and confessing. Something about the way Deucey had looked was playing on her mind, but she couldn't quite put her finger on it. Every time she tried, she just felt so sorry for him that she lost her train of thought. It was an inkling that came and disappeared before Maureen could grasp it. It wasn't helping that, every now and again, she was overwhelmed by the thought, *What in the name of God am I doing here anyway, with a bunch of boozebag losers, all going on about God or whatever?* Maureen just could not go God since she had effectively left the Holy Roman Catholic and Apostolic Church when she was thirteen years old, although, just to keep the Sarge off her back, she continued to pretend to go to Sunday Mass, or bits of it anyway, at least until she'd met Dicey. She'd been forced to leave God and the Church when it became clear to her that there was no hope of redemption—not for her. She'd stolen so much makeup from Woolworths, she knew that, even if she went to confession, she had no hope of absolution, because the priest would insist that she pay back the store for all the stuff she'd robbed. She would never have that much money, and so she would never get forgiveness. And if she didn't get forgiven, then she couldn't get absolution. And if she couldn't get absolution, then she couldn't take Communion. So every Sunday, she would have to sit jarred up in the pew by herself as everyone else went up to the altar rails to receive the body and blood of Our Lord Jesus Christ. She'd have to sit there like a mook and everyone would know she was in a state of sin, so how could she go to Mass? Not going was another mortal sin. Maureen's milk bottle, which in the *Baltimore Catechism* stood in for the immortal soul, was once only spotted with venial sin, but it had become coal-black. Her eternal soul was destined to burn in the heat and the darkness and stench of hell for eternity—not much to look forward to, Maureen thought.

When Verna was called on to speak, Maureen got out of herself and into the meeting. She could hear Verna's story about how far down her boozing had taken her, how she lost everything, her house, her youngsters, and how, finally, she even lost herself, and how she didn't care, not even then, and how she figured she was born an alcoholic, because when she was little, long before she'd started drinking, she'd felt so cut off from everybody else, so different. Verna said that she was so grateful for the program of Alcoholics Anonymous, because not only did it get her off the booze, but it showed her a way to live, and it meant that she was alone no more. She said that the God of her understanding was definitely not the God she'd been terrified by at Presentation Convent. The God of her understanding just stood for Good Orderly Direction. She said she'd read this in the Daily Reflections but that she wanted to share it, and she read out from a book, "Still a child, she cries for the moon, but the moon, it seems, won't have her." That's how she'd spent her life, she said: uselessly crying for the moon.

But how else are you supposed to get the moon? Maureen thought.

The next fella that spoke was from somewhere up the Southern

Shore. The crowd from the Southern Shore all had a way of talking that Maureen found captivating, and buddy was no different. He said that all the time that he'd been drinking, his life had been like a boat that was out on the wide sea, but it was a boat that had no charts or radar or navigation of any kind aboard, and because he had never learned to navigate by the stars, he was all the time lost, lost out on an ocean of trouble. He said that getting in the program had been like getting on a big boat with a crew of people on board with charts and radar, and he was even learning to use the stars to set his course so that in real bad times, when he couldn't see the charts or there was something wrong with the navigation equipment, he could always depend on himself.

Verna and buddy seemed to be talking directly to Maureen. It was like someone had come in and told them all about her, how she'd always felt like she was all by herself, out on a dark spit of land with the wind roaring and the rain spilling down while everybody else was warm and cozy in a room together, dry and happy, and it was Christmas and Easter and all the High Holy Days of Obligation all glommed into one glorious, adorable family get-together. Every day, Maureen felt so lost and she never knew which way to go, and even when she did decide on a direction, it always led to disaster. On top of that, for as long as she could remember, Maureen had known that everything she felt was the wrong thing to feel, and she never knew what to feel or what to do or even what to think, and she'd often find herself thinking when she was faced with a problem, *What would a real little girl do? How would a real little girl feel?* Because although Maureen fought savagely to be seen as a grown-up, whenever she thought of herself, she saw a lost little girl, a little girl who didn't have access to that wonderfully clear map that everybody else used to navigate through ordinary days.

The last one they asked to speak was Dicey. Maureen had been praying that Dicey wouldn't, but she said her name, her real Patsy Anne name, and said she'd only been sober for six days and that she'd always known that she drank too much, but she didn't think she was an alcoholic until she found out she was pregnant. Maureen gasped and looked at Dicey, who looked down and continued, ". . . and so I was so sick from being pregnant that I didn't want to drink, and I wasn't going to drink, but it ended up all I did *was* drink. I just stayed on it steady from stars in the sky morning till stars in the sky night. I don't remember where I was, I can hardly remember where I went, and I just slept wherever sleep overtook me, and when I finally went home, I was so sick, I was as sick as eight dogs. I decided right then I was never going to drink again. That was a Monday, and by Friday, I was right back on it. That week, I knew I was going to die if I kept drinking, but if I didn't drink, I knew I would just as soon be dead anyway, and to tell you the truth, at that point I didn't care. And then I found out that the baby's father was dead." She paused, almost looked over at Maureen but didn't. "I've been coming to a meeting every day for the last six days and I haven't had a drink."

Maureen was afraid to look at Dicey. *And then I found out that the baby's father was dead.* Who was the baby's dead father? Maureen looked at Dicey, but she wouldn't look back. Something about the way Dicey wouldn't look at her made Maureen feel half-sick and scared. She had to get the fuck out of this meeting. She stood up to go, but Dicey reached out and took her hand, and Maureen had to sit back down. She sat there and didn't say anything and finally Dicey whispered, "I'm so sorry, Reenie."

"Sorry for what, Dice? Shure I don't care that you're pregnant. I mean I care, of course, but, you know"—she pointed at herself—"I was in the same boat." From the way Dicey was holding her hand and avoiding looking at her, Maureen felt she'd better keep talking. "The dad, the father, buddy who you're having the baby for, is dead?" A creeping sense of dread settled in the pit of Maureen's stomach, but still she went on: "Who is it, Dice? Or is that a bad question to ask, 'cause you know . . ." Maureen realized that her volume control button had drifted up and she wasn't whispering anymore. Someone in the front was sharing about how when he first came into the program, they'd said there was always hope from the ocean but there was no hope from the grave, and though he still was lost on an ocean of trouble, the grave was where he'd been headed if he kept on drinking the way he'd been drinking. Maureen could hear him but she couldn't stop talking. Dicey was trying to shush Maureen, but she was afraid that if she stopped talking, she wouldn't be able to breathe. She knew, as much as she didn't want to know, but she couldn't believe it. She wouldn't believe it. It was unbelievable.

"You and Bo?" she managed to croak out. Dicey just nodded her head silently. Maureen was so shocked. How could she not have known? How could she have been such a fool? A kind of dry sobbing overtook Maureen. There were no tears, just gasps and hiccups. It was like she'd used up her daily dose of tears and now she was a desert.

Dicey finally looked at Maureen and said, "I don't want this baby. I'd rather die than have it."

Maureen couldn't stop the dry weeping, which, without the water, really hurt. Her lungs were burning and she was hiccuping hard.

"I never told anyone. I'm living with Sam and her boyfriend. I never even told them," Dicey said.

"What are you going to do?" Maureen choked out.

"Bo was gonna give me some money so I could, you know . . . go up to Montreal and take care of it. I can't tell anyone. I don't know what to do." Dicey was crying too, but with real tears, big fat ones, that rolled down the middle of her face.

"Well . . . I don't have any money, so . . . ," Maureen said lamely.

"I wasn't askin' you for any."

"Oh, okay. Are you gonna be all right?" Maureen said. She felt so sorry for Dicey, but at the same time, she was so angry that Dice would have slept with Bo behind her back like that. Not that she'd ever expected anything better from anyone, but it was such a cliché.

"Why? Why'd you do it, Dice?"

"Oh, we were at it this good while. A long time before he got together with you. The last year he was with Fluff, it was just . . . I don't know." Dicey really did look lost for an answer.

"I don't have anywhere to live. I'm just staying with someone, or else you know . . . ," Maureen stammered out. A part of her wanted to help, but another part wanted to beat up something, to turn over something, to put the place up on stilts, to act out so she wouldn't have to feel so . . . hurt. She thought, *I'm not so stupid as to be hurt, am I?*

Dicey said, "No, I am grand with Sam and Dominic."

"Yea, I'd be afraid if you moved in, you'd be puttin' the makes on my boyfriend, George. You know what you're like." Maureen was trying to joke, but it just came out all bitter and angry.

Dicey was still crying, but Maureen was determined to not spill any more tears that day.

CHAPTER THIRTY-ONE

ESPITE HER RESOLVE, MAUREEN WAS CRYING AGAIN AS she knocked on George's door. There was no answer. She knocked harder, banging away with her fists. Someone on the third floor opened a window and looked down on Maureen and yelled, but Maureen just kept banging. Then she kicked the door. She kicked it till her feet hurt, and then she banged with her fists till they ached. She was still kicking when a cranky-looking George answered the door.

"What? What is it?"

"I need to come in."

"Far out," George said dryly as he stepped back, making a sweeping gesture into the squat little vestibule. Maureen headed right up over the stairs to George's apartment.

"So," George said, pretending normalcy. "Where've you been since last night?"

Maureen didn't answer. She didn't have the strength to go through it all. She just flopped down on George's beanbag chair, the only slightly comfortable piece of furniture other than the bed in George's whole apartment.

"You leave last night to go meet someone downtown, and then you come back here almost twenty-four hours later, looking the worse for wear, and you don't have an explanation for that?"

Maureen was tempted to start a fight along the lines of "Who the fuck are you to demand an explanation from me?" But the effort required to say that was beyond her. She was worn out, worn down, worn to a thread.

George stood there with his arms crossed and looked sternly down at her in the beanbag chair.

"What? What do you want?" she said, looking up at George. "What do you want from me?" Maureen didn't have the patience to deal with George right now. What in the name of God did he want? Probably what they all want. She might as well give it to him just to get him off her back. "Do you want to do 'it'?"

"'It,' Maureen?" George was not relenting. "What 'it'?"

"Jumpins, George, you know: 'it.' 'It.' Don't be such a crucifier, George. You know what 'it' means."

"Well yes, of course, as a red-blooded young man of twenty-one, a believer in free love and peace and unending grooviness, I always want to do 'it,' but maybe the more interesting question, Maureen, might be, do you?"

"Not really." Maureen sighed, looking down at the floor. "But it might . . . you know . . . stop you being mad at me and help get my mind off stuff."

"Yea, great. That's just great. Whenever you need to get your mind off all the important stuff, you can just—"

"Geez, what are you getting mad about, George?" Maureen

looked at him in surprise. "And what? Are you just going to talk normal from now on?"

"I'm upset, I guess."

"You're upset?"

"Yea, I'm upset. You leave last night to go meet someone; the cops are looking for you; a criminal consortium, who you believe might have murdered your ex-boyfriend, are looking for you; and you don't come back and you don't call." George was looking more and more upset. "You don't even bother to explain where you were. And the way I've been feeling about you, Maureen—"

"No! No! George, NO. Don't start with me about feelings; I don't want to hear it. I got too many feelings already, and they're all crashin' around in here." Maureen whacked herself on the head much harder than she'd meant to. "And sometimes staying up all night, AND GENERALLY DRIVING ME NUTS." Maureen managed, through the propulsive power of spite and fear, to gracelessly extract herself from the beanbag, and she paced away from George across the small living room.

"Maureen, sit down. Everything's okay. I'm not mad, I'm just worried. And even if I was mad, that'd be okay. Feelings are okay, everyone's got them—they come, they go, they change all the time."

"Look," Maureen said, turning on George. "Don't talk to me about feelings, okay? I got enough on my mind today without taking on old feelings." She spat out that last word like it was poison. "What is the fucking point of feelings and all that old nonsense anyway?" Maureen walked toward George. "Let me say this very clearly, just once: I don't want to talk about feelings 'cause half the time, I don't even know what it is that I am feeling, but the only thing I'm sure of is that I am sure I'm feeling the wrong thing."

"Just try to breathe," George said.

"I am breathing, for Christ sakes. If I wasn't breathing, I wouldn't be able to pace around your front room." Maureen paced herself into the bedroom and fell straight back onto the bed. George came in.

"Dicey is pregnant," Maureen said.

"Dicey?"

"Yea, Dicey Doyle, the Three Musketeers Dicey."

"Well, so?"

"So. She's knocked up with Bo's baby."

"Oh," George said. "How do you know?"

Maureen explained it all. ". . . So, I'm a little bit upset because Dicey's just where I was a few years ago."

"How so?" George said, sitting down on the bed.

Maureen didn't want to do it, but with as few words as possible, she told him about the pregnancy and how she now knew that the baby was in Montreal and how she was going to go to Montreal to get her baby back.

George wasn't as shocked as Maureen thought he might be. She guessed that being knocked up was no big deal for the molls in all those hard-boiled detective books he read.

"And that's all I need now. My best friend and my boyfriend. Turns out Dicey was 'woman enough to take my man.'"

"You're still calling Bo your man?"

"No, it's a Loretta Lynn song: 'You Ain't Woman Enough (to Take My Man).'"

"And Dicey? She's your best friend?"

"Well, I really didn't have any friends when I was with Bo. He didn't like—"

"It's fascinating," George said, looking at Maureen. "Your mind actually *does* kind of work like a country and western song, doesn't it?"

Maureen was lost in thought and ignored George's patronizing remark about the way her mind worked.

"And something weird is going on with Deucey, too," she said. "I don't know. I can't quite put my finger on it, but something's not adding up. And Fox said something . . . I don't know . . . strange to Jack."

"Strange like what?" George said.

"I don't know. I remember thinking, *What's he mean by that?* but I was so freaked out where he had me tied up and all."

"He had you WHAT?"

"Tied up," Maureen said, losing patience. "Yes. It was pretty bad for a while, but it's fine now. We made a deal, and then they reneged on that, and now, I don't know . . . I don't know where we stand."

Maureen collapsed back on the bed and found herself crying again. Turns out, it was true what she'd always feared: once you started with that crying shit, there was every chance you might not ever be able to stop.

George stood by the side of the bed and looked down at her. "I could just lie down on top of you if you want."

"Oh yea, right, *that*," Maureen said, dismissing the idea.

"No, no, not *that*, as you so disdainfully refer to the act of love. I could just lie on top of you so you'd feel grounded. You know, so you'd have something heavy on top of you, so you'd feel more connected to the earth like . . . It's worked for me a couple of times."

Maureen thought it was a stupid idea, but she let him do it, and it did make her feel a bit better, heavier, like she wouldn't just float off and disappear. It made her feel more real, like there was more to her. They lay there like that until finally, Maureen, still crying, drifted off to sleep.

THE LOUD RING OF THE TELEPHONE WOKE HER UP. IT WAS after one in the morning. She stumbled out to the hallway and answered.

"A collect call from Carleen Maynard from the Tanguay Detention Centre for Women, Montreal. Will you accept the charges?"

Oh Jesus, Carleen. All her chickens were coming home to roost. For a brief, cowardly instant, Maureen thought she might just hang up, pretend the connection was cut, but her better nature forced her to say, "Yes, operator, I'll accept the charges."

There was a long pause and then Carleen's voice, unmistakable, said, "Hi, Reenie. It's me, Carleen."

Maureen just laughed and said, "I know. I'd know your voice, Carleen, if you were boiled."

Neither of them spoke for what seemed like an age.

"Carleen, how did you know I was at this number?" Maureen finally said.

"Joycey sent it to me. Oh God, Reenie, I just got here to Tanguay. The boys made it happen, and oh, I would've just died down there in Jamaica, and Joycey told me how you didn't go to the cops about the boys."

"Yea," said Maureen, "but that was nothing. It was—"

"Reenie, you always had my back. If I only listened to you that time and came home with you from Montreal."

"Carleen, I didn't—I should've—"

"You were so right."

"Oh, Carleen, don't say that."

"Why not? It's only the truth. I always knew I could count on you. Look, Reenie, I don't have much time, but Joycey told me all about how you're coming up here to find your baby. And when you're here, will you come and see me? I'll put you on the list."

"That's all different now, Carleen. I don't know now if I'll be coming up or not." At that, Maureen started to cry and Carleen tried to comfort her as best she could until she had to get off the phone because another prisoner wanted to use it. Carleen sounded scared when she said, "I'm done anyway. I was just getting off," which made Maureen realize the ridiculousness of Carleen comforting her when it was Carleen who was locked up in a detention centre, surrounded by a lot of bad and dangerous women.

Well maybe, Maureen's mind said, *all those women aren't bad and dangerous. Maybe they are women like Carleen, who just wanted something different, something better for themselves. Maybe they were a little bit naive, too, like Carleen.*

God, why does Carleen have to be so grateful to me for being her friend? 'Cause no matter what Carleen thought, Maureen knew the rights of it. She'd never had Carleen's back—not because she didn't want to, but because she couldn't. Maureen always believed that it took everything she had just to look after her own self. How could Carleen not know that Maureen was too fucked up to be anybody's friend really and have anybody's back?

Well, who ever had your back? Maureen's mind said defensively.

"Nobody—that's who," Maureen said out loud, but she couldn't quite get herself worked up like she usually could about how unfair everything was for her.

Maureen's mind mocked her: *You always get a raw deal, and nobody cares about you, and nobody loves you, and everybody hates you, and you're gonna eat some worms.*

Oh, fuck off, Maureen said to her mind. Just fuck all the way off.

CHAPTER THIRTY-TWO

THE NEXT MORNING, GEORGE AND MAUREEN WOKE with a start. They could hear footsteps—loud footsteps stomping up over the stairs and in through the apartment door. Maureen threw on George's shirt from the day before and George stood there in his boxers. They rushed into the hall.

Jack Dunne was striding through the apartment, barrelling through, rage coming off him in waves. Maureen was terrified. He stomped past her into the kitchen and sat himself down at the table. Maureen and George followed after him and stood dumbfounded. Looking at Jack, Maureen wanted to say something, but she was speechless.

"Nice of you to drop by, Jack, but really, it's a little early for a social call, isn't it?" George said.

Jack sat there and looked at them with such resentment and anger, looked at them as though they were the cause of all the problems he might have in his life.

George was making a determined effort to act normal. He filled up the kettle, put it on the stove and said, "Tea, Jack? Slice of toast?"

Jack just kept looking straight at them.

"No? Not a breakfast man, then? . . . They say it's the most important meal of the whole day."

Jack still said nothing.

George, standing next to the stove, waiting for the kettle to boil, said, "Look, Jack, you can't be here. You've got no right."

Jack stood up and walked slowly and deliberately toward George and stopped in front of him in what could only be described as a threatening manner.

George seemed to flounder a bit, but he said, "This is private property. You have no right to be here. I—I will call the police if I have to."

Jack turned on his heel and began walking out of the kitchen. "No need for that," he said. "I'm leaving now anyway."

Maureen followed him to the top of the stairs.

"How does everyone know I'm here?" she managed to croak out.

Jack looked up at her from the front door. "Oh, we got ways. Don't you worry your pretty little head about that, Mo-reen," he said, echoing what lawyer Cramm had said to her in his office.

Maureen stumbled back into the kitchen. George put a big mug of tea in her hands, and she automatically lifted it to her lips and took a gulp and scalded the mouth right off herself. "Jesus, Jesus, Jesus Christ on a crutch," she sputtered, spilling hot tea down the front of George's shirt and burning her chest and the top of her feet in the bargain. George took the cup of tea out of her hands and sat her down.

"I guess hot tea is a bit too lethal in your condition," he said, handing her a glass of cold water. "If you spill this, it will only help take the heat out of the burned bits."

George sat in the chair where Jack had been and said, "Maureen, what is going on?"

Maureen wouldn't look at him; she looked down at her feet, which were burning red from the hot tea, and mumbled, "Nothing."

"Nothing? Nothing? A drug-dealing murderer waltzes into my apartment at seven o'clock in the morning without so much as a by your leave, and all you've got to say is that nothing is going on?"

Before Maureen could answer, there was a knock on the front door. They looked at each other anxiously. Maureen instinctively reached out for George's hand. She stood at his side as he opened the door.

There stood Alistair Cramm, tall and stringy and straw-headed. Maureen gasped. Cramm stuck his hand out to George. "Alistair Cramm, Attorney at Law."

"George Taylor, graduate student."

"Yes, yes, and of course," Cramm said, nodding at Maureen, "I'm already well acquainted with our Miss Brennan. I am sorry for the inconvenient hour, but I have some information to share with Miss Brennan that I know she is anxious to have."

George stepped back and Cramm followed Maureen up over the stairs and into the kitchen. He took the same chair Jack had taken. Maureen and George sat down facing him.

Maureen said, "Jack Dunne was just sat in that very chair, threatening us, and I don't care, but we had a deal and unless you're here to—"

"Really? Jack Dunne? Here, threatening you? With what did he threaten you?"

"What?"

"What did he say when he threatened you?"

"Nothing," Maureen said.

"Oh."

"He just sat there," said Maureen.

"Just sat here?"

"Yes . . . but in a very, very threatening way."

"Oh, I see," said Cramm.

"Okay, you can drop the sarcasm, bud," George said. "The man marched into my apartment at seven o'clock in the morning and proceeded to behave in a threatening manner."

Cramm looked unimpressed. "Be that as it may, let us proceed with the reason for my unconscionably early visit. An acquaintance of ours in Montreal was able to, last evening, obtain the adoption records for one baby Brennan born April 10, Anno Domini 1968. He is presently abiding in Laval with a French-Canadian family, Jean-Paul and Lorrette LeBlanc. I imagine they are Acadian originally, from somewhere in the Maritimes. They have since had another child, a natural child, and Mrs. LeBlanc appears to be pregnant again." Cramm looked up from the pages in his blue lawyer file and said, "All the pertinent information is in here." And he handed the file to Maureen.

At first, Maureen was afraid to look down at the file she had in her hands because it contained everything she had wanted for so long. The information in that file was supposed to fill in the hole that Maureen had been carrying around inside her. But what if it didn't? What if there was never going to be anything that could fill that hole? Maureen felt dread when she imagined her life devoid of the hope that her determination to find her baby had given her. She knew she should be feeling deliriously happy, but instead, she just felt numb and at the same time terrified. And she wondered what the right, the correct, feeling would be. What would a real girl feel?

"Now what do I do?" Maureen blurted out.

"Well, that is entirely up to you, Miss Brennan. But now you do have the information with which we promised to provide you. Our part of that bargain you spoke of so passionately yesterday has been kept."

"But what about me appearing in court and the poisoning and trying to kill Bo and all and everything you were threatening me I had to do?"

Cramm looked at Maureen and smiled. "Don't look a gift horse in the mouth, Miss Brennan. Today is a new day, and my clients' needs have changed since yesterday. We . . . they now feel, at the urging of David 'Deucey' Dunne, that it would be more beneficial for us to remain with our original arrangement, for you not to appear in court but to take the information we've given you, leave the province, go to Montreal and stay there. We are going back to an original plan and no longer require your assistance." At that, Cramm turned on his heel, went down over the stairs and out the front door.

Maureen stood motionless. She couldn't seem to take it all in. She still didn't have the nerve to look at the blue file. Cramm's announcement had left her dazed.

"Well, doll," George said, turning to Maureen and looking happier than he had in days, "good news. It looks like it's nix nix on you going on the stand and having to blow the whistle on yourself or anybody else. So, maybe it's time, like the man said, for you to take a powder, blow this berg, cop the sneak, you know—"

There was another knock on the door and it was still well before nine in the morning. There were heavy footsteps on the stairs. Whoever was coming was not waiting to be invited in.

It was the cops, Kent and McCarthy.

McCarthy wasted no time: "There was chlordane on all the food in the fridge—everything covered with it—and the orange juice, full of it. So, missy, what do you make of that?"

Maureen, still bowled over by Cramm's news, didn't know what to make of anything really. Of course, the dark, hopeless side of Maureen had already suspected that getting what she wanted was not going to work out—nothing ever worked out for her.

But then another part of Maureen, acting without thought or plan, kicked in. Maureen's mouth opened up and out came, "Oh my God, he really did it. Bo always said he was going to kill me, and he went ahead and tried to do it. Is that what killed him? The poison? He tried to poison me. Oh my God, I can't believe it. Was there enough poison in the food to kill me?"

"No, maid. Just enough poison to make someone very, very sick."

"It's so hard to believe he would try to poison me . . ."

George was giving Maureen the oddest look. She raised her eyebrows and looked straight back at him, challenging him to say anything different. Then she looked at Kent.

"I'm just blown away by the thoughts of it. I mean, as bad as he was, I never thought he was a . . . poisoner."

Maureen, a person who had always blurted out the truth of whatever was on her mind, was now lying boldfacedly to the police. She really didn't know who she was anymore.

"What?" said McCarthy. "You're sayin' now that Trevor 'Bo' Browne poisoned the food in his own fridge and then sat down and ate the poisoned food?"

"I doubt he sat down. He usually just scarfed back his food standin' up in the kitchen. Maybe he put the poison on everything—or in everything." She looked quickly at McCarthy. "However it was he did it, I don't know, but maybe he did it when he was drunk—in a blackout, like."

"Did you see him standing at the fridge that night?" McCarthy asked.

"Well, I was kinda passed out on the floor in the living room, so I didn't see what he did—not after he wore himself out givin' me a shit-knockin'."

George put his hand on Maureen's arm, but she quickly shrugged it off.

Kent noticed the shrugging and said, "It's funny, Miss Brennan, that we could find no fingerprints on either the gallon of chlordane or on the Flit gun."

Maureen looked at Kent but she didn't see him. What she did see was a flashback of herself in the Livingstone Street apartment the night she crept back in and slept there. She remembered trying not to look at the chlordane but then really looking at it for a long time and realizing that her fingerprints would be all over the bottle—and on the Flit gun too. She saw herself getting a towel out of the hamper in the bathroom and doing a meticulous job of cleaning every inch of those two objects.

"God, he thought of everything," she said. "I guess he really meant to kill me."

McCarthy looked unconvinced. "I think it was you, miss—you who poured the poison in the orange juice and then sprayed it all over the food in the fridge, because you knew that your lover, Trevor 'Bo' Browne, would get up in the morning with a wicked hangover—"

"Nice theory," George said. "You hammers and saws, you're always trying to put a Chinese angle on everything, but in this case . . ."

McCarthy and Kent looked confused by George's words, but George continued.

"Why don't you two bulls just take it on the heel and toe?" said George.

McCarthy and Kent looked at Maureen.

"I think he means, 'Why don't you leave?'" Maureen explained.

"Unless you're going to pinch the frail—"

"Oh, for God's sake, George, stop. I mean it. Seriously. I can't take it anymore. You've got me addled," Maureen said. She tried to smile at the two cops.

"Jingle-brained," George said, almost under his breath.

"STOP," Maureen yelled.

"Miss Brennan," Kent said, "if I could get you to focus for a minute."

Maureen looked at him.

"Now, is it your contention that the deceased tried to poison you by putting chlordane in the food he knew you would be eating?"

"Yes," Maureen said. "Bo always swore he was gonna kill me if I ever tried to leave him, and who else woulda . . . coulda done it?"

"Well, Miss Brennan, as Sergeant McCarthy has already said, you might have done it."

"Yea, I might've, but I'm not a vicious, violent—I don't know a word bad enough to say what he was—am I? I am not the one who was taken down to the cop shop two or three times to stop me from laying any further brutal beatings on my girlfriend, am I?"

Maureen was beginning to feel a rising sense of indignation at the injustice of it all. Imagine! Blaming her—the victim. It was so wrong . . . Well, of course, it was her, but they didn't know that.

"I think it would be better if you guys left now," Maureen said, standing tall on her outraged victim act.

"We'd like you to come down to the station with us," Kent said.

"Why?"

McCarthy shot Maureen a look. "Why? Because we know you put the poison in the food, missy, but being a couple of easygoing guys, we figure that maybe if you came down to the station and told us everything you know about DAFT and so on, we could go a little easier on you."

"Go easier on me? I didn't do anything! Are you arresting me?"

"Unless you're gonna put her in bracelet and haul her down to the hoosegow—"

Maureen stopped George with a look. He quickly composed himself.

"I think our business here has come to an end, gentlemen," George said.

Maureen started to show them to the door.

"It's not over yet, missy," McCarthy said, way too close to Maureen. His breath stank. Maybe it was a tooth, maybe he had some stomach problems or maybe something had crawled up inside of him and died, but something was rotten inside Sergeant McCarthy.

Maureen stepped back. "Certs: it's two, two mints in one. It's a candy mint and also a breath mint. You might want to try one, Sergeant McCarthy." She wasn't sure where this saucy-as-a-shitfly person was coming from today, but she was enjoying her.

McCarthy turned away in disgust.

When they had left, George said, "I don't even know who you are anymore."

"Neither do I," Maureen replied.

CHAPTER THIRTY-THREE

W HEN ARE YOU GOING TO STOP BEING SUCH A STUPID
little fool and start growing up?" The Sarge was right up
in Maureen's face, spittle flying, eyes flashing in fury. Maureen had
gone to Princess Street to say goodbye to Kathleen and promise
she would bring Kathleen up to Montreal to live with her as soon
as ever Maureen got settled away. But in her new guise as saucy-
as-a-shitfly Maureen, she'd opened her mouth and boasted to the
Sarge that she'd found her baby. Now she was paying the price for
that boast.

"That youngster was adopted, and the ones that adopted it,
they're protected from foolish-arse teenage girls stupid enough to
open up their legs to the first fella who asked them and get caught
in the bargain. Oh, get a dust of sense, for God's sakes. Even you
can't be that stupid as to believe that if you, nothing but a chit of
a child yourself, got that youngster back then everything is going
to be hunky-dory and all your dreams are going to come true. Oh,
give your head a shake, you stupid little moron. Open up your eyes
and take a fuckin' look around. If having youngsters was the key

to happiness, then wouldn't I be cagged off on cloud nine? 'Oh, if only I had my little baby, everything would be all right.'" The Sarge minced about doing a not bad imitation of Maureen if, in fact, Maureen's voice was up five or six octaves and she was severely delayed in her brain function. Normally, at this point, Maureen would have cracked right the fuck up and been reduced to a flurry of useless oaths, but today she stood her ground.

"Like I said, I already know where my baby is and I know where the people who got him live."

For a moment, the Sarge seemed to be thrown, but she quickly rallied with, "Yea, that's what you think, you mindless little retard."

"Maureen's not retarded; I'm retarded. Mom said." Kathleen piped up from the sidelines.

"Shut up!" the Sarge snarled at Kathleen. "Those adoption papers, they're sealed, legally sealed for the life of that youngster. Nobody can get at 'em, nobody can unseal them, not the mother, not the youngster, not anyone."

"Yea, well someone did," Maureen said.

"Oh, don't be a bigger fool than you already are, Maureen. It can't be done, I'm telling ya."

"Yea, and I'm telling you that it can be done. It can be done and it is done."

Maureen's mother moved in on Maureen, poking her in the chest, driving her back against the wall. "You don't tell me anything, you little shitfucker."

Maureen's father almost walked into the room, but thought better of it and pitched against the archway between the front hall and the front room. He said, "Now, Edna, that's not the best. Reenie's only visiting . . ."

Maureen's mother didn't even dignify him with a scornful look, let alone an answer. Raymond came in the front door, took one look at the crowd in the living room and beat it up over the stairs. The Sarge bawled up at him, "And what in the name of Christ do you think you're doin' trackin' dirt up over those stairs? Get down here and take off them dirty big boots before I blinds ya."

Raymond skulked back down and, hoping to get the Sarge's attention off him, chimed in with "What was the old man just saying about Reenie?"

The Sarge turned a look of withering scorn on Maureen's father and said, "What odds now what that was saying. That should just keep its mouth shut if it knows what's good for it."

"Mom, I got a flight booked for Montreal tomorrow, and I'm gonna be on it."

"Yea, not if I throws you down over the stairs first and breaks both your legs you won't be on it."

"Yes, I will so," said Maureen. "Even if you blind, cripples and crucifies me, I'm still going to Montreal, and when I get there, I'm going to find my baby."

"Yea, Montreal," the Sarge spat out. "That's the proper place for the likes of you. That's all you need now, up sluttin' around Montreal, welcoming flags of all nations, and don't you for one second, my dear, think that you can come crawling back here again when you gets yourself in trouble. Don't think you can sashay in here so as I'll take care of you and whatever new little bastard you got streeling in after ya. I got enough to look after here, weighted down with a bunch of"—the Sarge took a look around the room, searching for a word low enough to describe her children—"bitch's bastards," she finally said.

"Mom, mom, mom, are we the bastards? Mom, mom, mom, but if we're bastards—are we the bastards, Mom? 'Cause if we're the bastards, that means you're the bitch."

The Sarge took a step toward Kathleen. Maureen stepped in between them. The Sarge kept coming, but Maureen didn't do her usual back-down. The Sarge was now in Maureen's face, giving her a hard look, then she took a step back, quickly deked to the side, got behind Maureen and gave Kathleen a vicious punch on the fatty part of her upper arm. Kathleen cried out in pain.

"What did I tell you about getting your mouth going? Did anybody ask you to get your big stupid mouth going?" the Sarge said.

Kathleen started to answer but instead rubbed her arm where it had been punched. The Sarge threw Maureen a triumphant look over her shoulder and went to stand beside Raymond and Maureen's father, both of whom shifted uncomfortably, wanting to get away but apparently lacking the guts to make a decisive move.

"Well, I wouldn't come back here to this hellhole anyway no matter what," Maureen said.

"Oh yes, you're all talk now, but you'll be down on your knees begging to come back to this 'hellhole.' But I'll tell you right now: you won't be getting in, Miss High and Mighty. You think you're so much better than everybody else, looking down your nose at everyone, and you're nothing more now than a common slut. Knocked up, beat up, fucked up altogether."

"Edna, for the love of God, you don't have to talk to the girl like that."

The Sarge turned on Maureen's father. "And whose fault do you think it is that she's going around Miss Snooty Snoot with her nose so high up in the air it's a wonder she can breathe at all? Whose fault is it? Yours, that's whose fault it is."

"Now, Edna, you don't mean that. You're just sorry she's going."

"Sorry she's going? When I see the back of that little cocksucker, I never want to see the front of her again. She's dead to me."

That last remark pretty well put a stop to all conversation in the front room. Maureen was struck dumb. Even Kathleen had nothing to say. Maureen managed to push past Kathleen and the Sarge, Raymond and her father and sail out through the front door. Because Maureen wasn't paying attention, she missed the second step down from the storm door and fell smack on her arse. She whipped her head round to see if any of them had seen her, but thanks be to God, they hadn't. She picked herself up, dusted herself off . . . *and started all over again.* The song kept going through Maureen's head all the way up Princess Street, faster and faster, picking up speed, over and over and over in her mind. It was like what had just happened in the front room had been too much even for Maureen's relentless mind, and it had just given up and put on a song loop.

Someone touched her shoulder. Maureen screamed and turned around. It was her father.

"I only got a minute, Reenie, 'cause herself will have my hide if she catches me, but you know that's your home back there and it'll always be your home, no matter what."

Maureen exploded. "Oh, what bullshit, Dad! The only person whose home that is, is the Sarge's. Look, I gotta go."

"Wait. I know your mother is . . . well she's a hard bit of business."

Maureen snorted.

"But she loves you, Maureen."

"Yea, right."

"She does."

"Yea, well she got a queer way of showing it."

"That's just her way, Reenie. It comes out like she's mad all the time, but really she's scared. She's afraid all the time, and that's how her scared comes out. See, she wants so much for you, Maureen, for all of ye, but . . ." Maureen's father broke off. "Oh, what's the use of talking? Shure talking never did no good anyhow."

"Right, and I don't even know what you're talking about anyway, Dad."

He put his arms around Maureen, pulled her into him and just held on to her. Maureen had never felt so awkward in her whole life. Her father had never, as far as Maureen could remember, put his arms around her, and it was so . . . embarrassing. She stood there for what seemed like hours but was only a couple of seconds. She didn't want to offend the old man, but she wanted to get away from him. She tried to gently pull away, but her dad just kept holding on to her. Finally, she said, "Dad, I gotta go."

The old man said, "It's all right, Reenie. It's okay, everything is going to be all right," and he just kept holding on to her and patting her on the back.

Some tiny thing inside of Maureen just let go—it snapped, because it felt like an elastic that had been stretched to its limit had just broken. With that, Maureen put her head down on her father's wide, bony shoulder.

She didn't know how long they stood there like that on the corner of Princess and New Gower Street, but when he finally let her go, she felt her legs give way, and she was afraid that some really necessary part of herself might have let go. If that was true, how was she going to get through everything now? She looked at her old man and said, "Daddy," and just saying the word made her feel even more exposed and helpless.

"It's all right, Maureen. You're all right, my darling. Shure you're as strong as an ox, just like your mother." Maureen started to protest, but he went on. "Yes, you're just like the Sarge: determined. Go through a brick wall to get what you wants, don't let nothing stop you."

Jesus, Maureen thought, *why are we out here in the middle of the street having the only talk we've ever had?*

"Dad, I'm not the one bit like her," Maureen said to her father.

"Oh yes, and that's what you are, my love, just like your mother, afraid of everything, afraid of being afraid. Afraid you've got to control everything and if you don't control everything, it will all fall abroad. And afraid 'cause you know deep down that you're not up to the job of controlling *anything*, but you're too afraid to let it go. You got no faith, my love, and very little hope, and what charity you got is way too thin on the ground."

Maureen wanted to cry out against this pronouncement. Her

own father was accusing her of not having even one of the three virtues. *Of course, I have charity, but who would have faith? Faith in what? And hope? What's the point of hope?* When she was little, she had hoped things would be different, but she had given up on that.

"Look at me, Reenie. You already got everything you need. You got it all already in here." He tapped her on the forehead. "And in here." He tapped her on the heart. "It's all in there waiting for ya. You just gotta start using it. Oh yes, it's all gonna be all right in the end. Oh, lots of times your life's tough and nasty and dirty but still all right for all that. Your Nan used to say, shure it's always all right in the end, and if it's not all right, then it's not the end yet."

"But sure, you always said Nanny died cursing Poppy and screaming out in her death agony."

"Yes, and then it was over. And when she was gone, her face had a look of peace and she looked thirty years younger, and it was all right then because it was the end. What's coming is coming, Maureen, my love. We didn't cause it mostly, and we mostly can't cure it or control it, so—"

"Dad, why didn't you ever pick up for us with Mom when she was going at us?" Maureen had been wanting to say that for a long time.

Her father looked at her for a moment, sighed and said, "Well, Maureen, sure that'd only make her worse if she thought we were all in it together against her."

"Against her? But sure, Dad, we're her youngsters."

"But when you've been steeping and stoopin' up to your eyeballs afraid of everything, my Jesus, sure, the people you love, like your youngsters, they're like the Viet Cong, Maureen my dear. They sneak up on ya when you least expect it and wipe you out completely."

"Are you drinking, Dad?"

"Oh, I had a couple of beer at the Ritz Tavern on my way home from the wharf. Only old bellywash, beer is."

"Oh."

"Overtime cheque, Maureen. The old woman didn't know I had it." He took off his cap, the old-timey St. John's tweed cap he always wore, and took sixty dollars out of the inside hat band. "And what the old woman doesn't know won't hurt her. Here now, you take this, it's all I got, but at least it will be some help to you up in Montreal. And when you find the baby, by that time, she'll be over it and you can come back home."

"She might be over it, Dad, but I'm not. I'm never going to be over it."

"Oh, Maureen my love, never is a long, long, long time."

"Good then, because even after a long, long, long time, I'm not going to be over it."

"Like I said, my lover, you're the face and eyes and hard-bitten heart of your mother."

"I'm going."

Maureen had to look away from her father then, because she saw in his eyes, for the first time, how he felt knowing that his youngest daughter had been treated like Maureen had been treated, how heartbroken he was by all the shit Maureen was in, and how painfully he wanted so much more for her, but how helpless he was to change any of it.

He had always just been the old man, silent until he had a few drinks in and then you couldn't shut him up. Once, Maureen's mother hit him on the side of the head with an iron frying pan. He went down but he did not shut up, not even then, flat out on the floor. He was still "rounding the Cape of Good Hope" and talking about the captain who did not give them their "one tot per day per man" that they were entitled to in the British Navy. There was a picture of Maureen's father, an old, old picture of when he was overseas in the Merchant Navy. He was heart-stoppingly handsome in that picture; he looked like a matinee idol. But now here he was, in his green work shirt and pants, his working man's tweed cap and his plaid slippers, a thin man on the verge of getting old, trying to do the best he could for a daughter who fucked up so much it didn't even seem like fuckups anymore, it just seemed like normal. Tears came to Maureen's eyes as she looked at her father, and he put his arms around her and pulled her into him again.

"Yes, my dear Maureen," he said, patting her on the back, "it's all going to be all right in the end, you watch and see."

Maureen pulled away from him and took off up New Gower, stumbling, blind from her tears, and she didn't even turn around and look back at him as much as she really wanted to, because to do that would seem too phony, too much like pretending, like she was in some shitty movie or something.

CHAPTER THIRTY-FOUR

WHEN MAUREEN GOT BACK TO GEORGE'S APARTMENT, Fox Albert was there.

"He said he had to give you something, so I let him in," George said apologetically.

"It's okay. What do you want now, Fox?" Maureen said.

"I got your ticket like we promised." He handed her an airline ticket and then tried to give her five hundred bucks, but Maureen wouldn't take the money.

"Why are you trying to give me money, Fox?" she said suspiciously. "What am I supposed to do for that money?"

"Nothing." Fox looked like he was about to say more, but then he looked at George standing next to Maureen and asked, "Maureen, is there somewhere we can speak privately?"

"Whatever you wanna say to me, you can say in front of George. He's my friend," she said, realizing it was the truth.

Fox looked uncomfortable. "The five hundred bucks is for the baby," he said.

Maureen didn't know what to say.

"Well, you know," Fox said, and nodded his head, just once, with intent.

Maureen was still not getting it.

"The baby. The baby? You and me—Montreal? Oh Maureen, even you cannot possibly be this stunned. The baby. Your baby could be . . . you know . . . my baby."

A tiny scream erupted from Maureen's mouth as she looked at Fox's flaming red hair and saw that dream again, of that little tuft of red hair all wrapped up in bunting being carried out of the delivery room in the nurse's arms.

George grabbed Fox by the arm and spun him away from Maureen. "Hey, bud, don't you think it's time for you to bounce?"

Maureen was grateful for the interruption.

Fox took a threatening step toward George and said, "I'm talking to Maureen, and I don't think it's any of your business."

"Yea," said George, "but it turns out you're gumming up my day, bud, 'cause you're not in some hash house now; you're in my joint. And I'm this close to throwing an ing-bing and getting the bulls on the blower. 'Cause ever since this whole jam started, I got the coppers on standby."

Fox shook his head in confusion and turned on his heel. As he left, he pushed the five hundred dollars into George's hands and said, "What is it with you two? Neither one of you are making any sense. Make her take this with her to Montreal."

When they heard the apartment door close behind Fox, George put his arm around Maureen and said, "What was all that about?"

Maureen tried to say, "Nothing," but she was voiceless. What was there to say? The baby was hers, nobody else's, and that was that. Silently, she reached out and took the five hundred dollars from George, grabbed her coat and walked decisively out the door. She didn't even turn around when George called out after her, "Maureen, where are you going? Maureen? Maureen!"

CHAPTER THIRTY-FIVE

Hello, Maureen. What are you doing over here? Slumming, are ya?"

Sam Fleming slouched against the door of her basement apartment in building 4A at Hillview Terrace apartments. The brave, saucy face Maureen had been wearing since the visit from the cops that morning melted and disappeared as soon as it was confronted by Sam's obvious hostility. Something about Maureen had always gotten right up on Sam's last nerve. Dominic Lewis, Sam's boyfriend, appeared behind her.

"Come in, come in, Maureen my love. Sam, what are you doing keeping sweet Maureen out in the hall?"

Dominic, the few times Maureen had met him, was always overly friendly and even flirty with her. She wished he wasn't. She could see, once again, it was making Sam mad making her dislike Maureen even more than she already did.

"Let me take your jacket, my love," Dominic was saying as he had his hands on Maureen's shoulders, acting way too familiar.

"Is Dicey here?" Maureen said, pulling away from Dominic's clutches.

"Yea—that's for me to know and you to find out," Sam said belligerently.

"Oh, Sam, I just want to see her," Maureen said.

"Well, don't start sooking, Maureen. Lighten up, girl. What's wrong with ya? I'm only giving you a hard time." Sam laughed at Maureen's discomfort.

The saucy Maureen decided it was time to take over, and she looked straight at Sam and said, "Well, I guess that's what's wrong with me. You're giving me a hard time and I don't like it and I got no time for it. Is Dicey here?"

"DICE," Sam bawled out, her eyes still locked with Maureen's.

Dicey appeared, ducking through the door into the low-ceilinged living room. It was dark in there, even though it was only early afternoon, and there was a musty smell in the apartment. The whole place made Maureen want to get out of there as soon as she could.

"Hey, Dice."

"Hey, Maureen."

"Whaddya at?"

Dicey just looked at her with a face that was possibly the saddest face Maureen had ever seen.

"Can I talk to you for a minute, Dicey?"

"Sure, Maureen, why not?"

"Can we go outside?" Maureen asked.

"Yea. Let me get my coat."

The room fell silent when Dicey left. Maureen smiled weakly at Sam and Dominic.

"What do you want with Dicey, Maureen?" Sam said.

"Well, that's for *me* to know and *you* to find out."

Sam gave Maureen such a threatening look, Maureen backed down and laughed nervously.

"I was just makin' a joke, you know, 'cause you said . . ." Maureen thought she might burst with discomfort, but then, thankfully, Dicey appeared and they went up to the parking lot.

Maureen wasn't sure how to proceed.

"Well," Dicey said, "you got me out here. What do you want?"

Maureen reached in her pocket, took out the envelope of cash and passed it to Dicey. Dicey was so down in the dumps, she seemed barely interested in what was in the envelope.

"Open it up," Maureen said.

Dicey opened it, saw the five hundred-dollar bills, and was confused.

"It's five hundred bucks. You can, you know, 'take care of things,' like you said."

"Why are you doing this?" Dicey asked.

For the life of her, Maureen didn't know. But because she was unable to duck a direct question, she said, "I want to do the right thing. Like they say in AA, do the next right thing. And the guy who might have knocked me up gave me this money 'cause I'm goin' up to Montreal and I'm going to find my baby, and he thinks it might be his, but that baby only belongs to me." Maureen kind of ran out of steam, but looking at Dicey, she knew she had to go on.

"And because you always liked me even though no one else did or even does, I guess. And maybe because Bo was gonna help you and he's gone now—and I'm not sorry about that, not the one little bit—but I am sorry that you, you know, are in the state you're in, and I never had a choice of what was gonna happen to me and my baby, and I'm just givin' you this money so you will have a choice—that's all."

Maureen realized she'd just said what she really did think. And for the first time in her entire life, when she wasn't drunk, she didn't wait for the other person to make the first move; Maureen just reached out and took Dicey in her arms, hugging her close.

"It's gonna be all right, Dice."

Maureen held on to Dicey longer than she was comfortable with, but she didn't care because the hug wasn't for her, it was for Dicey.

CHAPTER THIRTY-SIX

THE NEXT MORNING, MAUREEN TOOK A BUGDEN'S CAB to the airport. She wasn't feeling sad or even worried anymore. In fact, she couldn't seem to stop herself from feeling happy—which in and of itself was terrifying. Maureen walked through Torbay Airport clutching her boarding pass. The ticket Fox had given her was in Leanne Fardy's name—the one whose hair Maureen had gummed up at the Turtles concert. The youngest Vague Sister, apparently, had been planning to go to Montreal but had ended up on the locked ward at the mental. LSD had taken Leanne from vague to vacant. Leanne's cloud had turned out to be Maureen's silver lining. A lot of bad things had had to happen to a lot of people in order to get Maureen to the airport and on her way to Montreal to get her baby. Bo's death had only been the first in a cascading cluster of fucks. But Maureen wasn't going to start down that road of guilt and remorse, that long, long road that started with her getting knocked up in the first place and ended with her using poor old Leanne's ticket to finally find her heart's desire. No, Maureen didn't have time for all that, because today was a new day and she was headed out and headed back to where it all began.

Maureen hadn't asked Cramm how the boys had been able to get the documents—she'd been afraid to know. She tried just to be grateful that they'd done it, that they'd found her baby and a new line of defence—whatever it could be. But at least it didn't involve her humiliating herself on the stand. Sailing through the yellow dinginess of the Torbay Airport, past the big luggage carousel, Maureen was brought up short by the sight of McCarthy and Kent, who looked to be headed right for her. Maureen's eyes darted around desperately, looking for somewhere to duck into or something to squat down behind, but there was nothing in the big, open departure lounge. For one mad moment, she did think she could coopy down behind one of the vinyl seats, but she stopped before she made a total fool of herself. She was just straightening her knees when Kent said, "What are you doing here, Miss Brennan?"

"What are you doin' here? Why don't you leave me alone?"

"We're here on an entirely separate matter, Miss Brennan," Kent replied.

McCarthy chimed in with, "Now that we answered your question, why don't you answer ours."

"I'm going away."

"Where away?"

"Away away," said Maureen childishly, and then figured there was no harm in telling the truth now she was almost out the door anyway. "I'm going to Montreal."

"Montreal," McCarthy said. "Didn't you get in enough trouble last time you were up in Montreal, enough trouble to last you a lifetime?"

They knew she'd gotten knocked up. Maureen felt the blood rush to her face, but she calmed herself by thinking, *Of course, they've been investigating me.* By now, they pretty well knew everything there was to know about her, but thanks be to God, there was a lot of it that they couldn't prove.

"I'm going to Montreal to find my baby."

"You know, don't ya, that they're gonna let Jack Dunne get away with murder? Just charge him with manslaughter. And the way it's looking, he probably won't even do federal time. They're saying he was out of his mind provoked because of what your Mr. Browne did to Jack's brother, Deucey. Jack always looked after his little brother, but that time he went too far and he should be made to pay for it."

Maureen was looking at McCarthy and keeping her eyes as dead as possible because her mind was flying around like a rat on a wheel. Flying back to that time in the auditorium when Carleen had "the incident." She could almost hear Sydney Carton say, *It is a far, far better thing that I do, than I have ever done . . .* And Maureen remembered the weird thing Fox said the night they kidnapped her: he said to Jack, "You're not going to throw everything away again just . . ." And how Jack told Fox to shut up and how, inexplicably, Fox had done just that. Jack had given up his dreams of playing in the NHL because the scouts didn't want Deucey. She remembered what Cramm had said about Deucey almost dying for Jack, before they were born, and she remembered Deucey's eyes that day on the street when he said Bo's name. And suddenly, Maureen knew the

MARY WALSH

truth. All the clues pointed the one way, but Maureen had been too blind to see it. Now she knew, as sure as she was standing there, that it was Deucey who'd committed manslaughter. Deucey was the one who hated Bo so much, who'd been humiliated by what Bo had done to him, and in a rage, he had tied Bo up, put him in the back of the car and left him there. Jack was protecting Deucey. Jack was willing to give up his freedom for the brother who had almost lost his life saving Jack's.

How had she been so wrong? She had been so sure that Jack was nothing but a low-life skeet capable of the worst crimes. But despite how he looked, Jack had a noble nature. Shure he was just like Sydney Carton in *A Tale of Two Cities*.

"What?" said McCarthy.

Maureen snapped out of it. "Did I say something?"

"Yea, something about Sydney or something."

"Canadian Pacific Airlines Flight 647 departing for Montreal from Gate A, all passengers should now be on board Canadian Pacific Airlines flight 647 at Gate A . . ."

"Oh, that's me. I gotta go," Maureen said.

"So that's it, you're just gonna go, duck your responsibilities? If you do manage to find that youngster and bring it back, is that what you're gonna teach it? To let the crowd with all the money and the fancy lawyers get away with doing whatever they like to whoever they like whenever they like to do it, just so long as you get what you want, is that it?"

"I really, really, really got to go now," Maureen said, just as missus on the PA came on again. Kent looked at Maureen like she had disappointed him. Maureen wanted to explain that there was nothing she could do, when suddenly, there was George standing between Maureen and the two cops.

"Are you suggesting Miss Brennan has done something unlawful or there is some pressing criminal reason she should not leave this province?"

"Final call for Canadian Pacific Airlines Flight 647 to Montreal. All passengers should now be on board through Gate A."

"Well, then let it be on your head, Maureen Brennan, that this is the kind of place St. John's is now, the kind of place where murdering scumbags are getting off, and the kind of place where the people who could do something to stop it are doing nothing." McCarthy had to yell the last bit after Maureen and George started running toward Gate A.

"What are you doing, George?" Maureen was suspicious but also a little bit happy to see George there.

"Well, I'm going to Montreal."

"With me?"

"Well, more near you, I guess, because you didn't invite me for some reason."

"No, I didn't," Maureen said.

"Yea. I know."

They boarded the plane, and George, conveniently, had the seat next to Maureen.

"I guess it's pretty foolish of me, but I'm betting that if you don't ever allow yourself to get beaten down like that again, if you don't let anyone treat you like that ever again, if you take care of yourself, I am feeling pretty confident that you won't be putting poison in anyone else's orange juice ever again—at least that's what I'm counting on. I've got to tell you, though, I won't be drinking that much orange juice in Montreal—if I drink any at all."

Maureen punched him in the arm.

"I came along, Maureen, 'cause I got . . . feelings for you."

Maureen rolled her eyes but smiled secretly.

"I came along to help you."

"I don't need any help, George. I am doing good all by myself."

"Yea, so good. Oh, I can see that."

"When did you get so sarcastic?" Maureen said, not at all displeased with this new, snappier George.

"Who are you going to find to lie on top of you when you get anxious, to ground you out, if I don't do it? Who's going to constantly remind you that you have the right to remain silent even though you are totally incapable of exercising that right? Who's going to tell you the plot of all those movies . . ."

George had a whole list of things he was going to do for Maureen, but Maureen stopped listening. Her mind, which had been mercifully silent for so long, was back with a vengeance and was busy trying to undermine Maureen's entire plan. *What are you going to do when you get to Montreal? Even after you find the baby, he's already almost two and a half years old now. What can you do? You got no legal rights to him. What are you going to be, his babysitter? Be the maid? Move in next door? Live down the street?*

Maureen's mind was doing its best to confuse and confound and undermine her. For its pièce de résistance, it threw up a full visual of the Sarge saying, "Oh, give your head a shake, you stupid little moron. Open up your eyes and take a fuckin' look around. If having youngsters was the key to happiness, then wouldn't I be cagged off on cloud nine?"

To stop her mind from going cracked altogether, Maureen said, "I don't know what I'm going to do when I get there."

George said, "Well, we'll hidey-ho it on the public big car, take a powder to the—"

Maureen interrupted and said more to herself than to George, "I'll go visit Carleen. I'll try to see her as much as I can . . . But that's then and this is right now. And there's nothing I can do about what's coming. Like they say in AA, I can only live one day at a time. So the big question is, what am I going to do about right now?" For a moment, Maureen was stumped, but then, just like that, the answer came to her. "I should put on my seat belt, I guess. Buckle up. It could be a bumpy ride."

As the plane took off, George pretended he was the captain. "Captain George, making all the preparations to get this big bird off the ground." He did a couple of announcements from the cockpit, and by the time he'd finished, they were laughing and already in the air, and Maureen hadn't felt nervous at all.

Maureen looked out the window. They'd said on the radio that morning that fog was general all over the island portion of Newfoundland, and there it was, still rolling in, obscuring Bell Island, blanketing every part of the heath barrens, shrouding the treeless hills of the Avalon, concealing the vast emptiness of the interior. As she saw how the fog covered the island, Maureen felt downhearted, realizing how long she'd been living in a fog, and her usual feelings of dread and unease rose up in her as she thought of what was to come. How could she go forward? How would she know what to do with George? With her little baby?

Then the fog disappeared and they were flying above the clouds, racing across the clear blue sky, headed west, following the sun.

ACKNOWLEDGEMENTS

I am deeply grateful to all of the people who have helped me so enormously in the writing of this book.

I'd especially like to thank Perry Zimel, without whom there would be no book, and Iris Tupholme for her endless and constructive notes and all her gentle advice. And thank you to all the crowd at HarperCollins.

I owe a debt of gratitude to Monique Tobin for her encouragement and support, and all her hard work.

I'd also like to thank Jamie Pitt for her incredible assistance and for being my unflagging helper and mainstay.

An immense thank you to Jerome Kennedy and Rachel Huntsman for their advice on the law. I'd also like to thank Constable Mitchell Ryall. If there are any mistakes in the book regarding the law, they are entirely mine.

Thanks to Tamara Ross and the Banff Centre for the Arts, for giving me two glorious weeks in the woods.

And finally, to Aunt May for reading me all those books, on all those days and all those nights so long ago.